D0054597

GUNMEN OF THE DESERT SANDS

Ralph Cotton

A SIGNET BOOK

SIGNET
Published by New American Library, a division of
Penguin Group (USA) Inc., 375 Hudson Street,
New York, New York 10014, USA
Penguin Group (Canada), 90 Eglinton Avenue East, Suite 700, Toronto,
Ontario M4P 2Y3, Canada (a division of Pearson Penguin Canada Inc.)
Penguin Books Ltd., 80 Strand, London WC2R 0RL, England
Penguin Ireland, 25 St. Stephen's Green, Dublin 2,
Ireland (a division of Penguin Books Ltd.)
Penguin Group (Australia), 250 Camberwell Road, Camberwell, Victoria 3124,
Australia (a division of Pearson Australia Group Pty. Ltd.)
Penguin Books India Pvt. Ltd., 11 Community Centre, Panchsheel Park,
New Delhi - 110 017, India
Penguin Group (NZ), 67 Apollo Drive, Rosedale, North Shore 0632,
New Zealand (a division of Pearson New Zealand Ltd.)
Penguin Books (South Africa) (Pty.) Ltd., 24 Sturdee Avenue,
Rosebank, Johannesburg 2196, South Africa

Penguin Books Ltd., Registered Offices:
80 Strand, London WC2R 0RL, England

First published by Signet, an imprint of New American Library,
a division of Penguin Group (USA) Inc.

First Printing, November 2008
10 9 8 7 6 5 4 3 2 1

For Mary Lynn . . . of course

PART 1

PART 1

Chapter 1

Four gunmen stood in the shade of a flapping canvas overhang out in front of the Perro Negro Cantina. They stared silently into a wavering plane of heat, sand and glaring sunlight. They watched a thin black line twist and turn and finally squeeze its way out of some fiery netherworld and give birth to itself on the desert floor. At three hundred yards the thin black line began to evolve, taking on the shape of some strange, thin centaur. A wide rack of horns mantled the man-beast's head. Short billowing wings batted slowly at its sides.

Yet the four gunmen stared stony eyed, not the least surprised, each seeming to have seen his share of such creatures rise up from the hot swirling sand. Their eyes revealed a surly confidence—these men who knew of nothing the desert could conjure that couldn't be stopped short by the blast of lead or the slash of sharpened steel. Between them and the distant rider a hot wind howled and moaned, as if in grave anticipation.

Above the wind a Mexican gunman, Paco Ruiz, took it upon himself to say, "Rider coming," to his three companions, as if these *americanos* hadn't concluded as much on their own.

"We see him," a voice replied. Above them the wind caused the canvas to flap wildly in its frame. A dust devil spun its way down the middle of the empty street. The man-beast rode steadily closer, then stopped at a hundred yards and bowed its head slightly toward the ground; its short wings dropped and hung loosely at its sides.

"Ah, you look down and see the prints of our many horses riding into Agua Fresca, eh?" Paco said quietly to the distant figure. "And now you are asking yourself the question: Do you ride into Agua Fresca, here where the water is sweet and pure, but where you know there may be those who would kill you for your horse? Or do you ride on, to a place where the water is less cool and sweet, but where life is safer for you?" He smiled thinly to himself. "Are you bold of spirit, *mi amigo*, or will you prove to be faint of heart?"

"A gold buck says he rides on," said Bo Phelps, standing beside Ruiz, hearing Paco's quiet musings.

"Why do you think so?" Paco asked.

Phelps spat with contempt toward the distant manbeast and added, "He sees the odds on the ground at his feet. Water or no water, he'll ride on, 'less he's an idiot."

"I accept your wager," Paco said quietly, without

facing Phelps. *An idiot* . . . ? He didn't think so. He saw something in the bearing of the distant rider— this man-beast—something he could not explain, yet something he understood. Perhaps it was the way in which this creature of the desert straightened and stared toward them across the burning sand in spite of the many hoofprints on the ground beneath him. In his youth, Paco had seen wolves, big cats, other predatory creatures of the Mexican hill country carry themselves in such a manner. Usually they did so when prey had suddenly caught their attention, he reminded himself. A faint smile came to his lips.

"I say this one rides in," he said. He watched the man-beast scrape a restless hoof; then it straightened its horns and rode forward, as if on cue.

"Damn it," Phelps grumbled. "How'd you know that?"

Paco only shrugged without a reply.

Watching the rider approach, Phelps said, "Hell, for a gold buck, I'll kill the sumbitch before he gets here." He took a step forward, drawing a big .45 revolver from its holster.

"No," said Paco, "if you kill him now, you must still pay me."

"Like hell I *must*," said Phelps, a bit mockingly. "Where'd you get such a notion as that?" Yet, even as he questioned the Mexican, he lowered the .45 back into its leather.

"You tell him, Braden," Paco said to one of the other Americans, still without looking around at the three of them.

"You can't do something to tip the bet, Phelps, else

the bet's off," Braden Mann said, sounding put out with having to explain something so elementary. "You ought to know that without being told."

"Maybe I *did* know it," Bo Phelps replied in a gruff, surly manner. "Maybe I just wanted to kill the sumbitch, him costing me a gold buck." He stared out through the wavering heat, watching the coming man-beast change yet again as it grew closer to Agua Fresca.

"Kill him . . . ?" Paco Ruiz considered the coming rider for a moment with solemn speculation, then said to Phelps, "You owe me a gold buck. Do you want to make it double or nothing?"

Beside Phelps, Braden Mann chuckled. "Sounds like Paco don't think you *can* kill this hombre."

"Maybe Paco would like to know how it feels to get my boot toe jammed up his—" His words stopped short as Paco's dark eyes cut around toward him.

"Careful, my friend," Paco cautioned.

Phelps took it no further. He hadn't been riding with Quinn Madsen and his gang long, but he'd already learned that Paco Ruiz was a serious man, not one to tolerate threats, even ones made in a half-joking manner.

Looking away from him again, Paco reached a hand out to his side and said, "Give me my money."

Phelps fished through some loose change in his vest pocket, came out with a small thin gold coin and grudgingly laid it in Paco's palm.

"*Gracias,*" Paco said, slipping the coin into his trousers pocket without looking at it. "Now, what about double or nothing?" he asked.

But Phelps didn't reply. Instead, he watched the

approaching rider and said, "I best go tell Quinn we've got company coming."

The voice of Roscoe Turner, Quinn Madsen's right-hand man, said from the open doorway behind them, "Stay where you are, Bo, I'll tell him." He stood with his soiled rawhide shirt open at the chest, a bandolier of ammunition draped over one shoulder. With a hard gaze out across the wavering sand flats he said to the four, "Get rid of this jake." Letting out a puff of smoke from a cigar, he stepped back inside the cool darkness of the cantina walls.

"Can we have some fun with him first?" Phelps called out to the blue waft of smoke in the doorway.

But Turner didn't answer. He'd already returned to the bar, where he'd stood drinking with Quinn and five more hardened gunmen, all from along the Texas border.

"What have they got out there?" Quinn Madsen asked, swirling his wooden cup of tequila in his fist.

"A rider," said Turner. "Some flea-bitten drifter like as not." He picked up his own wooden cup of tequila and took a deep drink from it. "I told the new man, Phelps, to get rid of him. We don't need punk-wood drifters hanging around, stinking up the place."

Madsen nodded. "Unless you meant for Phelps to kill him, you should've made it clear." He shrugged. "Bo Phelps is a good man. But he's fast as lightning and he likes showing it." He grinned mirthlessly. "He's got a taste for blood. Hell, that's why I hired him."

"Want me to say something to him?" Turner asked.

"Naw," said Quinn, "let it go. It'll give you a chance to see him in action for yourself."

Lawrence Shaw had stopped the big buckskin only for a moment, looking down at the upturned sand. Beneath the ragged rim of his sombrero, his eyes had followed the horses' tracks, seeing them meander in and out of sight across the rise and fall of the desert floor. He knew who'd made those tracks. There were two kinds of men who traveled in numbers on the badlands floor, *federales* and banditos, he told himself. He hadn't seen any *federales* on the badlands in months.

Squinting ahead through the white glare of sunlight, he'd nudged the buckskin forward onto the path. These were gunmen, banditos, desperados, he told himself idly, gazing ahead, the buckskin moving at a restless bounce, knowing water lay waiting ahead. But it didn't matter to Shaw who they were or what they were. He and the buckskin needed water. He needed other things too—ammunition, food, coffee. But first things first; he and the horse needed water.

Beneath the ragged blanket that he'd cut a hole in and now wore draped over his shoulders as a poncho, Shaw's right hand rested on his lap, only a nerve twitch away from the butt of the big Colt standing hidden beneath the poncho in a tied-down holster.

Upon seeing the dusty, ragged figure ride onto the windblown street and then to the well, Bo Phelps said to Paco in a confident tone as he stepped past him, "Yeah, what say we do make it double or nothing?"

"You're on," Paco replied. He didn't move; he only watched as Bo Phelps and Braden Mann stepped out from under the flapping canvas.

"Get my money ready," Phelps said. He and Mann walked toward the stone well where Shaw had stepped down from his saddle and let the thirsty buckskin have at the cool water. Beside Paco, the fourth gunman, a hard-bitten badlands outlaw named Drop the Dog Jones, studied Shaw's face closely for a moment until recognition set in. Then he whispered, "Oh, hell, boys," and backed away.

"Do you know this man, Dog?" Paco asked, glancing over his shoulder as Drop the Dog shied farther back into the shade.

"No, I don't what you call 'know' him, but I sure as hell know who he is," said Jones.

"Oh?" Paco turned his gaze back to Shaw. "Did I make a foolish bet?"

"No," said Drop the Dog, "but you might have a hard time collecting."

At the well, Shaw had seen the two coming, walking with a few feet between them. But he ignored them as he picked up a water gourd from the stone wall, dipped it into a clay urn filled with water and sipped from it. When he heard a voice call out, "Hey you, hombre," he paid no attention. Instead, he continued drinking as he turned slowly, taking in the small town of Agua Fresca.

"Look at this," Phelps said to Braden Mann, as if in disbelief. "This jake must be deaf or something." Then he shouted at Shaw from only a few feet away, "Hey, you! What's wrong with you anyway?"

Shaw finally turned to them, lowered the drinking

gourd slightly and looked himself up and down. "Nothing, why?" he replied dryly. As he spoke he slung a few remaining drops of water from the gourd and laid it back on the stone wall.

" 'Why,' he asks," Phelps said to Mann with contempt, both of them stopping a few feet away.

"Because that's our water you're drinking, you ignorant saddle tramp," said Mann.

"You should've spoken sooner," Shaw said flatly, wiping a hand across his lips.

"You've got some gall, hombre," Phelps said to Shaw. "You ride in here and drink our water, you and your buzzard bait cayouse." He gestured toward the buckskin. "Now we're going to have to make an example of both of you, right, Braden?"

"Sounds right to me," Mann said, his hand poised near his gun butt. He looked the unsuspecting buckskin up and down as if deciding how best to punish the animal.

Shaw only stared, knowing this game by heart.

Phelps gave a dark chuckle. "I hope you're wearing a gun, hombre," he said. "A man shouldn't go around, him and his horse swilling other men's water, 'less he's packing some iron. You packing iron, drifter?"

At the open doorway of the cantina, Quinn Madsen, Roscoe Turner and the rest of the men stood watching. "All right, watch this," Madsen said to Turner, standing beside him. "This is going to be good."

At the well, Phelps and Mann both looked surprised when Shaw flipped the corner of his poncho back and revealed the big, clean, shiny Colt standing in its holster. "Whoa," said Phelps, giving a smug grin. "Where'd you manage to steal a gun like that, hombre?"

At the doorway, Madsen said to Turner, "Here we go, keep your eye on Phelps' hand. He's fast."

But suddenly, Shaw's Colt was out, up, cocked and pointed at Phelps, who stood with his mouth agape, his hand not even making it to his gun butt.

"Damn *Phelps'* hand!" said Turner. "The drifter has him cold. I never saw *anything* that fast!"

Stepping in close to Phelps, the bore of the big Colt staring him in the eyes, Shaw said calmly but with no trace of doubt, "Your next move will get you buried." He didn't seem at all concerned with Braden Mann, who stood frozen in place, his hands having managed to go chest high in reflex and stop there in a show of submission.

"Pull that trigger, they'll all kill you," Phelps managed to say, gesturing a nod toward the cantina. His face turned ashen as Shaw reached down, lifted Phelps' .45 revolver from its holster, cocked it and backed away a few feet.

"We'll see," Shaw said, keeping Phelps covered now with his own gun. "You," he said to Mann, pointing Phelps' cocked .45 at him, "loosen your gun belt and pitch it over here."

Mann gritted his teeth in rage and humiliation, but did as he was told. When the gun belt landed at Shaw's feet, Shaw stooped down, popped six bullets out of the belt and began sticking them into the cylinder of his Colt, careful to keep the .45 pointed and ready.

"Say!" said Phelps, watching Shaw load the Colt. "Your gun wasn't even loaded!"

"It is now," Shaw said, clicking the Colt shut and cocking it alongside the .45.

From the cantina doorway, Turner said to Madsen. "Did you see that?"

"I saw it, but I don't believe it," said Madsen. To the men gathered around him, he said, "All of yas spread out. When I say so, kill this fool. Nobody is going to blow into town and ride roughshod over my men."

"Quinn," Paco said over his shoulder, "Drop the Dog says he knows this hombre."

"Yeah?" said Madsen. "Who is he, Dog?"

"He's Fast Larry Shaw," Dog said, keeping his voice low, lest Shaw hear him. "Me and Lying Earl run into him when we were riding with the Barrows brothers. He killed Titus Boland in the street, him with his right arm in a sling. *Generalisimo* Sepreano's whole army stood looking on."

"Fast Larry Shaw, eh?" Quinn said with a short grin, staring out to where Shaw stood with both Phelps' and Mann's guns under his control, Mann's gun belt hanging from his shoulder. "I've heard of him," he added in contemplation, rubbing his chin. "I thought he was dead."

"Say the word, he *will* be," said Turner. He stared out at Shaw with a scowl, his hand going around his gun butt.

"Naw, let's not kill him just yet," said Madsen. "Call him over here, Paco. Let's hear what he's got to say."

"Are you sure about this, Quinn?" Paco asked, checking to make certain.

"If I was *you*, I would never ask *me* something like

that again," Madsen said, a cool and dangerous tone coming to his voice.

Without hesitation, Paco called out toward the well, "Hey, you, hombre, come over here. My *jefe* wants to talk to you."

"Not today," Shaw said, turning toward them with his Colt cocked and pointed. "Tell your boss I'm only passing through."

"Listen to this arrogant fool," Madsen said to Turner, all the while managing to keep a thin smile on his face toward Shaw. "Stand where you are," he called out. "I only want to talk to you. Don't make us kill you."

Down the dirt street, from a crack in a weathered door, a young girl watched intently. When it looked as if the danger of a gunfight had passed, she turned and hurried to the bed where her mother lay holding a wet cloth to her battered, swollen face. "*Madre, por favor*, wake up, come quickly!" she said. She held her small hands out as if to shake her mother, but dared not, considering the woman's condition.

"Stay away from the door, little one," her mother moaned through her battered face.

"But, *madre*!" said the girl. "You must come see. It is a miracle! The angel we have prayed to the Holy Mother for has come to us!" She crossed herself quickly. "He stands in the street at this very moment!"

Chapter 2

On the street, Shaw stopped at the buckskin's side and stood watching as Madsen and his men walked forward from the cantina. A few feet away, Braden Mann and Bo Phelps stood seething with rage, both of them realizing how bad this made them look to the others. "Surely you're not riding out of here with my gun!" Braden said, humiliated.

"No," Shaw said. He unloaded Braden's Colt, pocketed the bullets and pitched the empty gun to him. "Just your ammunition."

"Just my—!" Braden looked down at the gun lying in the dirt, then at his gun belt hanging over Shaw's shoulder. But in his helplessness he only cursed under his breath.

"What about me?" Phelps growled. "Give me *my* gun and I'll cut you in half—I swear to God I will!"

Without reply Shaw opened the big revolver and let the bullets fall into his hand. He dropped the bullets into his trousers pocket, then pitched the gun into the dirt three feet in front of Phelps.

"It's not loaded," Phelps snarled, clenching and unclenching his gun hand near his empty holster.

"Load up," Shaw said flatly. He seemed not to even notice the rest of the men walking toward them along the dirt street from the cantina.

Madsen and the others slowed to a halt, seeing what was going on. "Easy, men," Madsen said, stopping them with a raised hand. "It looks like Phelps is still in this game."

"Then he's a fool," said Turner.

"He might be," said Madsen, "but we're going to let him play it out."

Phelps jerked bullets from his gun belt and hurriedly shoved them into the .45. "You just made a bad mistake, drifter," he said, getting his confidence back now that he had his gun in hand. He might have let this man get the drop on him the first time, he told himself as he slapped shut the Colt's cylinder and gave it a spin, but it wouldn't happen a second time. He slipped the gun down into its holster.

Shaw, watching, waiting calmly, looked him up and down and said, "Are you ready?"

"Am I *ready*?" said Phelps. "You're mighty damn right I'm *ready*." He half crouched, his gun hand poised near the butt of the .45. "You best ask the devil's blessings, drifter. I'm sending you straight to—"

Shaw's shot hit him solidly between the eyes, picked him up and hurled him backward in a spray of blood, bone and brain matter, before Phelps' hand even touched his gun.

"Good Lord!" Madsen said, having still seen only a blur as Shaw's Colt streaked up and fired.

Braden Mann stood stunned, staring down at Phelps' body.

"Well?" Shaw said to him.

"Huh?" Mann looked at him.

"Do you need to load up?" Shaw asked in the same flat, smooth voice.

Mann held his hands chest high, looking to Madsen for some sort of help. "Quinn?" he said.

Near Madsen and Turner, a gunman named Dick "the Hatchet" Shuller said, "We've got to kill him for this."

"Everybody stand down," Madsen said, ignoring Shuller. He said to Shaw, "I've got a man here who tells me you're Fast Larry Shaw. Are you?"

Shaw shook his head no. He spun his Colt backward into his holster almost as fast and slick as he'd drawn it. "Fast Larry is dead."

"He's lying," said Drop the Dog, keeping his voice down behind Madsen.

"What is your name, then?" Madsen asked.

"I don't use one," Shaw said. He looked at the buckskin, who had continued drinking thirstily through the sound of the gunshot. The big horse, having drunk its fill, stood looking at him now with water running from its muzzle. "Are you through?" Shaw asked the big sweat-streaked animal. The buckskin nickered under its breath and stood watching as if it understood.

Madsen tried again. "Mister, you just killed one of the fastest guns I've ever known."

"So?" Shaw said.

"So I think I've got a right to know your name," Madsen insisted.

"I told you, I don't use one," Shaw repeated, his voice letting Madsen know there was no point in asking again.

Madsen let it go. "All right, No Name," he said. "I don't know *you*, but I believe you know who we are. I'm Quinn Madsen. These are my *compañeros*. One word from me and they'd chop you to pieces right there beside Phelps."

Shaw looked down at Phelps' body, then looked back to Madsen. "Oh . . . ?" he said, sounding as though he either didn't believe it or didn't care one way or the other.

Madsen shrugged a shoulder. "What do you expect? You cost me a good man."

"If he was good he'd be alive," Shaw said.

"Yeah, well, anyway," Madsen went on, "now I'm left a man short. Killing you would be a terrible waste of talent." He pointed a finger at Shaw for emphasis. "Bad for business, far as I'm concerned."

Shaw only nodded and looked back and forth from one stone-hardened gunman's face to the next. The only man he recognized was Drop the Dog Jones. He had seen him at a gunfight he'd had less than a year ago at a place called Hell's Gate, the hideout for a band of killers known as the Barrows Gang. "And?" Shaw said.

"*And* I always need men who are good with a gun," Madsen said pointedly, "men who don't mind taking what they want and to hell with anybody who

tries to stop them." He gave a nod of his head
toward the gun belt hanging from Shaw's shoulder.
"Sort of like you just did here."

Braden Mann's face reddened. "I still want my
damn gun belt back."

"Hear that?" Madsen chuckled. "He wants his gun
belt back." His smile vanished as he turned on his
heel, drew a Colt from his belly holster and shot
Braden Mann in the chest.

The men all flinched in stunned surprise. But Shaw
only cast a glance at Braden lying in the dirt clutching his shattered chest with both hands. "Now you're
two men short," he said quietly.

At the crack in the weathered door, the bruised
and battered woman had joined her daughter. The
two had been watching when Shaw shot Bo Phelps.
The woman winced at the sight, and made the sign
of the cross on her bosom. Backing away from the
door a step, she said, "No, little one, this is not the
angel we have prayed for the Holy *Madre* to send to
us. This is a bad man, just like the rest of these murderers. The Holy *Madre* would not send such a terrible angel as this to do what must be done here—God
forbid."

"But, *Mama*," the little girl said, "this must be the
angel the Holy Mother sent to get rid of these men."
She nodded toward the street beyond the closed
door. "Two of them are gone already."

On the street, Madsen gestured for Drop the Dog
and a Colorado gunman, Filo Hewes, to drag Braden
Mann to the side, out of the street. "Either choke him
to death and finish him off, or stick a rag on his
chest, give him some water or something," Madsen

said. He tossed the incident aside, then turned back to Shaw with a cold, narrowed stare, not liking his attitude.

"Being two men short is bad right now," he said. "I've got gun work waiting to be done. I've gone along with you shooting Phelps because I saw him come looking for it. But now let's get down to some business, talk about what we can do for each other." He nodded over his shoulder toward the cantina. "I could use a drink, myself. What about you?"

"Yeah, why not?" said Shaw. He looked to the side of the street where Filo Hewes put away a coin he'd just flipped, then bent down over Braden Mann and clamped his fingers around his throat.

"All right, get your horse and follow me," Madsen said, turning back toward the cantina. "Paco, you and Jones stick with him, see that he finds his way."

Drop the Dog Jones shied back a few feet, but Paco stepped forward and said to Shaw as Madsen and the others walked back across the dusty street, "All right, *Anónimo*, you heard him, get your horse, let's go."

"*Anónimo*, hell," said Drop the Dog. "He's no more nameless than I am. You can ask Lying Earl Sunday when he sobers up. He'll tell you—this *is* Fast Larry Shaw."

Paco said to him, "Was it not you who told me to believe nothing Lying Earl says?"

"Yes," Jones replied, "but if he tells you this is Fast Larry, you *can* believe him."

"I will call this man *nameless* until he asks me to do otherwise," said Paco. As he spoke he stepped over to Phelps' body, stooped down and fished the coins from his vest pocket. Looking up at Shaw, he gave a half smile and said, "I had a wager with this man. He lost."

As Paco stood up and stepped away, Shaw bent down, loosened Phelps' ammunition belt, pulled it from the dead man's waist and slung it up over his other shoulder.

"Hey, you can't do that," Jones said, getting bolder, testing Shaw a little. "Who says you can take the man's bullets?"

"Who says I *can't*?" Shaw responded.

"Nobody says you can't," Drop the Dog said, backing off from the matter. "But it don't seem right. You killed him, now you're taking his ammunition?" He looked to the Mexican for support.

Paco shrugged and said, "Bo Phelps has ammunition he no longer needs, eh? What do I care who takes it?"

"If nobody else cares, neither do I," said Jones. He looked back and forth sourly between the two. Grumbling under his breath, he turned and walked away toward the others as the men filed into the cantina.

With two belts full of bullets over his shoulder, Shaw turned and picked up the buckskin's dangling reins. *Water, ammunition . . .* He took stock of himself. All he needed now was food and some coffee and he'd be on his way, having done what he rode in to do.

As if hearing Shaw's thoughts, Paco said, "You have done well for yourself, eh, *Anónimo*? For one who has only just arrived here." He took two thin black cigars from his shirt pocket and held one out to Shaw. "Take it, *por favor*," he said with a thin smile.

Shaw took the cigar, sniffed it and stuck it into his shirt pocket. "*Gracias*," he said. "But why so generous?"

Paco shrugged. "I saw how quickly you killed Bo Phelps. I can afford to be generous to one so deadly with a gun. If you ever draw your gun on me, I hope you will remember it was I who befriended you. Perhaps it will throw off your aim."

"I respect a man who knows the value of a good cigar," Shaw said.

Paco chuckled under his breath. "So, what do you say? Will we be riding together, you and me, for Quinn Madsen and his border raiders?"

"I wouldn't count on it," Shaw said. "I have business waiting on me in Durango."

"Business in Durango?" Paco looked him up and down, his ragged poncho, his battered and frayed sombrero, his run-down boots.

Hearing the doubt in the Mexican's voice, Shaw gazed straight ahead, saying, "Like I told him, I'm just passing through."

"Ah, but if I were you I would think about his offer most seriously," Paco said, the two of them speaking back and forth from beneath the shade of their broad sombreros. "Now, while his offer is friendly and generous, you should take it as graciously as you took the cigar I gave you."

"Or else?" Shaw said, knowing there was an *or else* waiting in the conversation.

Paco gazed also ahead toward the cantina. "Quinn

Madsen will not give up until he finds what it takes to make you ride with him—to do his bidding," he said, his expression turning grim. "He will first offer you much money." Paco shrugged. "But if that does not work, he will find another way. Do not think that just because you are so fast with a gun he will not try to kill you."

"Haven't thought it," Shaw said, taking in the Mexican's words for consideration.

Paco looked him up and down, recounting what he'd just seen happen to Bo Phelps. "I am not saying he *can* kill you, *mi amigo*, only that he will do his best to kill you."

"You have to admire a man who does his best," Shaw said flatly.

Paco stared at him, Shaw's dry humor and lack of concern taking him a moment to understand. Finally a thin smile came to his lips. "Ah, *Anónimo*, my nameless friend, I think I like your style. I think you and I would ride well together, eh, amigo?"

Shaw didn't answer. They walked on.

As soon as the two men had walked out of sight into the cantina, the young girl stepped back from watching them through the crack in the door and turned to where her mother had seated herself stiffly at a wooden table. The woman sat with her bruised and battered face bowed, a wet cloth pressed to her swollen eyes. "You are hungry, *Mamá*," the child said. "I must go to the cantina and bring you some food."

"No," the mother said, casting a sore glance at her from beneath a shroud of glistening black hair. "You stay away from the cantina, and keep a safe distance from those men. I will go find food for us."

"But, *Mamá*," the child insisted, "he has warned you, you must stay inside until your face is healed. You cannot leave here!" She turned to leave quickly before her dazed mother could continue her objection. But her mother managed to catch her by her arm and stop her long enough to say, "Listen to me, little one. Do not think that because you are a child these men will not do to you what Quinn Madsen does to me! These men are animals, do you hear me? *Animales!*" She shook the girl a bit as if for emphasis.

"I—I know, *Mamá*," the child replied, pulling away gently as she spoke. "But you must eat if you are to regain your strength so we can run from here, *sí?*" She dared not tell her mother that one of these men had already tried to do those things to her. But she had managed to slip free from his drunken grip while he'd held her down with one hand and fumbled with his trousers with his other.

"If anything were to happen to you, little one . . ." Her mother let her words trail as she reached out a hand and brushed a silken strand of hair from her young daughter's face.

"Don't worry, *Mamá*," the child said, "I run faster than the hare . . . *un liebre.*" She managed a slight smile.

"I know this," said her mother, "but even the fastest hare can be caught. Take no chances with these men. Do not go to the cantina for food. Go instead to the old woman's *choza* and tell her what we need." She raised a finger and wagged it to make her point. "Only to her hut, and nowhere else."

"But, *Mamá*. Now that the angel from the desert is here, he will not allow anyone to—"

"Do you understand me?" Her mother cut her off. "Only to the old woman . . . no one else. She will do whatever she can for us. There is no angel coming to help from the desert. There never will be. Get such notions from your mind, little one."

"But, *Mamá*," the girl said in a broken tone, "why have we been praying so hard for an angel if there is none?"

Her mother felt her swollen eyes begin to well under the weight of her despair. "We pray because it is the *only* thing we can do for ourselves."

"But don't you see, *Mama*?" said the child, a look of hope in her innocent young eyes. "We prayed for the angel and he is here. What good is it for us to pray if we cannot see when our prayer has been answered?"

"Go, little one," the woman said, too exhausted, too hurt and broken to discuss the matter. "Bring us some food. When I am able, we will escape from this monster and his evil men. Until that time, let us not waste time talking about such foolishness. There are no angels coming . . . at least none to help us."

"You are wrong, *Mamá*. You must believe with me that our angel is here," the child whispered under her breath, backing away. Turning and leaving through the small door at the rear of the shack, she absently crossed herself. "We must believe in those things we pray for."

Chapter 3

Inside the cantina, Quinn Madsen and Roscoe Turner looked up as Shaw pushed the dusty blanket aside and stepped through the doorway of the Perro Negro Cantina. Paco stepped in right behind him, followed by Drop the Dog Jones. Watching them walk toward the bar, Madsen said to the owner of the shadowy cantina, "Rodero, open a couple of new bottles—mescal and tequila. Welcome our new friend to the ole Black Dog." He lifted a wooden cup of tequila toward Shaw and Paco, then tossed back a drink.

"Yes, of course," said Sepo Rodero, hurriedly grabbing fresh bottles from beneath the wet, battered bar top. "Welcome to my Perro Negro Cantina—the Black Dog Cantina," he added quickly, translating his words into English.

"*Gracias,*" Shaw said. Then he asked the man in Spanish where he might get his horse fed and billeted out of the sun.

Rodero looked first at Madsen for approval. When Madsen gave it with a nod of his head, the cantina owner gestured a hand toward a thin young man at the far end of the bar. "Carlos, see to it this man's horse is grained and aired. Put him in one of the stalls out back."

"Which horse is yours, senor?" the boy asked, stopping in front of Shaw with his hand extended.

Shaw produced a small coin from beneath his ragged poncho and dropped it into the boy's hand. "The buckskin at the end of the rail," he said. "Grain him slow—this much." He made a fist to show the boy the amount of grain. "Then rub him down and feed him that much again."

"Enough about the horse," Madsen said in a gruff but friendly manner, "let's get some of this *loco medicina* in you, make you feel more sociable, eh?" He stuck the bottle of tequila out to Shaw and swished its fiery golden contents. "I'm still determined to get you to ride with us."

Turner stood back, watching in silence, measuring Shaw up closely.

Shaw ignored the tequila bottle stuck toward him and said to Rodero, "What have you got to eat back there?" He nodded toward a blanketed doorway at the rear of the cantina.

"Plenty of *frijoles* and *asó cabra*," the owner said.

"Beans and roasted goat," Shaw said, translating the man's words. "How quick can I get it?"

"*Mas pronto*," said Rodero, already turning and heading toward the back doorway.

"*Bueno*," said Shaw. "*Andole, por favor.*"

Not wanting to be ignored and made to look bad in front of Turner and the rest of his men, Madsen said, "Hey, Shaw, I'm talking to you." He started to swish the bottle toward Shaw again, but before he got a chance, Shaw grasped the bottle quickly from his hand and threw back a long swallow. *"Gracias,"* he said, as soon as he lowered the bottle from his lips and ran the back of his hand across his mouth. "I feel more sociable already."

Seeing that Shaw had begun to settle in and drink with Madsen and the others, Drop the Dog Jones eased away, slipped out the front door and hurried down the dusty street to the trash-littered yard of an adobe that he and some of the men had taken over for their living quarters. Inside the adobe, he walked to the snoring man lying sprawled on a blanket in a rear corner. "Lying Earl! Wake up!" he demanded, kicking the sleeping figure in the thigh. "Come on, damn it, wake up. We got trouble coming our way."

"Huh?" Earl Sunday shook his head and wiped a hand down his face, trying to come awake. "Trou-trouble?" He looked all around bleary-eyed as if expecting something terrible to befall him before he could manage to defend himself. His hand grappled for a black-handled Colt lying on the dirty blanket beside him.

"Don't grab your damn gun, Earl," said Jones, kicking his hand away from the Colt. "Wake up and listen to me. Fast Larry Shaw is here."

"Shaw! Jesus!" said Earl, sobering up and coming awake quickly. "Where is he? What's he want?" He looked all around as if Shaw might be lurking nearby.

"I don't know," said Jones, "but he was dang sure sided with those two lawdogs, Dawson and his deputy, last time we saw him."

"Yeah," said Earl, "and he killed Titus Boland

right in front of our eyes." His brow furrowed with the bad memory. "We were both dang lucky to get away with our lives."

"Yep, and you've got to help me tell that to Madsen. He's trying his best to get Shaw to ride with us!"

"Ride with us? Oh, hell no," said Earl, coming to his feet, his knees still a little wobbly. "If Shaw's in, I'm out." He snatched the black-handled Colt from the blanket, shoved it into his holster and tucked his wrinkled shirttail down into his trousers. "Make room, I'm coming through," he added with determination.

"Whoa, hold on," said Jones, grabbing his arm as he turned to head out the door. "I didn't mean for you to tuck tail and run! I need you to stand with me and tell Madsen what we both saw at Hell's Gate."

"You can tell him," said Earl. "Besides, you're all the time telling everybody how much I lie. You've got the whole gang calling me Lying Earl."

"You earned yourself that name long before we ran into each other," said Drop the Dog Jones. He turned loose of Earl's forearm, seeing the man had stopped heading for the door.

"Right enough," said Earl, "but you could have let it die, instead of telling everybody. Who's going to believe anything I've got to say?"

"Madsen will, I hope," said Jones. "Leastwise, to save our own necks we've got to do our best to tell him." He gave Earl a slight shove toward the doorway. "If he won't listen to us, we'll both start looking for a chance to skin out of here together. I've got a notion that wherever Shaw is, Dawson and his dude deputy won't be far behind. We're going by the livery barn and see what Shaw's got in his saddlebags. He left them hanging behind his saddle."

"He did?" Earl considered it, then said, "What good will that do us? If he had anything of value, he would've slung them over his shoulder."

"Don't be contrary with me, Earl," Drop the Dog warned. "I ain't in the mood for it." He jerked his head in the direction of the livery barn. "Let's go."

When the two had left the adobe, the young girl raised her head and peeped in carefully above the windowsill where she had been crouched down listening from outside. Seeing that the men had left, she clutched the small empty food basket to her chest and hurried off along the alleyway that led to the rear of the cantina.

Out front, on their way to the livery barn, Jones and Earl Sunday stopped short as three riders came into town on a back trail and turned onto the main street. "*Hola*, boys," said the rider in the middle, a rough-faced young Texan gunman named Cero "Double Aces" Stewart. "What's the serious faces all about?" As the young gunman asked, he and his two companions stepped down from their saddles and stretched and slapped dust from themselves.

"Aw, hell, Aces, I'm glad to see you," said Jones, speaking for himself and Earl. "We've got big trouble in the making. If you ever needed to use that fast draw of yours, today is the day."

"Hey, come on," said Cero, giving the two other riders a bemused look. "Whatever's wrong, you tell ole Double Aces about it." His Colt came up lightning fast and spun on his finger. "I bet it's nothing I can't fix."

"Fast Larry Shaw is in town," Earl blurted out. "He's threatening to kill the first man who—"

"That's a lie," said Jones, cutting Earl off and shaking his head. "Damn, Earl, you can't help yourself, can you?"

"Fast Larry Shaw?" said Cero, his Colt stopping sharply on his finger, his thumb over the hammer as he glanced along the dusty street.

"That part's true," said Jones. A grave attentive look come upon Cero's craggy face. "He's at the cantina talking with Madsen about riding with us."

"You don't say . . . ?" Cero turned his Colt back and forth in his hand as he continued looking along the dusty street toward the cantina. "I've always wondered how Fast Larry and I would get along, both standing on the same stretch of ground." He grinned at the two riders standing beside him. "Indian, you're always freely spilling your opinion. What say you? If me and Shaw threw down on each other, who'd die with his guts bleeding?"

"You," Indian Coyle said bluntly. He stared at Cero Stewart with resolve.

"Hey, where's your faith, Indian?" Cero snapped, swinging the Colt quickly, cocking it with the tip of the barrel beneath Indian Coyle's chin.

"You need me to ask him again now that you've pulled your hammer back, Double Aces," said Tommy Layton, himself a renowned Texas gunman. "Maybe his opinion has took on a whole different outlook."

"Is that right, Indian?" Cero said with a dark, devilish grin, rubbing the tip of the gun barrel back and forth beneath the Indian's chin. "Should I ask you again, this time with a little stronger conviction?"

"Ask me forty times," said Indian Coyle, standing rigid with a flat look on his dust-streaked face, "forty times I'll tell you . . . face Shaw, you're dead."

Cero gave a chuckle, lowered his Colt, uncocked it and spun it backward and into his holster. "You're no fun, Indian. What makes you say that about me anyway? You've seen me shoot. Hell, you've won money on my shooting."

"I've seen Shaw shoot too." Indian Coyle shook his head slowly. "You want to sit this one out."

"Yeah? I'll keep that in mind." Cero seemed to take his words seriously, owing to the look on Indian's face and the fact that in such matters he'd never known Indian to be wrong.

"I've seen him shoot too," Earl cut in. He gestured toward Jones. "Me and Drop the Dog watched him kill Titus Boland deader than a—"

"Is he lying, Dog?" Cero asked Jones, staring hard at Lying Earl. "Because if he is . . ."

"No, this time he's telling the truth," said Jones. "We both saw it. Shaw is fast. But hell, I never seen anybody that couldn't meet their match, have you?"

"Good point," Cero replied. To Indian he said, "See? Why couldn't you have told me something like that? Instead of having me dead and buried before I've even said howdy to the man?"

Indian Coyle only stared blankly.

"I've seen Shaw some other places too," said Lying Earl, taking advantage of having someone believing him. "I saw him kill two men in Eagle's Nest, three more in Hyde City."

"Is that a fact?" said Cero, looking past Earl and

seeing Jones shaking his head no, discrediting every word Earl said.

Unsuspecting, Earl continued. "I seen him shoot his way out of a saloon in—"

"All right, that's enough," said Jones, cutting him off gruffly. He looked at Cero. "We're headed for the livery barn. I want to get a look through Shaw's saddlebags."

"That's where we were headed," said Cero, turning, his reins in hand. "I think we ought to just mosey over there with yas. Get an idea what this big, bad Texas gunslinger has been up to lately."

At the bar, Shaw stood finishing his plate of beans and goat meat and wiping a piece of bread around on the empty plate.

Beside him, Madsen cast a glance at Roscoe Turner, then continued speaking to Shaw as he had been all the while the gunman ate his fill. In a voice that barely hid his impatience, Madsen said, "I understand how a man like yourself wants to be a lone wolf. Time was when I myself felt that way. But things have changed. Times have gotten tight. Every day, there's troops showing up along both sides of the border, trying to hold down ole boys like us, get us under their boot, so to speak."

Shaw swallowed the last bite of bread and wiped a hand across his mouth. "I'll take my chances," he said. "I'm not looking to make new friends."

Madsen felt a surge of rage in his chest, but he kept it in check. "And I'm not used to having an offer of friendship thrown back in my face, Shaw."

Before Shaw could reply, his attention turned to

Cero Stewart, who walked into the cantina with Lying Earl and Jones right behind him. "Shaw! I'm looking for you," Cero called out. At the bar, Madsen gave Turner and the others a nod, telling them to spread away and see how Shaw would handle a top gun like Double Aces Stewart.

"Maybe you should have taken my offer while you had a chance, Fast Larry," Madsen said in a half threat. "I don't know if you've met Cero Stewart. He's from Texas, same as you."

"I've heard of Double Aces," Shaw said, already knowing where this was headed. He gave Stewart a cold, flat stare. "I hear you're real fast."

"You better believe it, *Deputy* Shaw," said Cero, returning the stare. To Madsen he said, "I found this in his saddlebags." He pitched a tin badge to Madsen. "I figured you might want to take a look at it, before you go letting this snake in our midst."

Madsen caught the badge, looked at it in surprise and turned it back and forth in his hand. "Well, well, look what we have here."

Turner stepped in beside Madsen for a closer look, his hand resting on his holstered Remington revolver. The rest of the men saw the badge and stood tensed, ready to reach for their guns at Madsen's command. "Tell us what you want, Quinn," Turner said quietly, his eyes riveted on Shaw.

Chapter 4

Madsen considered the consequences of his men shooting it out with Shaw right then and there. He'd already seen enough to know that Shaw was not an easy man to kill. He also knew that with his being the leader of the gang it stood to reason that he would be Shaw's first target. With all this in mind, plus the fact that he still needed men like Shaw riding with him, Madsen looked around slowly and calmly at the situation.

"Everybody take it real easy," he said, raising his hand for emphasis. "I want Shaw to tell us who this piece of tin belonged to before we go shooting one another full of holes over it. For all we know Fast Larry might have killed the lawman who was wearing this badge. What about it, Shaw?" he asked.

"Yeah, Shaw," Cero cut in, standing well poised for a gun duel. "Let us hear you deny it's yours."

"I don't deny it," Shaw said matter-of-factly. "That badge belongs to me. I took it off the day I caught up with Titus Boland and killed him." As he spoke, he looked past Cero Stewart at Drop the Dog Jones.

"See? I told you," said Jones, "he killed the Barrows brothers too. Me and Earl here saw it!"

"That's right," said Earl. "He shot them both down, took out a knife and commenced to scalp—"

"No, he didn't do *all that*," said Jones, cutting off Earl before he could go any further with his tale. "But he did kill them, and now that I see that badge, I understand why he did. Fast Larry has turned straight-up lawdog!"

Madsen looked at Shaw. "What have you got to say for yourself, Shaw? Are you a lawdog?"

"No, I'm not," Shaw replied, his right hand hanging loose but ready at his side. "But it's all true what Jones said. I took on a deputy badge because it was the best way for me to hunt down Titus Boland after he murdered a woman I cared for. As soon as I killed him, I took off the badge."

"You're saying you *was* a deputy, but now you're not?" Cero asked with a sly grin. "That sounds awfully peculiar. You just put on a badge and wear it so long as it suits you?"

"Believe what you want," said Shaw. "I'm through talking about it. If you plan on pulling iron, get to it." He stared hard at Cero.

"Whoa, hang on," said Madsen, keeping everybody at bay. Then he said to Shaw, "You say you only become a lawman long enough to kill Titus Boland? That must've been *some* woman you cared about."

"It was," said Shaw, without taking his eyes off Cero Stewart.

"But what about the Barrowses?" Madsen asked. "Why'd you kill them?"

"The Barrowses just happened to get in my gun sights," Shaw said coolly. "So did a few *federales* before it was over." He continued staring at Cero Stewart. "What about it, Double Aces? Are you going to draw that six-shooter, or has the room grown too small for you?"

Stewart sneered. "You son of a bitch."

"Wait!" Madsen shouted at Stewart, seeing the gunman begin to make his move. But Cero had gone too far to stop himself. He snatched his Colt from his holster.

Shaw's response came fast, catlike. His colt streaked up from his holster; his bullet hit Cero in the heart before the gunman got off a shot. But Shaw didn't stop there. A child's voice shrieked from the rear of the cantina, "Look out, senor!"

Shaw spun away from the bar on his heel. He turned in time to see Tommy Layton leap forward from beside the rear door with a rifle leveled toward him.

A shot from Shaw's Colt slammed Layton back against the wall. Layton's rifle flew from his hands; he slid to the floor onto his knees clutching his bleeding chest. Shaw fanned the Colt back and forth, searching for his next target. Turner and the rest of Madsen's men stood tensed, ready to reach for their guns. But Madsen stood with his hands spread, showing Shaw he wanted no fight with him. "It's over! Everybody stand down!" he shouted at both Shaw and his men.

Shaw stood expressionless, his Colt cocked and ready.

"None of us had anything to do with this, Shaw," Madsen said, gesturing toward Tommy Layton lying dead by the rear door. "If it's more killing you want, so be it. But this was Cero and Layton's doings, not mine."

"I believe you," Shaw said. He glanced across the men and saw they had eased down under Madsen's order. He lowered his Colt a bit in reply. Then he looked along the rear wall and found the owner of the voice that had called out a warning to him. "Who's this?" he asked, seeing the young girl huddled down beside a broken table in the far corner.

Madsen also saw the girl, and he gestured one of his men toward her as he replied to Shaw, "This is Francisca."

"You know her?" Shaw asked, slipping his Colt into his holster as the man pulled the child up and led her toward the bar.

"Her mother is a friend of mine," said Madsen. "A really *good* friend, if you understand what I'm saying." He reached down for the child to come to him. "What are you doing here, Francisca" he asked. But the girl passed him without so much as a glance. Instead she hurried to Shaw, looked him up and down and said, "You—you are not hurt, Mr. Angel?" Then before he had time to answer she said quickly, "I knew you would not be hurt. I knew they could not harm you—"

Mr. Angel . . . ? Stooping down to her, Shaw said, "Whoa, little lady, my name is Mr. Shaw, not Mr. *Angel*." He looked at her closely. "No, I'm not hurt, thanks to you." He brushed a strand of hair from

her cheek. *"Gracias, usted niño bello."* For a fleeing
instant he felt as if his life was worth saving, something he had not felt in a long time.

Madsen appeared uncomfortable at the sight of
Shaw and the young girl talking so easily. "You're
right, Francisca is a beautiful child," he said, translating Shaw's words. As he spoke he reached out a
hand and drew the girl away from Shaw. "You run
along now, sweetheart. Mr. Shaw and I are busy
men."

When the girl resisted, Madsen squeezed her
shoulder a little tighter and pulled a little harder.
"Go fill your basket and get home," he said, keeping
his voice from growing gruff with her. "Or maybe
you'd like me to have Deacon Lucas come along to
help you?"

Shaw saw the child's eyes fill instantly with fear.
"No," she replied, giving in quickly and stepping
away, "I will go! My *Mamá* is expecting me." Even
as she spoke her dark eyes stayed on Shaw's.

"Rodero," Madsen said to the cantina owner, "take
her out back to the *cocina,* send some food home with
her." As Madsen pulled her farther away he patted
the girl's shoulder, but Shaw saw that it was only
for appearance's sake. He also saw that the child was
not accustomed to the gesture, and that she resented
it. "I can't have *either* of my girls going hungry, now,
can I?" Madsen said with a false-looking smile toward
the child.

The girl's eyes lingered on Shaw a moment longer
until Rodero came behind the bar and ushered her
along with him toward the rear door, the two of
them having to veer around Tommy Layton's body

still lying where he'd fallen. What had he seen in her eyes? Shaw had to ask himself. Fear? Yes. Despair? Yes. Hopelessness? Yes, but it was hopelessness giving way to something. *But what? Faith . . . ?* Yes, he decided, he believed it was. But faith in what? In him . . . ? No, he told himself, that couldn't be it.

"Who is Mr. Angel?" he asked Madsen, as interested in studying the expression on the outlaw leader's face as he was to hear his answer.

Madsen shrugged. "Who knows, with this kid? Probably some make-believe friend of hers." He stepped closer to the bar, picked up the bottle of tequila and poured some into Shaw's wooden cup. At the same time he motioned for some of the men to get the two bodies up and out the door. "I don't have much to do with the girl, to tell you the truth." He gave a short sly grin. "It's her mother I'm interested in."

"I see," Shaw said contemplatively, staring toward the rear door, unable to get the girl's eyes out of his mind.

Studying Shaw's expression for a moment, Madsen read it completely wrong, and said in a lowered voice between the two of them, "She's a little young, but not *too* young. She's growing up every day. Just because I'm with the mother doesn't mean you couldn't—"

"Forget it," Shaw said, cutting him off. Madsen's words caused anger to well up in his chest. Anger was something he hadn't felt for a long time, in spite of all the killing he'd been a party to.

"No offense," said Madsen, pushing the wooden cup closer to Shaw's hand on the bar top. "That just goes to show what I'm willing to give, just to get you to ride with us."

Shaw threw back the shot of tequila and set the cup down on the battered bar top. "Do you have to have an answer right now? If you do I have to tell you *no*."

Madsen asked with a curious look, "Why would waiting for an answer make any difference?"

"Right now I'm tired and cross, and I've spent a lot of my time shooting your men," Shaw said. "Maybe I'll change my mind after I get a little rest, and get to know more about the men I'd be riding with."

Madsen stuck a fresh cigar into his mouth, lit it and blew out a stream of smoke. He considered Shaw's words carefully for a moment. Finally he said, "I'll tell you what, Fast Larry, I'm still waiting for a few of my regular men—they've been off here and there, on small jobs across the border. You take a few days until they get here. Let Paco show you around. Enjoy yourself, get drunk, find a woman, do whatever you like. When I get ready to ride, you give me your answer . . . and let that answer be our final word on the matter. What do you say, have we got a *deal*?"

"I say that sounds like a good way to leave it for now," Shaw replied, touching his hat brim on the matter. "Yes, we've got ourselves a deal."

Madsen turned to the others, who had gone back to drinking even as they kept a cautious eye on Shaw and Madsen during their conversation. "All right, men, listen up," said Madsen, raising his voice for everybody's sake. "Until everybody gets here and we're gathered up and ready to ride, consider Shaw here as my personal guest. Treat him like he's one of us." He raised his wooden cup as if in a toast. "I'm hoping that he *will be* soon enough."

No sooner had Paco led Shaw out of the cantina to show him where he'd be bunking than Turner sidled up closer to Madsen. "I saw how fast he is, but do we really want a man like him riding with us? He's never going to follow anybody's orders."

Madsen gave a crafty smile. "I know that. But you saw what a fighter he is. When the time comes that we need to leave a man behind between ourselves and the law, Shaw's the man. He won't do it if he thinks he's following orders, but he'll do it if he thinks it's his own idea."

"I don't trust him," Turner said.

"Aw, hell, neither do I," said Madsen. "He's a belligerent, headstrong son of a bitch. But he didn't get the name *Fastest Gun Alive* sitting home smoking a pipe. He's a straight-up killer who doesn't give a damn if he lives or dies." He threw back a drink from his wooden cup and added, "I'm always looking for that kind of man."

Turner nodded. "I admit he is one hell of a gunman. The fastest I've ever seen. If the time comes we need to leave a man behind to protect our backs, he's got my vote. The problem is putting up with him until that *time* comes."

Madsen poured more tequila for them both. "Don't press me for details, but that time might come sooner than you think, Roscoe." As he picked up his wooden cup he said, "Meanwhile, why don't you get

Bert Sibott to lean on Shaw a little? We know how
good Shaw is with his Colt. Let's find out how he is
with his fists."

"Against Sibott?" Turner gave a bemused look.
"Are you sure about this, Quinn? Bert Sibott was the
French bare-knuckle champ. He'd likely kill him if
Shaw was stupid enough to fight him unarmed."

Madsen gave Turner a cold stare. "Roscoe, if you
think you're going to question everything I say,
you're wrong. Now tell Bert you want him to get in
Shaw's face. The next thing I want to hear from you
is how it turned out. Do you understand me?"

"Clear as a bell," said Turner, seeing he'd gone
too far on the matter. "I'll get Sibott right on it." He
stepped back and walked toward the big Frenchman
standing bowed over his drink at the far end of the
bar. When he drew closer and the Frenchman took
note of him, Turner motioned toward the rear door
and said quietly, "Bert, come talk to me out back.
I've got a job for you. . . ."

Out in front of the cantina, Shaw and Paco had
walked to the livery barn where Shaw checked on
his horse and picked up his saddle, bedroll and saddlebags. Leaving the barn at Shaw's side, Paco shook
his head and said in a lowered, guarded tone,
"Amigo, I have to tell you, I have never seen Quinn
Madsen treat anybody so special, the way he is treating you."

Shaw only gave him a sidelong glance and asked,
"Do you trust it?" He listened closely for Paco's answer, knowing that his words would reveal just how
much he could trust the Mexican as well.

With no hesitation, Paco said quietly, "No, I do

not trust it. If I were you I would not be deceived by Madsen's hospitality. But for now I would take advantage of it and rest my horse in his shade." He grinned. "Your horse will thank you for it." He shrugged. "Anyway, you are fast enough with your gun that you do not have to be in a hurry to please anyone."

They walked on along the dusty street toward the small adobe where the men stayed. Shaw considered Paco's words and decided the Mexican was being honest with him. "What's the story on the girl and her mother?"

Paco gave him a serious look, seeing that there was more there than curiosity. "Please listen to me carefully, my friend. The girl Francisca and her mother belong to Madsen. There is nothing to be done for them. I must warn you not to think of them or get involved with them in any way."

As they talked they had walked to the adobe and stepped inside. Shaw looked around at saddles lined along the floor with blankets rolled up lying beside them. In a small hearth a bed of embers still glowed beneath a blackened tin coffeepot. "All right, you've warned me," Shaw said. "Now tell me about them."

Paco sighed and again shook his head. "I will tell you, but only because I try to be your friend, and I know if I do not, you will find out some other way. So what I tell you must be in secret between us, *comprende?*"

"Understood," said Shaw. He dropped his saddle beneath a window ledge and looked at Paco expectantly.

Paco looked all around as if to make sure no one

was listening. "The woman stays with Madsen because he holds her husband prisoner. He will kill her
husband if she does not go along with whatever he
demands of her." Paco shrugged. "What can she do?
Madsen knows that she cannot go to the *federales* for
help. Even if they cared enough to help her, she
knows her husband would be dead before the *federales* could find him and set him free."

"And the girl knows this?" Shaw asked.

"*Sí*, I think she does," said Paco. "She knows her
father is gone. She knows her mother lives with Madsen. What more does a child see?"

Shaw considered it for a moment, starting to understand the look in the girl's eyes. "Mr. Angel . . . ,"
he murmured under his breath.

"*Sí*, Mr. Angel," said Paco. "When I first came here,
she called me Mr. Angel. But she stopped when she
realized that I am only another of Madsen's outlaws."

"The best hope for these people is for Madsen to
tire of the woman, release her husband and ride
away," Shaw said. "But there's lots of other ways
things like this can go . . . none of them good."

"And now you see why I have done nothing," said
Paco. "Any move I would have made would only
have gotten the child's father killed, eh?"

"You don't have to explain yourself to me," said
Shaw.

Paco fell silent for a moment, then said, "I am not a
good man. I am a bandito and a gunman. I left this
life of rags and hunger. I owe these people nothing.
Her husband chose to be a sheep instead of a real man
who stood up for his wife and child. What am I to do?"

Even as he spoke, Shaw could see that he was talking harshly in order to hide his shame. "Like I said, you don't have to explain yourself—"

Shaw's words were cut short by the booming voice of Bert Sibott, whose huge frame filled the doorway. "Well, well," he said, with only a trace of a French accent. "It's a good thing I got here when I did. You just threw your saddle down in my spot, Shaw. I can't have that, now, can I?" He stepped inside, his sleeves already rolled up, his gun belt missing from around his waist.

Shaw looked at Paco, then down at the saddle on the floor beneath the window ledge. "You must believe that I knew nothing of this, my friend," Paco said in a lowered voice. "This is Madsen's doings."

"I understand," Shaw said, watching Drop the Dog Jones and Lying Earl lurking outside the front door. To the big Frenchman he said, "Suppose you pick up my saddle and move it out of your way?"

"I came here to bust your head, gunman," said Sibott with a wide, cruel grin, "not to carry your lousy saddle for you." He cracked his big round knuckles, raised his fists into a fighter's guard and stalked forward.

"I didn't think so," Shaw said. "Let's get this over with." He took off his gun belt, let it fall atop his saddle on the floor, then took off his sombrero and dropped it atop his gun. He moved cautiously sideways until he stopped and stood a few feet in front of the hearth, casting a quick glance toward the iron poker leaning against the wall on the other side.

"I see what you're thinking, gunman," said Sibott. "Make a move for that poker and I'll just have to beat you that much harder."

Shaw stopped dead still in front of the hearth, as if the big man had read his mind. "There's no fooling you," he said.

"Not when it comes to this, gunman," said Sibott. "I've been in too many fighting rings . . . this is *my* game."

Chapter 5

Outside the small adobe, Drop the Dog Jones and Lying Earl watched in rapt fascination as Sibott moved in a wide circle, drawing ever closer to Shaw. "The big Frenchy is going to kill him for us, Earl," Jones whispered.

"Thank goodness," said Earl. "I was afraid we'd never get rid of him. Did I ever tell you about when I was in Kansas? There was this big fellow—"

"Stop lying, Earl," Jones said, cutting him off. "Shut up and watch the fight."

Inside, Sibott spoke to Shaw as he readied himself to charge forward. "Do me a favor, gunman," he said. "If you're still able to talk, tell me when you've had enough, so I don't have to wear myself out beating on you all day." He gave a wide, mirthless grin. "I hate getting my fists all bloody because some jake is too proud to admit he's done in."

"I'll tell you when," Shaw said flatly. "You be sure and do me the same favor."

"Ha," the big man scoffed, towering above Shaw by a full ten inches. "You've got a strange sense of

humor going for you, gunman." The brawler had
tried to keep him talking as he set up a fast attack.

But Shaw stood his ground in front of the open
hearth, well prepared for the big fighter to make
his move.

Suddenly Sibott shouted, "Take that!" He lunged
forward hard and fast, feeling confident, knowing the
fight would be over once his powerful swing con-
nected.

But Shaw knew better. As the big man made a
long roundhouse swing, going for his one-punch
knockout, Shaw ducked to one side and stuck out
his foot into Sibott's path, tripping him.

"Oh, no!" Jones said from outside the doorway as
the big Frenchman hurled headlong into the open
hearth where Shaw had deliberately positioned himself. Shaw didn't have to lay a hand on him. Instead
he dropped his guard and watched the bare-knuckle
brawler rumble past him like a derailed freight car.

Sibott bellowed fearfully as he saw himself flying
into the open hearth. But there was nothing he could
do to stop it. Paco winced at the sight of the big
man's head smashing the pot of hot coffee and rip-
ping down the iron frame supporting it. With a loud
painful grunt the Frenchman slammed into the rear
of the stone hearth before landing in a puff of smoke,
sparks and hot ashes.

"Holy Mother . . ." Paco whispered to himself,
feeling the small adobe tremble from Sibott's impact.

As hot coffee and bits of charred wood reined
down about the adobe, Shaw stepped over to a table,
picked up a gourd full of drinking water and walked
to where Sibott lay struggling, his broad shoulders

wedged into the open hearth, his right arm having jammed deep up the chimney. "Have you had enough?" Shaw asked flatly.

"You son of a— Yiiiiii!" Sibott had started to curse him, but his profanity turned into a shriek of pain and fear as the embers already burning his chest suddenly caused his shirt to burst into flames. "Get me out! Get me out!" he screamed and sobbed, flames spreading all over his large torso.

Shaw reached in with the large gourd and poured the water down over him, turning smoke, flames and glowing embers into a dark sizzling cloud. "Are you sure you've had enough?" Shaw asked again, stepping back from the rising billowing cloud of steam.

Sibott coughed and gurgled and sobbed. "I'm— I'm stuck!" he gasped, struggling with his shoulders and right arm.

Shaw nodded for Paco to help and the two of them took the downed Frenchman by his boots and pulled and jerked until his right arm dropped down from the chimney and his shoulders came unstuck from the hearth. When they dragged him free of the steaming embers, Paco picked up a canteen lying next to a saddle on the floor, opened it and poured the contents over the Frenchman's singed and smoking head. A smell of burned hair loomed.

"Oh, God . . . *thanks* . . . Paco!" Sibott managed to say in a raspy voice between coughing and gasping for breath. "I—I thought I was . . . going to be . . . roasted alive!"

"You would have been, you fool," Paco said. "But don't thank me, Bert, it was Fast Larry here who poured water on you and put out the flames."

"He—he did?" Sibott looked puzzled by such an act of mercy coming from an opponent. He looked at Shaw, who had walked over, picked up his gun belt, buckled it around his waist and tied the rawhide string around his thigh. Through watering red-streaked eyes the Frenchman rasped, "Shaw . . . much obliged. I—I don't know . . . what to say."

Shaw picked up his sombrero and looked at drops of coffee on its brim—coffee that had sprayed all the way from the mashed pot in the hearth. He brushed the drops off with his hand and set the sombrero loosely atop his head. Without replying he walked over, reached a hand down to the big Frenchman and helped him rise wobbly to his feet. As soon as Sibott turned loose of Shaw's hand he wiped a hand down his wet, scorched face and staggered a few feet to the table and slumped down onto a straight-backed chair.

"I never should have agreed to do this. It didn't feel right, me, a professional fighter taking advantage of a man much smaller than myself." He shook his big disheveled head in shame and added, "I'm sorry, Shaw."

Paco and Shaw gave each other a bemused look. "Don't mention it," Shaw said quietly.

To Paco, Sibott said, "What am I going to say when Madsen asks me about the fight?"

Paco and Shaw looked at each other again. Paco replied as he stared hard at Jones and Lying Earl, who stood watching through the doorway, "Tell him there was no fight. I will tell him the same thing, that I saw no fight. Which is the truth, *I didn't see any fight*. I only saw you fall into the fire," he added, hardening his stare at Jones and Earl. "Did either of you see a fight?"

"Well, no," Jones said, "come to think of it."

"No fight as far as I could see," Lying Earl added. "If you want to hear about a fight—"

"Shut up, Earl," said Jones.

"You'd do that for me?" Sibott asked Shaw. "Not let Madsen know what happened here?"

"I won't if you won't," Shaw said quietly. He turned a cold stare to Jones and Lying Earl. "If he hears about it we'll all know who told him."

"It won't be me," said Jones. He gestured toward Lying Earl and said, "Madsen won't believe nothing he tells him anyway."

"Then we all have a secret, don't we?" Shaw said, looking from one to the other.

"We sure do," said Jones, "and don't go thinking you need to kill us to keep us quiet, Bert," he said to Sibott. "I swear nobody is going to hear about it from us. You've got our word on it."

The three watched as Jones and Lying Earl backed away from the doorway, turned and disappeared out of sight. "What do you think, Paco?" Shaw asked.

"I think they are both too afraid of either of you to say anything unless Madsen presses them real hard," Paco said, liking the idea of Shaw asking for his opinion. He turned to Sibott and saw a new respect for him reflected in the big fighter's eyes. "And you," he said with authority, "if he asks you what happened, tell him you were on the way to find Shaw when you fell into a fire out back. I will say I saw you fall. All right?"

"All right." Sibott stood up, his eyebrows gone,

his shirt full of burn holes, his big lumpy face smudged and glistening with burns and blisters. "I— I owe you one, Fast Larry," he said sincerely.

Shaw only nodded.

Once Sibott was also out of sight, Paco said to Shaw, "If you're all through making new friends, I will finish showing you around the village."

"Yeah, let's go," Shaw said. He stepped toward the doorway and said, "Show me where the girl and her mother live."

Paco raised a dark eyebrow. "It will make no difference if I tell you that going there is a bad idea, will it?"

"Not a bit," Shaw replied.

"I thought not," said Paco, striding past him in order to lead the way.

As the two stepped out and walked along the dusty street, Shaw asked, "Who is Deacon Lucas?"

"So, you heard Madsen threaten the girl by telling her Deacon Lucas would take her home, eh?" Paco said.

"Yep, I caught that," said Shaw. "Who is he? Where will I find him?"

"He is not here right now, but he will be coming back any day," said Paco. "Deacon Lucas Leeman is the leader of the Leeman Gang. They started as scalp hunters for the Mexican government years ago, but now they ride the border with us."

"What kind of man is he?" Shaw asked, having heard of the Leeman Gang but wanting to hear Paco's opinion.

"Deacon Lucas is not a man, he is a low, rotten devil," Paco said, spitting as if to get the name Deacon Lucas out of his mouth. "I believe even Madsen fears him."

"Why is the girl so afraid of him?" Shaw asked, feeling as if he already knew the answer.

"Because she knows he wants to get his filthy hands on her, if he has not done so already. If he has not, I have no doubt he *will* do so before we leave here."

"Had you planned on doing anything to stop him when that happens?" Shaw asked bluntly.

After a silent pause, Paco said, "Yes, I will shoot him. I did not think about it before, but now that you bring it to mind, yes, I would have shot him already if I found he laid his hands on her."

"That's good to hear," Shaw said flatly.

"I mean it," said Paco. "I know that I have done nothing so far, but then, neither has he. If I caught him trying to harm the girl, by the saints I would stop him. This I swear to. That pig." He spat again.

Shaw looked at him. "So, me being here brings out your better nature, eh?"

Paco looked embarrassed, but then he smiled. "I must admit, I have thought little of the girl and her mother because this is how things are done in my land. The strong only take . . . the weak only give. This is why I live the life I live. I decided to be one of the ones who take, eh? Much like yourself?" He searched Shaw's eyes for some sort of approval. "Am I wrong to make such a choice, in a land where choices are so few?"

"Believe me, Paco," Shaw said, walking on, "I'm not the one to ask."

"I understand," Paco replied. He grinned as they

walked along, "I know it will be 'interesting' riding with you."

Only moments after Shaw and Paco had left the cantina, Madsen pushed his empty wooden cup away and told Turner, "I'm going to take care of some *personal* business." He gave Turner a knowing wink. "You and the boys drink up. I'll join yas later. Until then, I don't want to be disturbed."

Turner nodded. "But you'll want me to send for you if Deacon Lucas and his men show up?"

"Yeah, in that case, *be sure* and send for me," said Madsen, before turning and walking out the back door.

He walked through the littered alleyway with deliberation, a black cigar clamped between his teeth, his fits clenched loosely at his sides. When he arrived at the small adobe where Francisca and her mother lived, he didn't bother to knock. Instead he shoved the door open and barged in, knowing the fear his sudden presence caused in the woman. "Where is that little *nit* of yours?" he demanded, glaring at her, liking the startled look of terror that always came to her dark eyes at the sight of him.

"Who, Francisca?" The woman rose from the table and stood shakily, her face still bearing the painful reminders of his last visit.

"Hell yes, Francisca," Madsen said. "Who other little nit would I be talking about?"

"I—I don't know where she is," said the woman, looking all around as if the child might be hidden somewhere in the small, sparsely furnished room.

"She brought food from the cantina." She gestured at the basket sitting on the table. "But then she left again. Is something wrong?"

"Damned right there's something wrong," Madsen said gruffly. As he spoke he took off his hat and hung it on the wall peg inside the door, the spot where only her husband's battered straw sombrero used to hang. "She damned near got her stupid little head shot off a while ago. Didn't you hear the shooting, you stupid woman? Or were you too deep in enjoying another siesta?" he asked with contempt, unbuttoning his shirt as he spoke.

She didn't answer, because no answer would be the answer he wanted to hear; yet any answer could send him into a rage and make him beat her. Instead she bypassed his question and inquired cautiously about Francisca. "She was in danger? At the cantina?"

"What did I just say?" he replied gruffly, taking off his gun belt, draping it over a chair back. He jerked his shirttails from his trousers, unbuttoned his shirtsleeves and held his arms outstretched on either side. "A couple of my men were faced off against a killer who rode in off the desert. She warned him . . . stuck her nose right in where it didn't belong. I'm thinking about carrying her over and tying her to a post, leaving her there for Deacon Lucas when he gets back. He's been pressing awfully hard for her, you know."

Again, she knew better than to answer. He didn't want an answer. She had learned that much of what he said was only meant to frighten and torment her.

She knew why he was here and what he wanted from her. She also knew better than to resist. She stood waiting, dreading, knowing what came next.

"Get over here, Ramona," he demanded. "Take these clothes off me." He leered at her. "Mescal and tequila make me as randy as a range stallion."

She did as she was told. While she undressed him, Madsen looked down at her trembling hands and said in a kinder voice, "You've done all right by me, Ramona. Thanks to your *hospitality* I've seen to it that Nito has had the best food and care of any man in the mines." He grinned. "My work can be awfully demanding. Keep taking good care of me and I'll keep taking good care of Nito. In fact, I'll be bringing him home to you real soon."

"You—you will?" She dared not act too happy, show too much emotion.

"That's right," Madsen said. "I'm taking off the rest of what he owes me based on how well you take care of me these next few days." He grinned and pressed her down onto her knees in front of him. "Now put your heart into it and show a little appreciation."

Outside, the girl remained partially hidden by a stack of firewood she had ducked behind as soon as she'd spotted Madsen headed toward her house. She had seen what went on when he was there and the memory of it made her skin crawl. Besides, she reminded herself, after what had happened earlier at the cantina, it would be better to stay out of his sight. He was certain to be angry with her.

She stood crouched, watching the house so intently

that she did not see the gunman, Jake Matthews, until he had crept up close in the empty alleyway and grabbed her firmly by her shoulder. "Got you!" he said, turning her to face him so quickly that before she could bolt and run, he had managed to get an arm around her waist and pull her against him tightly.

"Let me go, please! Let me go!" she said, struggling, kicking and clawing at his chest.

He shook her roughly. "You best settle down. Don't make me cuff you around, little darling," he said with a dark chuckle, bowing his face close to hers. "What are you doing here, spying on your ma and Madsen?" He looked toward the small adobe, then down at Francisca with a drunken grin. She smelled his strong sour breath on her face. "You're wondering what's going on in there? Hell, I can show you, come here."

"Please, let me go! Stay away from me!" Francisca struggled, but to no avail.

"This won't take long," Matthews said in a slurred, drunken voice. He dragged her farther back behind the wood pile, fumbling with his trousers while the girl continued struggling against his grip.

"Turn her loose," Shaw said, he and Paco having hurried forward along the alleyway when they'd seen Matthews approaching the girl from behind.

"Yeah, who says?" demanded the gunman, turning toward them with the girl held tightly against his chest.

But before he got a good look at the two, Shaw's fist shot out and flattened his nose against his face.

The drunken gunman flew backward, releasing his

grip on the girl. He grabbed his gun, but before he could draw it, Paco stepped forward and clamped a boot down onto his wrist. "Shame on you, Jake," he said. "You better hope Quinn Madsen doesn't hear about this." He took his boot off the man's wrist slowly, allowing him to remove his hand from his gun and loosen a bandanna from around his neck.

"Damn it, I know it." The gunman hacked and gurgled, cupping his bleeding nose into his wadded-up bandanna. "I'm just drunk. . . . Can't you see that? You don't have to tell Madsen about it." He turned his eyes up to Shaw. "And you didn't have to break my nose, Fast Larry!"

"Next time I'll kill you," Shaw said flatly, holding the girl, who instead of running away, had thrown her arms around his waist for protection. "Get out of our sight," Shaw added, letting the girl hide her face against him.

Seeing Shaw's hand poised near his gun butt, Matthews raised his gun hand in submission. "Okay, okay, I'm gone." Without another word he eased away a few cautious steps, then turned and hurried away, cursing under his breath.

"Are you all right?" Shaw asked.

Instead of answering she nodded her head and clung to him, her thin arms wrapped tightly around his waist. Shaw gave Paco a look. Then he reached down and gently but firmly pulled her arms from around him. "Young lady, I was just on my way to your house, to thank you for saving my life."

"You cannot go there," the girl said, "nor can I." She gave a look of loathing and shame toward the adobe. "Not while *he* is there. Not until the devil is finished with what he does to her."

Shaw glanced toward the adobe, then looked at Paco. The Mexican only gave him a shrug of helplessness.

"Take my mother and me away with you, Senor Angel, please," the girl pleaded. "I beg of you."

"I'm afraid I can't do that, child," Shaw said, patting the top of her head gently as she clung to him.

"Then kill him for us," the girl sobbed. "Please kill him for us. It is what I have prayed for you to do. . . . My mother and I both have prayed for you to come here and kill him for us. This is why you are here! To kill this devil!"

"Careful what you say, little girl," Paco warned her, letting his words also serve as a reminder to Shaw that he rode for Madsen.

Shaw understood. He stared down into her tearful dark eyes, beginning to get a glimpse of what was going on in her mind. "No," he said with gravity, "killing Madsen for you is not why I'm here. You have this all wrong. I'm no angel. I'm not the answer to anybody's prayers. I rode here to gather supplies and water my horse. Anything else that's happened was just coincidence. Do you understand me?"

The child only stared up at him.

No, she did not understand, Paco thought, watching in silence, seeing something at work here, something that he knew instinctively could bring trouble for him if he wasn't careful. There were dark places in his new *friend* Shaw, places filled with pain and regret. He wasn't sure if Shaw was a troubled man searching for some spark of goodness left in this stark desert world, something to make him want to continue living. Or, he wondered, seeing the child look up at Shaw with eyes full of hope, was *the Fastest Gun Alive* only searching for something worth dying for?

Shaw looked to Paco for help, a way to make the girl understand and give up any foolish notions she had of him. But Paco only shrugged and shook his head.

After a moment of silence, Shaw peeled the girl's arms from around him and asked, "What is your name, young lady?"

"Francisca," she replied quietly.

"Well, Francisca," Shaw said, glancing in the direction of the cantina, where music and drunken laughter spilled out onto the street, "this is not a good night for a young lady to be out on your own. Is there a place where you stay when you can't go home?"

"*Sí,*" Francisca said. "I have a place where I go when I cannot go home." She pointed toward a weathered cross standing above the rooftops at the far end of the village.

"Well then," Shaw said, "if you'll allow me, I'd be honored to escort you to church." As he spoke he took off his hat in a gesture of courtship.

"*Gracias,* Senor Angel," the girl replied, taking his forearm.

Paco remained a step behind them as the two walked along in the grainy evening light.

Chapter 6

On their way along the dusty alleyway, Francisca looked up at him and said, "When I told my mother that I saw the angel we had been praying for, she looked out and saw you and said that you are no different than the other men who ride with Madsen and the deacon. That I should stay away from you. But I told her she was wrong." She gave Shaw a soft, hopeful smile.

"I think you should listen to your mother, Francisca," Shaw said. Paco walked along behind them, listening in silence.

"I told her that I saw your wings as you rode off the desert floor," Francisca said without seeming to hear him try to dissuade her.

"My wings?" Shaw looked puzzled.

"I know what she saw," Paco offered, stepping up on the other side of the girl. "In the heat and wind, your poncho looked like wings batting at your sides." He gave a thin, sly grin. "To us you looked like a demon from hell." Referring to the three men

Shaw had killed, he added, "To Bo Phelps, Cero and Layton, you *were*."

Ignoring what Paco said about him killing the three men, Shaw said to the girl, "Hear that? Paco and the others saw me as a demon. You saw me as an angel. I expect people see what it is they want to see."

"I saw the angel we have all prayed for, and that is what you are," she said firmly, looked straight ahead as she walked on.

Shaw stopped her, stared down at her and said, "Look at me, Francisca. How old are you?"

"Before this summer ends I will be fourteen years old," she said, turning her eyes up to him, looking at him with conviction, knowing he was out to change her mind. "My mother says it is then that I will become a woman."

"Then you're old enough to know that there are no angels traipsing around out there in the desert sand," Shaw said, not wanting to be harsh, but not wanting her to fool herself about him.

"That is also what my mother told me when we spoke about you," Francisca replied.

"Your mother told you right," Shaw said.

"Then what they have taught me is not true?" She gestured toward the weathered cross standing atop the small church.

Shaw felt pressured for a way to answer. "It's not that it isn't true, it's just that . . . it's not the way things are. It's the way we might like for things to be."

"If it is not the way things are, that is the same as it not being true." She stared at him.

He looked again to Paco for help. Again Paco only looked away.

"I'm sorry, Francisca," Shaw said, gesturing her forward toward the church. "These are questions that I can't answer for you."

When they arrived at the small room attached to the rear of the church, Francisca knocked quietly and stood facing the door until it creaked open and an aged priest stood holding on to it for support. Looking first at the girl and then at Shaw and Paco flanking her, he asked in a weak and ill-sounding voice, "Child, what are you doing with these two?"

"Padre, this is the angel I told you about," Francisca said, motioning toward Shaw. "Can we come in?"

"Angel?" The old priest looked both Shaw and Paco up and down, a skeptical expression on his pale, drawn face. "Child, you must stop this foolishness. This man is no angel, he is a murderer." His gaze fixed on Shaw. "I watched from the rooftop as he killed three men in the street today." He moved his gaze to Paco. "And this one, he rides with the desperados! I have seen him many times with them. Shame on you," he blurted at Paco with a cold stare. "You are one of us, and yet you reject us and ride with these desperados."

"*Sí,*" Paco said, stepping forward, "I ride with these men. I will ride with them so long as it suits me. I do so without your permission, and without accepting your judgment of me, old one." His hand grasped his gun butt instinctively. But then he caught himself and stood back.

"Padre, please," Francisca said quickly, "Senor Angel was kind enough to bring me here."

"Senor Angel indeed," the old priest said, his weak voice seeming to find strength in his anger.

Ignoring the old priest's manner, Shaw stepped forward and cut in, saying, "Padre, I didn't come here to argue with you. The streets are not safe for a young girl alone tonight. Francisca can't go home just now." He gave the old priest a knowing look.

"Enough," the old priest said with a wave of his ancient hand. "I know why she cannot go home. It is because one of your kind has destroyed her family. This is the sort of thing men like you bring to our doorsteps."

"I only arrived today, Father," Shaw said. "I brought nothing to your doorstep. When I leave, I hope to leave your doorstep in the same manner."

"Three men you have killed!" The old priest held up three knotted fingers. "Death is what you brought. Murder is what you brought!"

"Death, yes," Shaw said in a mild tone. "But not murder, Father." He shook his head slowly. "Those men wanted to kill me. I killed them first. Is that murder?"

"Murder or not, what you did is a *sin*," the priest retaliated.

"What would you have had him do, Padre, let them kill him without defending himself?" Paco cut in and asked, Shaw not seeming interested one way or the other in what the priest had to say on the matter.

"With faith, God would have protected him," the priest said.

"Ah, I see," Paco said, leaning in closer, right in

the old priest's face. "God protects those of us fortunate enough to have such faith. But for us less fortunate whose faith is lacking, we must stand up and protect ourselves."

"Blasphemer! Get away from this holy place!" the old priest shouted angrily. "This is God's house and you defile it." He hurriedly pulled Francisca inside. To Shaw he said in a harsh tone, "If you *were* an angel, as this poor child thinks you are, you would go! You would ride away, leave our village and allow God to work things out for us as he sees fit!"

"Please don't go, Senor Angel!" Shaw heard Francisca cry out just before the door slammed in his face.

"Well," Paco said with a slight chuckle, "I have done my job showing you around. You have seen both the good"—he gestured a hand toward the closed door of the church, then in the direction of the cantina, where music and laughter loomed above the street—"and the evil. What do you think?"

"I think it would be hard for one to get along without the other," Shaw said. He turned from the door of the church and walked away in the darkening night.

Walking beside him, Paco said, "Believe me, if you were to go in and kill Quinn Madsen tonight, it would not solve the girl's and her mother's problem, it would only change it. The mother would be free from Madsen, but her husband would be dead."

"I wasn't thinking about killing him," Shaw said. "But it appears the thought might have crossed your mind."

"Me?" Paco grinned. "No, amigo, I have not

thought about killing Madsen. I ride with him for *money*, and I mean for *big* money. It would be foolish for me to think about killing him, even if I *could*."

"Where does Madsen keep the girl's father?" Shaw asked quietly.

After a silent pause as Paco looked all around the encroaching darkness, he said, "The man's name is Nito Gomez. Madsen owns interest in the Luzzo tin mines fifty miles east of here in the hills. He had Nito taken there to work off some trumped-up debt he claims the man owes him." He paused again, then said, "It is an old game the Spanish dons used to play with their peasants. The husband is no more than a prisoner. He cannot leave. Yet Madsen tells the woman he will keep the husband fed and well treated so long as she submits herself to whatever he wants from her. It brings shame to the family, and in the end the husband always dies."

Shaw looked at him. "Sounds like you've given all this some thought."

"*Sí*, perhaps," Paco conceded with a slight shrug. "But I am sure Madsen has told the man that if he tries to escape his wife and daughter will be killed. So there is no way out for any of them."

"Not so long as Madsen is alive," Shaw offered. "The girl is right. Somebody needs to kill Madsen."

"Yes," Paco agreed. "But not one of us. Much better if the angel she prays for *does* ride in off the desert floor and kill him." He grinned.

"Yeah, some desert angel," Shaw said, gesturing back toward the weathered church, "not a couple of *sinners* like us." The two walked on in the darkness toward the light of the cantina.

"No, my friend," Paco agreed, sounding relieved, "it is not a job for sinners like us."

After a silence Shaw asked, "Do you still think it would be interesting riding with me?"

Paco smiled, staring straight ahead. "Not only will it be interesting," he said. "I believe it might be a little dangerous." He paused, then said, "You have something in mind regarding the girl and her mother, eh?"

"That's right," said Shaw. "I'm going to take a little ride for a couple days. I want you to cover for me while I'm gone."

Paco hesitated. "I know where it is you go. You go to free Nito and reunite him to his family, all this because the girl thinks you are an angel."

"Yeah," Shaw said in a wry tone, "I've always wondered how it feels, being an angel."

"And you want me to lie for you?" Paco added. "Cover for you while you ride to the mines?"

"Yep," said Shaw.

"You ask so much from one who hardly knows you. Why do you think I would do that, risk my neck for you?"

"Because you've been seeing what goes on with the child and her mother, and you've wished yourself that some angel would ride in and do something for them."

Paco let out a breath. "I hope you are not about to do something that will get me killed."

Julimez, Mexico

The face of Wild Dick Bernie appeared briefly in the darkened open window until a rifle shot ex-

ploded from across the empty street and sent a bullet
thumping into the adobe. "Damn it," he shouted,
dropping down out of sight. "Why doesn't Deacon
come on with our horses?" Five feet away on the dirt
floor a half-naked prostitute lay dead in a pool of
blood. Near her side lay a naked outlaw named Orville Nolan. Dark blood surged from his gaping
mouth as his body twitched and struggled against
death's cold embrace.

On the dirt floor, a gunman named Sonny Engles
looked at the third gunman and said, "Tell him,
Hatch."

Morgan Hatch levered a fresh round into his rifle
chamber and said, "Deacon ain't coming, Wild Dick.
They've left us jackpotted." In a far corner two other
young prostitutes huddled with their arms around
each other, sobbing in terror.

"The hell?" said Wild Dick. "I've never known
Deak to jackpot a man."

"This law posse has dogged us nearly a full week,"
said Hatch. "Deacon's had plenty of time to decide
who to give to them while him and Charlie Bone and
Blackie save their own skin."

"I just don't believe it," Wild Dick persisted. "Bone
or Blackie maybe, but not Deacon Lucas." Another
rifle shot exploded from across the dark street. The
bullet sliced through the open window above Wild
Dick's head and thumped into the far wall.

"Oh?" said Sonny. "In that case, you tell us where
our damn horses are. We've been pinned here too
long. Deacon and Bone have hightailed it on us."
Two more shots resounded.

"We never should have left our horses so far away," said Wild Dick. He brooded for a moment, then relented and said, "Maybe they did jackpot us, but this is not the time to jaw about it. What do we do now?"

"We grab these whores for cover, shoot our way out of here and keep moving," said Morgan Hatch. The two women in the corner jabbered and sobbed more intently upon hearing his words. "The longer we wait here, the worse this little shindig is going to get." He rose onto a knee, fired a quick shot out through the window and ducked back down as a volley of rifle fire responded. "I don't know about you two, but I'm about as mean as a damn rattlesnake when I'm cornered," he said with bold defiance. As he spoke he raised a Colt from its holster, checked it and put it away.

Wild Dick and Sonny Engles looked at each other in the blue darkness. "Hell yes, so am I," said Sonny.

Wild Dick levered a fresh round into his rifle chamber and said, "Me too, let's let 'er buck."

Hatch looked over at the two frightened young women and said, "Girls, we're going to have to impose on yas to help us out here. . . ."

Outside in the darkness across the empty street, Lon Bixby watched the surrounded adobe building as he spoke to one of the seven men lined along the street beside him. "We shouldn't be doing this at night."

"Oh? What are you, Lon, an Apache now? You don't fight at night?" said Odell Macky.

"Maybe the Apache knows something that we don't," Bixby countered. "Anyway, I'd feel better if we waited until Dawson and his deputy show up."

"Damn it, Lon, there's seven of us here, eight counting Jimmy Peck," said Odell Macky. "We're all primed and loaded. I'll be plumb ashamed to face Dawson and his man if they see us hunkered down here like a pack of rabbits. Let's flush them out. We've already started the fight with them. They know we're here."

After a moment of tense silent contemplation, Lon Bixby rose and said, "Boys, let's put it to a vote."

"A *vote*?" Macky said in disbelief.

"Hell yes, a vote," Lon replied indignantly. "It was the way our forefathers did things. It was good enough for Ben Franklin. It's damn well good enough for me." He stood up more and looked along the line of men lying behind firewood, water troughs and shipping crates. "I want everybody who thinks we should charge in and take these men on our own to signify by saying—"

His words stopped short as a bullet ripped through his forehead.

"My God, Lon's dead!" Mason shouted, wiping Bixby's warm blood from his eyes as the three outlaws came spilling from the adobe, their rifles blazing in the darkness, the young women screaming as the gunmen held them tightly to their chests.

"Don't shoot, they've got hostages!" one posse man shouted. But in spite of his words, along the street the other posse men returned fire as the three gunmen hurried along the street toward the hitch rail where they had left their horses.

Seeing the empty hitch rail awaiting them in the pale moonlight, Hatch shouted above the gunfire, "The horses are gone!" He shoved the limp, blood-slick body of one of the prostitutes away from him and fired back toward the riflemen.

"What now?" shouted Sonny, the young woman screaming and struggling madly against his chest as he returned fire with bullets zipping past them.

Wild Dick bellowed loudly and began a crazy broken dance as bullets nipped and sliced at him.

Grabbing the badly wounded gunman and giving him a shove, Hatch shouted to Sonny, "We take *these* sons a' bitches' horses!"

Seeing the men and their remaining hostage head for the posse's horses standing between two buildings a block away, Odell Macky shouted as he fired, "They're going for our horses! Stop them! Give Jimmy some help!"

In the alleyway between the two buildings, a young man named Jimmy Peck fired bravely at the charging gunmen while he held the reins to the posse's horses wrapped together in his gloved hand. But he was no match for the desperate outlaws. A bullet from Hatch's big Colt slammed into his chest and sent him sprawling back among the frightened animals, his hand still gripping their reins, the horses spooked, on the verge of bolting away.

"Get on!" shouted Hatch, grabbing the reins to two horses from Peck's dying hand and shoving Wild Dick up onto a saddle.

Sonny pushed the screaming young woman away from him and grabbed the reins to two of the horses as the others streaked past him. "You are one lucky whore!" he shouted at the young woman, who huddled down into a ball against the side of the building. He turned and fired at the posse men, who had stood up from their cover and come running forward, firing wildly in an attempt to save their horses.

"Can you shoot?" Hatch asked Wild Dick, who lay forward, holding on to his saddle horn, his chest, back, shoulder, legs and head covered with blood. The upper half of one ear had been sliced off by a bullet graze. "It looks like you took the brunt of it."

"I did, but hell yes, I can shoot!" shouted Wild Dick, bullets nipping against the walls and zipping through the air around him. "Give me a good slap and stand back!"

"See you in hell, then," Hatch bellowed, slapping the horse solidly on its rump.

As the animal bolted away amid a volley of rifle fire, Wild Dick wobbled in his saddle and fired steadily toward the oncoming posse men. "Come on, Hatch, damn it!" shouted Sonny, throwing the reins of one of the horses into Hatch's hand.

Hatch leaped up into the saddle and started to bolt away. But then he stopped and looked at Sonny as bullets sliced through the air close to his head. "To hell with them. I'm taking down as many of them as I can!"

"Are you loco?" shouted Sonny. But before the words left his mouth he saw Hatch slap the horse's rump with his rifle barrel and send the horse straight into the rifle fire.

"Hell, why not?" Sonny growled under his breath. He nailed his spurs to the animal's side and raced out into the fray, his Colt blazing in his hand.

Chapter 7

Odell Macky stood in the middle of the street watching the two horsemen come charging toward him from behind exploding blossoms of gunshots. "My God, does nothing stop these devils!" he whispered to himself. The dark street had become lit by streaks and flashes of gunfire coming from either end. At the far end of the street, Wild Dick had stopped and looked back, realizing that Morgan Hatch and Sonny Engles had turned and ridden into the fight. Lying limply forward, hanging on to his saddle horn, he said in a rasping voice, "Boys, you ain't leaving me to die like a gut-shot dog."

On the street, a bullet from Hatch's gun hit Macky high in his shoulder and spun him in a full circle before flinging him backward off his feet. A posse man named Ed Whitfield rushed over in a crouch, grabbed Macky by his coat collar and began dragging him to cover as the two charging outlaws bore down upon them.

"Sa-save yourself, Ed," Macky said, his boot heels plowing two long streaks in the dirt behind him.

As a bullet whistled past Whitfield's head, he stopped dragging Macky long enough to return fire toward the coming horsemen and said, "I fear I'm unable to save either of us, Odell."

No sooner had he spoken his words than a wild bullet from the remaining posse men lifted him out of his crouch and slammed him to the dirt. Above Macky, Hatch stormed past, the horse's hooves coming dangerously close to slamming down on the wounded man's chest. Only a second behind Hatch, Sonny Engles raced along. Lying off onto his horse's side, Lakota-style, he fired from under the horse's neck, shrieking out a war cry.

Under the fierceness of the two outlaws' attack, the posse men ceased firing and fled the wide-open street for cover. One, a former Pinkerton detective, stood his ground until a bullet from Engles punched through his heart and flipped him backward. Another posse man ran into the firelight of a street torch just long enough for both Hatch and Engles to see him clearly. Hatch jerked his rifle around toward the man, but before he got off a shot, a bullet from Engles' Colt nailed the man in his back.

"Lord! It's like fighting the savages!" said a wounded posse man, seeing Engles streak past in the shadowy darkness.

"Kill 'em all, Sonny!" shouted Hatch, sliding his horse down to a halt and spinning it around in order to ride back through the posse men again. Engles came right behind him, straightening up in his saddle. "Are you hit?" Hatch asked, holding his horse back for a second, just long enough to check on the other outlaw. On the street the firing had stopped.

"Yeah, but not bad," said Engles, slinging blood from his left hand, blood that had run down from the bullet hole in upper arm. "You?"

"A couple nicks," said Hatch, levering his rifle one-handed, ready to get back into the fight. "I'll make it."

The two started to spur their horses forward at the same time. But before they got the chance, a voice called out from the darkness between two adobe buildings, "We've had enough! We give up."

Hatch and Engles looked at each other in surprise. Engles gave a dark chuckle. "The hell is he talking about?"

"You can't *give up*, you sons a' bitches!" Hatch called out to the dark silent street. "This is not a kids' game."

"Ride away," the same voice called out, trying to sound strong, but not doing a good job of it.

The outlaws sat in silence for a moment; then Hatch called out, "We've killed all of yas, ain't we?"

"No," the voice said, "there's still some of us left."

"If there is, they're wounded all to hell," Engles said quietly. "Let's ride back and finish them off. This is too good to let go of."

Hatch spat and considered it. "What about Wild Dick? Did you see him anywhere back there?"

"Naw, I didn't see him," said Engles. "I think he was too shot up to make the run with us. I think he probably rode on. He was in bad shape, last I saw him."

Back along the street, the two heard Wild Dick let out a rebel yell. "That's him now!" said Engles, the two staring stunned at streaks of gunfire zipping off right and left while they heard hooves pounding along the middle of the street.

Engles laughed and shouted loudly, "Give 'em hell, Wild Dick!" Only a few return shots resounded from along the edge of the street. As soon as Wild Dick rode past wobbling in his saddle, the street fell silent behind him.

"Easy," said Hatch as the hoofbeats drew closer. "The shape he's in, he might start shooting at us."

"Not a chance," said Engles. He called out, "Over here, Wild Dick."

A gunshot exploded; the bullet whistled through the narrow space between the two outlaws. Hatch jerked his horse to the side. "I told you," he said to Engles.

"Damn it, Wild Dick, it's us!"

The hoofbeats slowed to a quick walk; the horse circled into sight in the grainy darkness. "Pards, I'm sorry," said Wild Dick, "I can't see shit for all this blood." He wiped a bloody hand over his bloody eyes.

"Aw, man," said Engles, looking at Dick Bernie, who sat covered with blood, "he's ruined."

"I'm not ruined," Wild Dick said, his voice sounding pained and weakened from loss of blood.

"Yep, we've got to get him patched up before he bleeds out on us," said Hatch.

"Ah, hell, listen to you," said Dick, batting his bloody eyes, looking back and forth, trying to locate Hatch from the sound of his voice. "All I need is some mescal and a little rest. I'm a West Texas bearcat, pards. We don't topple over easily."

"There he goes," said Engles, watching the wobbling gunman pitch out of his saddle and land face-down in the dirt.

"Ah, hell, see if his heart's beating," said Hatch, seeing Engles step down and hurry over to the downed gunman. He stared back toward the dark street and said over his shoulder to Engles, "Well, is he alive?"

"Yeah, but he's sliding off. We've got to slow down this bleeding."

"Yeah, I see that," said Hatch. Then he called out to the dark, silent street, "Listen to me, posse man. You want to live, you get your ass out of town now!" He paused, listened, then followed up. "Do you hear me? Clear out, else we'll shoot you out!"

"Give us five minutes! We've got wounded," said the same voice that had been speaking all along.

"You've got three minutes," said Hatch, "and I ain't carrying a watch."

"We're going," said the voice. "But there's two wounded men here that can't be moved. They need tending. I won't leave them unless I know they'll get tended to. I need to hear somebody's word on it."

"All right," said Hatch, "you've got our word on it. They'll get tended to. Now get going, before we change our minds and make another *charge*." As he said the word "charge," he looked over at Sonny Engles with a grin of satisfaction.

On the dark street, the posse man, Randall Wynn, who'd been talking to Hatch stepped inside an adobe building where a candle glowed on its wooden stand. Looking down at two wounded men who lay on the floor against a wall with a bloody body staring up blankly between them, Wynn tried putting on a cheerful face and said, "Fellows, I've got good news."

"Are you . . . being funny?" a former railroad detective named John Willis asked grimly, blood running from the corner of his lips.

"No, not at all," Wynn said, getting rid of his cheerful expression. "But listen to this. They gave me their word. They'll get you both tended to just as soon as I ride out of here."

Willis coughed wetly and said through the bubbling blood on his lips, "Ride . . . out? You're going to . . . run off, leave us?"

Hearing his skeptical tone, Wynn said, "Fellows, I don't want to go, but I've got to go. I have to find Dawson and his deputy and get us some help here."

"We're dead, soon as you give us over to them," Willis said with resolve, staring at Wynn.

"No, no, no, I don't think so," Wynn insisted, patting the wounded man on his forearm. "There's no reason for them to lie about it. We put some bullets in them as well. All they want to do now is get patched up and get going. You'll be okay, I'm certain of it."

"Believe what . . . you need to believe," said Willis.

"Hot damn . . . you've . . . killed us, Wynn," said the other man, Ray Studdard, who lay with the muscle of his upper arm shot out and dangling bloodily onto his bare forearm. Two gaping holes in his bloody bare chest had been stuffed with the twisted corners of a bandanna.

"Ray, don't judge me for doing this," said Wynn, blood running down his left arm. "I'm hurt too . . .

and I'm all that's left standing." He rubbed his forehead anxiously. "I—I never seen anything like them in my life, and I fought against the heathen Sioux!"

"Don't credit them for . . . more than they're worth," said Willis, coughing as he spoke. "Like as not we all killed one another . . . out in the dark . . . cross-firing on each other." He managed to shake his head in disgust. "Most awful . . . mess I ever seen."

Wynn shook his head too. "Anyway, I'm sorry, I just can't do us any good here." He looked at the body lying between the two men, the gaping head wound, brain matter bulging, the dead blank eyes, a startled look on the dead man's face. "I'm only human." He swallowed the urge to vomit, and looked away, tears filling his frightened eyes.

Willis coughed up more blood and said, "Then get . . . your *human* ass . . . out of here. We know how . . . to die. Right, Ray?"

Ray Studdard spoke as if hearing them from some distant place. "I'll be in Illinois . . . near the creek . . . there at Pa's old place."

"What'd he say?" Wynn asked.

"He said to get the hell going." Willis coughed and rasped, growing weaker. "This is the most awful . . . mess I've ever gotten into," he repeated. "How'd they beat us, Wynn? How the hell . . . did they do this to me?"

"I—I don't know," said Randall Wynn, standing, backing away toward the door, no longer able to bear the sound of the wounded men's voices, the terrible sight of them.

*   *   *

As the sound of hooves faded away at the far end of town, Morgan Hatch and Sonny Engles put their horses forward at a cautious walk, Engles leading Wild Dick's horse by its reins. Wild Dick lay draped across his saddle like a dead man, sand caked on his bloody face from when he'd fallen to the ground. "That sounded like only one horse to me," Engles said, staring ahead into the distant darkness.

"I expect it was only one horse," Hatch replied. "If there was any number of them left, they wouldn't have given up." He chuckled under his breath, still amazed at the outcome of the gun battle.

Engles also chuckled. "I swear, I never heard of a posse trying to surrender. Have you?"

"No," Hatch said, his eyes scanning warily back and forth, his hand on his Winchester rifle, ready to raise it and fire if he had to, "but that doesn't mean it ain't happened." He paused, then added solemnly, "And we could still be riding into an ambush."

"I hear you," said Engles, growing serious again, the humor leaving his expression. his hand rested on the butt of the Colt in his holster. On the distant horizon, the first thin line of sunlight mantled a jagged hill line. He looked around at the bodies strewn on the ground.

In the grainy fading darkness they stepped their horses past bodies lying dead in the street. "Damn, we smoked them good," Engles said quietly.

"We couldn't have done all this," said Hatch. "These idiots must've shot the living hell out of one another."

"Far as I'm concerned we must've done all this,"

said Engles. "Maybe they splattered one another with a couple of stray shots, but damn, look at this." He gestured a hand around at the gory, bullet-riddled corpses. Turning in his saddle, he called out to Wild Dick, who looked more dead than alive, "What say you, Wild Dick? Did we burn a few down, or what?"

Wild Dick managed to squeeze out a deep mournful groan in reply.

"See?" Engles grinned. "Wild Dick agrees with me."

"I bet he does," said Hatch, veering his horse toward an open doorway, led there by two long smears of blood. He stepped down from his saddle and gestured toward the blood trails.

"I see them," Sonny Engles said quietly, also stepping down. He hitched his horse and wrapped the reins to Wild Dick's horse around his saddle horn.

The two drew their colts and stepped inside warily, hearing a labored cough through the open doorway where flies had begun to gather. "Don't . . . shoot, Mr. Hatch," John Willis murmured to Hatch in a weak and faltering voice. "We've neither one . . . got any fight left in us."

Hatch looked from Willis to Ray Studdard, his eyes going across the face of the dead man lying between them, seeing a fly walk across its blue lips. "How many are left in the posse?" he asked Willis. Studdard rolled his dazed eyes up at the sound of Hatch's voice. A string of red saliva bobbed from his chin.

"One," Willis said with a tone of regret and disgust.

"One?" Engles gave a bemused laugh. "Damn! What did I tell you, Hatch?"

Willis stared up into Hatch's eyes. "He said . . . you'd get us tended to?"

"Tended to? Sure enough," Hatch said dryly, "if that's what you want."

"You gave . . . your word," Willis rasped.

Hatch gave Engles a look. "Tend to them while I go get somebody to take care of Wild Dick."

"All right," said Engles. He cocked his Colt and stepped in closer to Willis as Hatch turned and walked out the door.

From out front Hatch heard Willis say to Engles, "You gave . . . your word."

"Oh, that," said Engles. "I think he was only funning."

Hatch heard the shot, then a short pause, then another shot as he stepped over and dragged Wild Dick down from across his saddle. "What's that?" Wild Dick asked in a pained voice, flinching at the sound of the gunshots.

"Just Sonny, making room for you," Hatch replied, looping the wounded outlaw's arm around his shoulder.

At the doorway, Hatch stepped to the side to allow Engles to drag the body of John Willis out into the street. "One coming in, more coming out," Engles said.

"Go around the *chozas*," said Hatch. "Find us a woman, one that knows how to clean and dress these wounds. We're not sticking around here. There's more law coming."

"I'm on my way," said Engles, ducking in past Hatch and Wild Dick, grabbing the body of Ray Studdard and dragging it out into the street. "I'll find the whore I grabbed earlier. She's quit shaking by now."

PART 2

PART 2

Chapter 8

U.S. Marshal Crayton Dawson looked down from the low hills east of Julimez. The village rooftops, glittering in early sunlight, had already begun to waver in the desert heat. "Whatever the shooting was, it's all over now," he said to his deputy, former undertaker Jedson Caldwell.

Deputy Caldwell stepped his horse over beside him and looked out and down onto the small gathering of adobes, huts, houses and outbuildings on an otherwise barren wasteland of sand, rock, brush and cactus. In the distance beyond Julimez a line of hills and mountains stretched as far as the eye could see, shrouded by rising heat and a silver-gray pall. "Maybe the posse fared better than we expected them to," he said. He pushed up his dusty, battered derby hat and crossed his hands on his saddle horn. The fingers of his black leather gloves had been cut at the knuckles, protecting only his palms.

"You really think so?" Dawson asked, looking him up and down, noting how the deputy's town clothes had gone to seed in these harsh Mexican desert badlands.

Caldwell sighed. "No, I'm just being optimistic. "We should have stayed together." As he spoke he glanced back at the three men in dark suits riding up to them. "The quicker these *gentlemen* are gone, the sooner we can go about doing things the right way, as far as I'm concerned." At the center of the riders sat Samuel Messenger, American consulate to the Mexican government. Flanking him were two members of his border command, Ripley Tunis and Grady Carr, both former Pinkerton detectives.

"Yeah," said Dawson, also glancing around at the approaching riders. "I've learned that *government* works better when *government* stays home. But I've got a feeling they're not going to leaving any time soon."

When Messenger brought his horse to a halt, he sat for a moment gazing out in the direction the gunfire had come from during the night. Finally he said, "Marshal Dawson, I'll be taking my leave this morning. Agents Tunis and Carr have agreed to stay down here with you for a time, to lend you both a hand. I hope you'll take advantage of having this top-notch additional manpower."

Dawson kept his voice as courteous as he could. "We're most obliged, sir," he said, "but there's no need in keeping them from going on carrying out their ordinary duties on our account."

The silver-haired Washington diplomat saw right through his attempted civility. Almost before Dawson had finished speaking, Messenger countered sharply, "All I heard both before and after the gun-fight at Hell's Gate is how badly you need help out here." He gestured a hand toward the two agents. "Well, here they are."

"Yeah," Dawson said guardedly, looking the two men up and down, "here we are."

"You're damned well right, here we are," Carr said with finality. He glared hard at Dawson.

"They know nothing about how things are down here," Dawson said bluntly, ignoring Carr.

"What we don't know, you'll find we learn in a hurry, Marshal," Tunis said with a haughty confidence.

"People die learning out here," Dawson said, not giving in on the matter.

"Enough." Messenger raised a hand to cease any further discussion. "I vouch for both of these men. They are two of the nation's finest." He paused for a moment in reflection, then said, "Of course I realize they are both *sober*, willing and able to carry out orders, unlike your *other* deputy. I hope that won't put them at a disadvantage in your estimation. I recall how greatly you welcomed the services of Quick Lawrence Shaw."

"He goes by *Fast Larry* Shaw, not *Quick Larry*," Dawson said, correcting him.

"Whatever," said Messenger. "Tunis and Carr *will* be riding with you for a time, and that's final. I need *reliable* reports on the situation down here."

Caldwell cut in. "Are you suggesting the reports we've been giving you haven't been *reliable*, sir?"

"I hope I didn't give that impression," Messenger

said dryly, giving the two agents a knowing glance.
"But I do have to say it will be refreshing to get a
report *in writing* for a change."

Changing the subject quickly away from written
reports, Dawson said, "Shaw was sober the whole
time he rode with us. We never would have come
out of that gun battle alive had he not gotten to Hell's
Gate ahead of us and done what he did."

"Yes, yes, of course," said Messenger in the same
dry skeptical tone, dismissing the matter with the
toss of a gloved hand. "Shaw was a virtual one-
man army."

"You're damn right he was," Dawson said, getting
more and more irritated at Messenger's smug re-
served manner. "I wish he was riding with us right
now." His eyes went across the two agents. "He's all
the help we would have needed. We would have
Lucas Leeman and these border raiders down over
their saddles this morning instead of riding down
there to see how many dead they left behind."

"Shaw is a drunken joke," said Grady Carr, a look
of defiance on his red moonlike face. "I'm sick of hearing what a top gunman he is. All that talk about being
the fastest gun alive sounds like something he dreamed
up on his own, to keep him in drinking money."

"He *is* a top gunman," Dawson shot back at him.
"Only a coward and a braggart shoots his mouth off
about a man who's not standing in front of him."

"Which are you calling me, Marshal?" the big red-
faced lawman asked, stepping his horse closer to
Dawson.

"Take your pick," Dawson said in a harsh tone,
not backing an inch.

The two glared hard at each other, but Messenger cut his horse in between them before the argument could build any further. "Gentlemen, there'll be plenty of fighting to go around when you catch up to Deacon Lucas. Save it for the raiders," he said with authority.

"Yes, sir," Dawson said grudgingly, without turning his eyes from Carr right away.

"As far as Shaw goes," Messenger continued, "I don't give a damn if he's the *fastest* gun alive, or the *drunkest* gun alive. I've seen him fit both images. Either way, he disappeared on us. So forget him."

"He's out there somewhere," Caldwell said. "Don't write him off just yet."

"Right," Messenger said with sarcasm. "Shaw only joined us long enough to satisfy his personal vendetta against Titus Boland. Otherwise, he couldn't have cared less whether or not we took down Sepreano and the Barrows Gang."

Caldwell continued. "I still say, had he known there was more fighting to be done he wouldn't have left us—"

"Let it go, Jed," Dawson said quietly, cutting his deputy off. "Shaw did what he thought you wanted done, Messenger. If you want his badge back, I'll see to it he turns it in if we come across him. I doubt he's given that deputy badge much thought one way or another."

"Thank goodness it's only made of simple tin," said Messenger. "I'm certain if it had any value he would have traded it for whiskey by now." The two agents chuckled darkly at Messenger's remark.

Dawson looked away, out across the wavering

heart toward the village, in order to cut short the conversation about Lawrence Shaw. He and Shaw had been friends for too many years for him to listen to strangers belittle the man. "Are we ready to ride out there, see what's left of this place?" He nodded in the direction of Julimez.

Messenger sighed and slumped in his saddle for a moment, then said, "I'm needed in Matamoros. I'll be turning back right here. But yes, ride on. Your directive is to pursue these men until you have either *dispatched* them adequately, or they lead you on to Quinn Madsen and the rest of his gang."

"Don't worry," said Dawson, "as soon as we cross paths with them, they will be *adequately dispatched*." He touched his hat brim toward Messenger and nudged his horse forward. Caldwell swung his horse in beside him.

"Are they going to be too difficult for you two to deal with?" Messenger asked.

"We'll get along just fine, Samuel," Tunis said, daring to reply on a first-name basis, just to show Carr that he and Messenger went back a long way together. He turned his horse toward Dawson and Caldwell. "Carr here might have to whip them into shape, but I think they'll do well once we instill a little Washington discipline in them."

"Good luck," said Messenger. He backed his horse a step and added before they rode away, "If you do run across that drunkard Shaw, feel free to make it perfectly clear that the government neither wants nor needs his help any longer, if you get my meaning."

Carr looked back at him and nodded with a flat grin. "I get your meaning, sir. Don't worry, we'll find a way to make it very clear to him. I've never been too impressed by big-name gunslingers."

When the four men stopped their horses at a low sandy rise, seven hundred yards from the village, Tunis gave Carr a guarded look. With the trace of a smug grin he said to Dawson, "You know, Messenger didn't really make it clear just which one of us is to be in charge out here."

Sensing the agent was up to something, Dawson replied, "Do you suppose he had a reason for doing that?"

Tunis said, "I've known the man a long time. I've never seen him do anything without a good reason."

Dawson went along with the game, saying, "Maybe it slipped his mind."

"Slipped his mind?" Both agents chuckled. "That's most unlikely, Marshal," Tunis said. "I sort of know the way he thinks. I figure he decided that cream really does rise to the top. He figures whichever one of us proves himself most worthy is going to be the one the rest of just naturally want to follow. Does that make sense to you?"

Caldwell cut in. "This has been Marshal Dawson's command all along. I see no need in it changing. Had Messenger and you two listened to him when the whole posse had these men in our sights two days ago—"

"Never mind, Deputy," Dawson cut in. "Let's hear what Agent Tunis has to say before we discount him." He looked at Tunis and said, gesturing toward the village lying ahead, "Let's hear how you propose we approach Julimez?"

Tunis offered a slight grin. "Well now, let's see, Marshal," he said mockingly as if giving it long and serious thought. "A big decision like that I want to be sure I get it right." His mocking demeanor changed quickly. In a no-nonsense manner he said, "Don't treat me like I'm a fool, Dawson. There are no raiders left in Julimez, Marshal, no posse men either. Deacon Lucas and his men have done their worst and moved on. The posse will be right behind them. If we didn't need water for our horses, we could likely bypass this pigsty altogether. We could swing wide of this village and catch up to the posse."

"I see," said Dawson. "What about the villagers?" He had more to say, but Tunis didn't give him the chance.

"We have no time to attend to the villagers, Dawson," he said. "They'll have to fend for themselves. I say we ride straight in, water our horses, get ourselves supplied and keep going. We'll soon catch up to the raiders again. Next time I'll do the honors of placing Deacon Lucas' head on a stick for you." He gave Carr a grin of satisfaction. "That's the way we've learned to do business."

"That's your whole plan, eh?" Dawson asked.

"Yep, you've heard it," said Tunis. "Have you got any objections to it?" he asked in a confrontational tone.

Dawson didn't respond. Instead he swung down from his saddle and said, "If it's all the same with you, I'll rest here a few minutes and be along shortly."

"It's all the same with me." Tunis shrugged, feeling as if Dawson had already relinquished command to him. "I appreciate a man who knows his limitations." He gave his horse a nudge with his spurs and rode forward.

Carr gave Dawson a smug look and rode away beside him.

No sooner had the two ridden a few yards than Caldwell said to Dawson, "This is not going to work. I'm not going to take orders from a man like Tunis. He knows nothing about this desert and these people. What did Messenger mean, sending these two out with us? What was his reasoning?"

"These government officials don't always make decisions based on sound reasoning," Dawson said. "Their like whores. They're only interest is in keeping the person above them happy."

"I understand," said Caldwell. "That makes me wonder if these two are any good at what they do, or did they just happen to know somebody who got them appointed to their jobs?"

"I don't know," said Dawson, "but I'd trade them both for just one good seasoned Texas sheriff from anywhere along the border." As he spoke he lifted a canteen that hung from his saddle horn.

Caldwell nodded, considering it. "Was that a good idea letting them ride in to Julimez that way? Things can be tricky down here for a couple of *americanos* who don't know their way around."

Dawson shrugged. "We'll just have to wait and see. You heard Agent Tunis, what they don't know they'll *learn in a hurry*." He uncapped his canteen and swished the tepid water around, determining its low level. Then he led his tired horse over beside a large rock and sat down.

Caldwell followed him. "Yes," he said, "I heard him. That's what has me concerned."

"Like it or not, it looks like we're stuck with them for a while," said Dawson.

"Yes," said Caldwell, "and like it or not, we've got to ride into Julimez for fresh water. These horses won't make it past Julimez to the next water stop." He also took down a canteen of tepid water from his saddle horn, shook it to gauge its contents, then sat down beside Dawson.

The two sipped water sparingly and sat in silence for a few minutes until the sound of gunfire drew their attention toward Julimez. "Sounds like they've arrived," Dawson said flatly. He stood up, capped his canteen and hung it back around his saddle horn. He stepped back to his saddlebags, took out a folded white flour sack and shook it out. "Let's go see what they've learned so far."

Chapter 9

Tunis and Carr had ridden toward Julimez with bold determination. Two hundred yards from the main street running the length of the town, a voice had called out to the two agents from behind a weathered, broken-down mule cart whose wheels lay buried in sand up to their axles. "Throw down your weapons and step down from your horses," the voice said in stiff English.

"Like hell," Carr replied. Both men drew their Colts. Carr fired a shot at the mule cart. His bullet sent a chunk of sun-bleached wood flying into the air. It also drew a heavy volley of gunfire, both pistol and repeating rifles, from behind the cover of cactus and low sunken rocks along a dry wash twenty yards to their left.

"Damn it, Carr!" Tunis shouted.

The pair spurred their horses and made a dash for town. But before they made it another hundred yards to the streets of Julimez, a second line of gunfire erupted toward them. This time they had to drop from their saddles and crawl quickly to a bald sunken rock, where they lay listening to bullets whistle past, inches from their heads.

"We were wrong, the raiders are still here!" Carr said in a frightened voice.

"No, you fool!" Tunis said sharply. "That's not Deacon Lucas and his men! If it was we'd be dead." He'd managed to snatch his rifle from his saddle boot before his horse bolted away.

"Then who the hell is it?" Carr asked. "It's sure as hell not the posse!"

"It's villagers—the town folks," said Tunis. He levered a round into his rifle chamber while he spoke. "This is why Dawson didn't ride in with us. He saw this coming. The son of a bitch let us ride right into it."

"Where the hell did these people get this kind of weaponry?" Carr asked without first thinking about it.

"Take one guess," said Tunis.

"Oh," said Carr, realizing the villagers had taken the weapons left by the dead. "But why are they shooting at us?" he asked. "What's got them so worked up?"

"Call it a hunch," said Tunis above the melee, "but after all that shooting last night, I expect they've had a bellyful of both the raiders and the posse chasing them."

"But it wasn't us," Carr insisted. "We haven't done anything to them."

"Keep that thought," said Tunis. "Maybe you'll be able to explain it to them." He rose only inches, just enough to get a quick glance at the terrain and fire a shot before dropping back down behind the rock as shots zipped past his face. Upon having seen the armed townsmen moving forward crouched low to the sand, he said, "On second thought, I don't think they're going to listen to anything we've got to say."

While the two lay pinned down by the advancing line of townsmen, Dawson and Caldwell slowly rode toward the first line of defense, who had turned and begun to close in on Tunis and Carr from behind. With the white flour sack tied to his rifle barrel, Dawson raised the Winchester and fired a shot in the air.

"Look at this, Mika," said one of the townsmen to a village elder as the armed townsmen turned around and stared toward the two riders seated beneath a white flag. "More of these gringo *bastardos*." He spat and started to raise a battered flintlock rifle to his shoulder.

"No, Fredo!" said Mika Endora, the village elder. "We must honor a white flag. We are not animals." He raised his voice loud enough for the others around them to hear.

"We are not animals, but they are," said the younger townsman. "You saw how they shot up our town, how they killed two innocent people."

"Yes, I saw what they did," said Mika. "But that was those men and the men chasing them. These two come in a show of peace. We will hear what they say. If they are like the others we will see to it they get what is coming to them." He looked toward the second line of townsmen, who were still firing on Carr and Tunis. With the wave of his arm back and forth slowly, the firing lulled, then stopped altogether.

Seeing the elderly Mexican bring the firing to a

halt, Dawson said sidelong to Caldwell, "Well, that's a pretty good sign." He nudged his horse forward at a slow walk. "Let's see how fast these two government *gentlemen* have learned not to rush into a town that's just been shot up all night by their fellow countrymen."

From their cover behind the low rock, Tunis and Carr quickly took note of the cease-fire. Tunis ventured a look back to where he spotted Dawson and Caldwell speaking to the elderly villager. "I'll be damned, it's Dawson and his deputy," he said, causing Carr to venture up beside him. "The marshal's waving a white flag."

Carr spat and said with sarcasm, "It looks like our U.S. marshal has surrendered us over to these peasant heathens. This is a fine image for us to be putting forward. What if word of this reaches the Mexican government? What if it reached people we know in Washington?"

"I don't give a damn about our image at the moment," Tunis said gruffly. "All I want right now is to get out from under these guns and get back on the trail."

But a full half hour passed before the elderly Mexican waved his arm to give his permission for Dawson and Caldwell to ride forward. Upon Mika's signal the Mexican townsmen eased back and allowed the two government agents to stand and meet Dawson and Caldwell as the two drew closer. On their way, Dawson took the reins to the agents' horses from a Mexican who had gathered the spooked animals. Arriving at the rock where Tunis and Carr stood brushing themselves off, Dawson handed them the reins. Without commenting on the incident that had just happened, Dawson said, "The posse and Luca's men shot it out last night, just like we suspected." His face took on a grim expression as he paused, then said, "The posse got wiped out."

"Wiped out?" said Tunis in disbelief. "What do you mean wiped out? You mean they got the worst of the figh—"

"I mean *wiped out*," Dawson said, cutting him off. "They're all dead." He gazed off into the distance. "They say one might have gotten away."

"Holy Joseph, only one man is still alive out of the whole posse?" Carr asked with a grimace.

"The wounded posse men that were left, the raiders killed in cold blood," Dawson said. He nodded at the horses. "Get mounted. It sounds like we've got ourselves a lot of burying to do."

Stepping into his saddle, Tunis looked all around as the elderly Mexican and the rest of the townsmen began gathering around them and heading for the streets of Julimez. "How the hell did you find all this out in this short time?" he asked Dawson under his breath. "How'd you keep them from shooting you both?"

Dawson didn't answer. Caldwell stepped his horse in close and said quietly, "It's all in how you treat people."

Carr gave the deputy a scorching look.

"Easy, Grady," Tunis warned Carr. "I've seen enough to know that we're walking on strange ground here. Let's both tread easy and get this job done."

Carr looked at him. "You sound like you're letting Dawson have charge."

"That's exactly what I am doing," Tunis said in a firm and serious tone. "We're not in Washington now." He nudged his horse forward and rode a few feet behind Dawson until they stopped on the main street and looked at the dead posse men lying in a row in front of the cantina.

Stepping down from his saddle, Dawson gestured back toward the elderly Mexican who led the towns-men onto the street behind them. "He said the gang split up when the posse got here. Deacon Lucas and some of his men rode away and left three of their pards to fend for themselves."

"Left his men to die," Tunis contemplated. "What kind of new wrinkle is that going to put on things?"

"Hard to say," said Dawson. "With them split up, it's going to be tougher on us chasing them down."

Tunis added, "But we'll have less guns aimed at us when we do."

"That's right," said Dawson, agreeing with him, noting how Tunis had seemed to settle down, as if he'd learned something important riding into the gun sights outside Julimez. "The next good water is going to be in Arajo, thirty miles across the flats. We need to press them just enough to keep them moving, but not so much that it keeps them on a killing spree."

"I say we go straight after Lucas, Charlie Bone and Blackie Waite. Forget the three they left behind until after we've finished with Deacon Lucas. He's the main snake we want."

"No," said Dawson. "For all we know this could all be a trap. We go after Lucas, these other three fall in behind us, pretty soon we're pinned down between them."

"Are you in agreement with him on this, Ripley?" Carr asked Tunis in a begrudging tone.

"That's right, I am," Tunis replied without a moment's hesitation. "I'm more interested in getting this job done than I am in who's in charge."

Before Carr could comment any further on the matter, Dawson said, "According to the old Mexican's description, these three sound like Wild Dick Bernie, Sonny Engles and Morgan Hatch. If that's so, we've got our hands full." He paused for a moment, then said, "Wild Dick is wounded. They have a woman with them, a young prostitute that Sonny Engles had held hostage. She cleaned and dressed all their wounds before they rode out with her."

"A hostage, eh?" said Tunis, considering it.

"I don't know for certain she's a hostage," said Dawson. "But unless something tells us otherwise, that's the way we'll play it."

Carr looked to Tunis for a response, having noted the way Tunis seemed more agreeable with Dawson.

"Yes, I understand," said Tunis. "Maybe she's a hostage, maybe she's a willing participant. We can't be sure." He looked around at the dead on the ground, grim reminders of what it cost to come up wrong or lacking against men like Deacon Lucas and the border raiders. "I suppose the sooner we get these posse men in the ground, the sooner we'll find out."

Twelve miles out of Julimez, two young German mine engineers had carried the body of their Mexican guide to a shallow grave they'd dug for him. They had been so attentive in their digging in the heat of the day that they hadn't noticed a high cloud of dust rising behind three riders approaching them from across the sand flats. When they finally did look up and see the horsemen riding in closer, one of them instinctively started to walk toward the wagon where he had leaned a long, ornately engraved rifle.

But as he neared the supply wagon a shot screamed in from one of the riders and thumped into the wagon's side rail, sending up a spray of dust and splinters. The young German stopped and stared out until the riders reined down only a few feet from him. Seeing the worried questioning look on the young German's face, Deacon Lucas Leeman gave a flat grin and said, "That would not be a neighborly thing to do, raising a gun on three unsuspecting pilgrims."

The young German stood erect and replied in an accent without apology, "I do as our guide, Pedro, has instructed us to do."

"Your guide, huh?" Deacon stood up in his stirrups and looked all around, seeing the other German and the body lying beside the grave. "Is that him on the ground?"

"Yes, he was bitten by a *winderside* rattlesnake two days ago. He could not recover."

"A *winderside* you say?" Deacon said mockingly, cutting a glance to Charlie Bone beside him. "They are rare in these parts." He gave a dark, short chuckle.

"He suffered," the German said, his English good but stiff and heavily accented.

"I'm broken up," Deacon replied flatly. As he spoke he gave a nod toward the other German.

Blackie Waite rode straight over and sat looking down at the swollen body for a moment.

"Hot damn, Luke, that snake filled him up good from the looks of him," Waite called out. Turning his attention to the German standing beside the body, Waite said cordially, "How are you today? Hot, ain't it?" He gestured a nod toward the short shovel standing beneath the man's right hand. "Drop it," he said.

The German raised his hand slightly and let the shovel fall to the sandy ground.

While Waite spoke to the other German, Charlie Bone circled his horse around the supply wagon and came back beside Deacon Lucas holding up a large half-full canvas water bag. "Look here, Deacon Luke," he said. He shook the canvas bag, sloshing the water around in it. "There's three more full ones too."

"Well, I'll be." Without taking his eyes off the young German, Leeman asked Charlie Bone, "Enough to keep us from stopping at Arajo?"

"I'll say, and then some," said Bone.

Leeman swung his horse around and circled the wagon to see for himself. Back beside Bone, he uncapped the water bag, took a mouthful, tasted it and smiled, water running down his dust-caked beard stubble. "My, my," he said to the young German, "I am so glad we rode in here for a visit." To Bone he said, "Take two bags with us."

"Wait," the German said, seeing Bone ride around toward the water bags. "You cannot take our water! We must have all the water for our mules and for ourselves, in order to cross this desert."

Leeman glanced at the four mules standing at the head of the supply wagon, then back at the pensive young German. Cocking his big saddle Colt as he raised it from its holster, he said with calm certainty, "You're not going to need it."

Chapter 10

Leaving Julimez, Morgan Hatch and Sonny Engles had followed the hoofprints left by Leeman, Bone and Waite. They pushed their horses hard, hoping to catch up to their companions, knowing the other three had no more than an hour's head start on them. At midmorning, when they'd heard the distant gunshot on the trail ahead of them, Engles and Hatch looked at each other. "That's them," said Engles. "I'd recognize Lucas' saddle Colt in a hail storm." Staring ahead, he asked Hatch, "Do you suppose that's a signal shot, Deacon's way of letting us know where they are?"

"A *signal*? Don't be simpleminded, Sonny," Hatch said, eyeing Engles skeptically. The girl sat slumped behind Engles, sleeping against his back. "Deacon ain't concerned about us. He thinks we're dead. They're up to something."

"I don't know," said Engles. "Maybe Dick was right. Maybe Deacon didn't *mean* to jackpot us. Maybe the way things happened he had no choice but to—"

Engles' words were interrupted by an outburst of pistol shots. At the end of the cacophony he said quietly with an embarrassed look, "Naw, I expect not. They're up to something, sure enough."

Beside Hatch, Wild Dick lay slumped onto his horse's neck, Hatch leading his horse by its reins. Dark blood covered the front of his chest, having seeped through the thick bandage the girl had made from a clean bedsheet. At the sound of the distant gunfire, the wounded gunman stirred, opened his eyes and mumbled something under his breath.

Hatch looked at him and said, "This ain't nothing. Go on back to sleep, Dick." But having looked at Wild Dick's chest, he said quietly to Engles, "He's bleeding again."

Engles asked, "Think we best prop him in some shade somewhere and go on? Riding's just making it worse."

Hatch stared ahead toward the sound of gunfire in contemplation. "Naw, not yet. Let's ride on up, see what they've got treed up out there. If he makes it to Arajo, we'll pay somebody to take him in."

"Ha," said Engles, "you called me simpleminded. You would trust these desert *peons* to take care of him?"

"I would," said Hatch, "after telling them we'll be back in two weeks. If he's dead we'll kill the whole village."

"The whole village?" Engles winced considering it, shaking his head slowly at the idea.

Hatch looked at him flatly for a moment, then said, "Let's go, Sonny. You're starting to aggravate the hell out of me."

They rode on, following the hoofprints to where they'd heard the gunfire. Unable, and unwilling, to push the tired, thirsty horses any faster, they arrived at the supply wagon almost a full hour later. Upon seeing the hoofprints leading away into the silver wavering heat, and seeing the three bodies lying on the ground, Hatch slipped his Colt back into his holster and circled the wagon. The four mules paid him no attention. They had stood dutifully in the same spot where the Germans had stopped them, having been unmoved by the gunfire, their heads lowered against the heat and the blazing sun.

"That son of a bitch, I'll kill him," said Hatch, stopping his horse and looking at two canvas water bags shot full of holes and hanging empty from the side of the wagon.

Easing his horse up beside him, Engles said, "But if he thinks we're dead . . ." He let his words trail.

"He doesn't know for sure," said Hatch. "He could have left something just in case we made it." He scowled at Engles as if the gunman were defending Lucas Leeman in the matter.

"Yeah, you're right, that son of a bitch," said Engles, realizing that thirst was beginning to make them both muddled and edgy. "I've still got half a canteen full of water," he offered.

"So do I," said Hatch, "but I can damn near hear it boiling." Letting his eyes follow the hoofprints off into the swirling heat, he went on to say, "It's for sure they're not going to Arajo now. They must've took on a good supply of water."

"Yep, enough to ride on and meet up with Madsen and the rest," said Engles. Looking around the barren sand flats, he added, "There's no cactus to cut up and chew." Behind him the girl awakened and pushed her hair from her eyes.

"Get down and check on Wild Dick," Hatch said to her gruffly.

Engles reached back and helped the girl swing down from behind him. "What about you?" he asked Hatch. "How're you making out?"

"Damn good," said Hatch. He touched a gloved hand to the dried blood on the side of his shirt from a bullet graze, then to another dried spot on the tip of his left shoulder.

As he looked down at his bloodstained shirt, Hatch's horse stretched its neck forward and nipped at the wetness still lingering on the empty canvas water bags. Hatch let the animal chew and pull and suck up the drop or two left in the bottom corner of the bag. Beside him, Wild Dick's horse ventured forward and licked at another water bag; Engles' horse stepped forward and did the same.

Hatch shook his head and swung down from his saddle. Looking at the four wagon mules, he said, "Let's poke these animals and see what they've got left."

Swinging down from his saddle also, Engles grumbled under his breath, "I hate a mallet-headed mule worse than any damn thing."

"I can't tell you how sorry I am to hear that," Hatch said with dry sarcasm. Helping Wild Dick down from his saddle and seating him in the sand in the narrow shade of the wagon, Hatch walked up to the mules while the woman and Engles took a look at Wild Dick's bloody chest.

Taking his Colt from his holster, Hatch walked up to the lead mule, raised its ear and slapped it loosely with his pistol barrel. The animal snorted and stomped its hoof. Then it settled and lowered its head. Hatch stepped back and poked the pistol barrel into another mule's side. The animal jerked quickly upright, its skin rippling in reflex. "Fresh as daisies," Hatch said, running a hand along the mule's coarse sandy rump. Looking off into the swirling heat, he said under his breath, "Deacon, you jackpotting bastard. I'm going to nail your rotten heart to a wall."

Arajo, Mexico

In the grainy evening darkness, less than half a mile from the small village, Hatch and Engles stopped the mules and stepped down from the animals' knobby bare backs. "Turn them loose, we're through with them," said Hatch.

"Hallelujah," said Engles, sliding off the mule in a spray of loose powdery sand. He drew his Colt, cocked it and leveled it close to his tired mule's head. "I've been waiting all day to do this."

"Put it away, Sonny," Hatch said. "We don't want to ride in there on the wake of a gunshot." He gestured a nod toward the sound of music coming from Arajo. "Hear that?"

"Yeah, I hear it, so what?" Engles said with defiance, hot, thirsty and cross from their desert trek.

"You'll stop hearing it once you fire that gun, and you know it," said Hatch, looking at the distant red and gold light from candles inside colored paper lanterns strung along the street of Arajo. "This town will turn dark as a tomb and you won't find a person stirring." Hatch turned a harsh stare to him. "We *do* want to get Wild Dick some help, a place to heal up, don't we?"

"Yeah, we do," Engles said, sulking almost child-like as he uncocked his Colt and jammed it down into his holster. "I could beat one to death—or stab one? That wouldn't be too loud, would it?"

Hatch didn't reply.

"This mallet-head nearly crippled me." Engles yanked his dusty hat from his head and slapped the mule's neck. The tired animal didn't even flinch.

Hatch looked at the woman seated atop a mule, her dress bunched up on her legs and tucked beneath her. "Keep yours," he said. "You'll need it to get home on." Hatch, Engles and the woman had ridden the mules from where they'd found them, but they had switched Wild Dick from horse to horse to keep the thirsty animals as rested as possible crossing the waterless sand flats.

"You are setting me free?" the young woman asked matter-of-factly.

"Soon," said Hatch. He took the reins to Wild Dick's horse from her, looked closer at her and asked, "You do want to go back to Julimez, don't you?"

She shrugged. "One place is as good as the next."

"Right." Hatch shook his head as he stepped back and looked at Wild Dick Bernie lying sprawled on his horse. He carefully shook Bernie's dangling arm to make sure the man was still alive. Wild Dick let out a pained moan. "He's still with us, Sonny," said Hatch.

"Hallelujah again," said Engles. He raised a big

knife from his boot well, reached out to the mule and slashed the length of leather wagon trace he'd tied around the animal's muzzle. "Get out of here, mallet-head," he growled, "before I open your guts up."

The tired mule didn't move. Engles drew the knife back and gave the mule's rump a hard slap with the flat side of the blade. Powdery sand dust billowed; the mule took a few short steps and stopped. "Leave him be, Sonny," Hatch called out. "Cut the other one loose and let's go."

"This mallet-headed son of a bitch," Engles growled under his breath.

Moments later Hatch and Engles led their thirsty horses onto the dark end of the street in Arajo and walked on toward the circling glow of light at the center of the small village. The two tired mules plodded along a few yards behind, drawn by the smell of water at the town well. "Looks like some kind of shindig they've got going on here," Engles commented as they walked on.

Twenty yards ahead, candles, torches and gaily colored cloth streamers lined the dusty street. The sound of guitar, accordion, flute and trumpet music swelled. Laughter filled the air as the villagers celebrated a piece of recent good fortune. Only three days before, the village leader had learned that a German and Swedish tin mining syndicate would be making the village a regular water stop on its shipping route across the desert from the hill country to Durango.

"Dios sonríe en nosotros!" the leader of the village cried out gleefully. He drank from a tall bottle of

mescal and waved his frayed straw sombrero. *"Dios en verdad sonríe en nosotros!"* he cried out again for emphasis.

"The hell's he carrying on about?" Engles asked as they stopped at the edge of the light.

"He's saying 'God smiles on their village,' or some such malarkey," Hatch replied, a stream of powdery sand dust spilling off his shoulder and running to the ground.

The village leader started to say something more, but his words stopped, as did the music and the laughter, as eyes turned toward the dusty, sweat-streaked strangers walking into their midst.

"Tell God not to stop smiling on our account," Hatch called out, his dusty gloved hand resting on the holster of his Colt. Beside him, Engles looked all around the circle of light, taking quick count of how many men were present, if any were carrying firearms. Seeing no weapons among the twenty or so men, other than an ancient flintlock rifle leaning against the well, he relaxed and gave a smile to a pretty young woman standing at her husband's side. Watching dust fall from Engles' leering, crusty face, the husband slid his arm instinctively around his wife's shoulders as if to protect her.

"Senors, welcome to Arajo," the village leader said in a quiet and subdued tone. He stared pensively as the woman walked into sight and stood only a foot behind Engles, the reins to Wild Dick's horse in her hand, Wild Dick lying limp in the saddle.

"Are you the *jefe* here?" Hatch asked.

In his native tongue, the man replied that yes, he

was the town leader, and assured them that if they needed help they would not be turned away.

Even though Hatch spoke Spanish, in order to gain control quickly, he shook his head vigorously and said, "Hunh-uh, mister. You're going to find that the quicker you start speaking English, the better we're going to get along. *Comprende?*"

"*Sí, compren*—I mean, *yes*, I understand," the town leader said, correcting himself as he saw Hatch's gun hand tighten around the handles of the Colt. As the two spoke, Engles eased over, took the reins to Hatch's horse from his hand and walked both horses to the well. He managed to put himself close to the rifle leaning against the low stone wall while the horses stuck their muzzles into a clay watering trough.

"Somebody getting married here?" Engles asked the faces standing nearby, looking him up and down. "If there is, I hope I can look forward to a nice piece of cake?"

"Oh no, Senor, it is not a wedding," said a young boy who stepped forward from the onlookers and spoke to Engles while Hatch and the town leader continued speaking back and forth in the middle of the street. "We are a regular stop for the wagons that carry ore from the tin mines." As he spoke he pointed into the darkness toward an unseen line of hills in the far distance.

"Boy! Talk about good luck," said Engles, managing to look as if he cared one way or the other. He watched townsmen ease Wild Dick down from his saddle and carry him off toward a small building just outside the circle of light.

"Sí," the boy said, rattling on excitedly. "We find this out the other day, and have waited for this holy day to celebrate. Two men from the mining peoples came here for water. They tell our town leader that as soon as they arrive in Durango they will tell the mine peoples about Arajo and make sure they send their wagons to us."

"Well, well," Engles said with a dark chuckle, recalling the bodies of the two young German mining engineers lying in the dirt. "Nothing like a good celebration to get things off on the right foot, I expect."

When the townsmen had eased Wild Dick down from his saddle, the woman led her mule and Dick's horse over to the well. On her way, she had heard the young boy explaining the villages' good fortune. When she stepped in beside Engles, she saw him chuckling under his breath. "Did you hear that?" he said in a lowered voice as she let the two animals drink. He picked up a gourd dipper, swiped it across the water and raised it to his face.

"It is not funny," she whispered sidelong to him. "Nothing good comes to these desert people. God has never smiled on them and he never will."

"Well, ain't you the gloomy one," Engles said. He drank from the gourd, shoved his hat back off his head and poured the rest of the water over his sweaty, dust-caked face. "Have you got a name, or is *Whore* all you go by?"

"Juanita is my name," she said, "but you can call me *Whore* if it suits you."

Engles swished a mouthful of water and spat a long stream back into the well. "Whore, it is," he said.

The musicians stood watching intently. As the townsmen carried Wild Dick out of sight into the adobe, they took it as their cue to began playing again. In the street, having heard from the village leader the same story the young boy had told Engles, Hatch grinned knowingly and dropped some small gold coins into the man's hand. "We're plumb honored as hell to be your first paying customers, *Jefe*," he said. "Won't be long, this place will be abuzz with industry."

"Yes, yes! To *industry*, and to *good fortune*!" the village leader said joyfully, sticking the bottle of mescal into Hatch's reaching hand. "*Dios sonríe en nosotros!*" he shouted, even louder this time, tossing a hand skyward.

Hatch winced and said, "Do not holler in my ear like that again, *Jefe*. God ain't smiling on you near as much as you think."

Chapter 11

Dawson and his party had approached the supply wagon warily, seeing the two bodies of the German mining engineers and their guide lying in the dirt. When they were satisfied that the area was safe, they holstered their weapons and stepped down from their saddles. "Good Lord," said Tunis, staring from body to body, noting the empty water bags and the lone mule standing close to the side of the wagon, taking shade from the evening sun. "Is there no letup in the killing?"

"Not down here," Dawson said, stepping over to where a shovel lay in the sand. "That's why they sent us to clean things up, both sides of the border." He picked up the shovel and stuck it into the sand, his hand resting on the handle for a moment. His eyes followed one set of tracks leading across the flats. The other set, now taking on the three mules, went off in the direction of Arajo. "Deacon Lucas took whatever water these men had, then killed them. Hatch and his pards knew they couldn't make it without water, so they headed for Arajo."

"Why didn't they try to catch up to Leeman?" Tunis asked, studying everything Dawson said, realizing that the marshal made sense.

Dawson nodded toward the empty canvas water bags with bullet holes in them, their edges chewed to shreds by the second party's horses. "Leeman and his men shot these other water bags up as a message to Hatch not to try catching up to them."

"Think there's bad blood between them?" Tunis asked.

"Who knows?" said Dawson. "If there wasn't bad blood before, there should be now—there would be if I were Hatch or one of his pards."

"But apparently these men cut one another's throats when it comes to their own survival," said Tunis, shaking his head in disgust. "I'm beginning to better understand the kind of men we're up against. They are all ruthless, savage and unpredictable. Would you agree that my summations are accurate, Marshal? I do want to be able to report accurately to Messenger when the time comes."

"You're getting there," Dawson said. He and Caldwell gave each other a knowing look.

Carr let out a breath of frustration. "When you report to him, mention that I'm getting tired of being a traveling burial detail for these outlaw sons a' bitches." Even as he spoke, he and Caldwell turned and walked over near the shallow grave. He took off his dusty riding coat, folded it neatly and laid it in the sand; then he picked up the other shovel and started digging, carving out a second grave beside the first.

By the time the dead had been buried, even though

the four men had enough water to make it on into Arajo, Dawson considered the risk of riding into the village late at night, on tired horses, knowing that the three men and their hostage had to have gone there rather than try to cross the flats the way Deacon Lucas' party had done. It had the ideal makings for a trap, and Dawson wasn't going to step into it.

With the wagon shading them in the pale purple moonlight, the men made a dark campsite, eating jerked meat and sparingly sipping tepid water from their canteens. They each took turns sitting up, keeping watch for two-hour intervals. Late into the night as Carr sat gazing out across the barren rolling flatlands, he saw the dark silhouette of a crouched man move toward them, zigzagging wildly.

"Wake up," he immediately hissed to the three sleeping men on the ground beside him. Rising to one knee, snatching his rifle up from his lap and clamping it to his shoulder, he leveled the sights onto the approaching figure and shouted out across the flats, "Halt!"

But the running figure didn't slow down. Instead it seemed to come straighter at him, more purposely. On the ground Dawson, Caldwell and Tunis had jumped up from their blankets almost as one, their guns coming up, cocked and ready. "Halt, or I'll shoot!" Carr shouted again, this time just as Dawson and the other two caught sight of the approaching figure.

"Damn it, Carr!" shouted Tunis, seeing the figure drawing quickly closer. "Don't make a threat! Shoot him!" As he spoke, Dawson saw them both level their rifles out across the flatlands. Yet something told him this was not one of the outlaws.

"Wait! Wait!" Dawson shouted, but it was too late. His words were drowned out as both agents began firing repeatedly into the purple moonlight.

"Don't shoot!" a voice cried out shrilly amid the din of rifle fire. But as the bullets sliced through the air, the voice turned into a painful scream. The figure dropped out of sight.

"I got him! I took him down!" Carr shouted with relief in his voice.

"Indeed, *we* took him down," Tunis called out, standing the rest of the way up and kicking his blanket aside. "Did you see him fall, Marshal?" he asked Dawson, levering a fresh round into his rifle chamber.

"Yes, I saw *somebody* fall," Dawson said, he and Caldwell hurriedly moving in beside the two excited riflemen. "Now hold your fire. Let's get out there and see just who it is you've shot."

Hearing the tone of Dawson's voice, Carr said, "It's one of them! I don't know which one, but it has to be one of them." He started forward with the others. "Whichever one he is, I'm the one who stopped his clock for him. You saw it, didn't you, Tunis?"

"I think we both shot him," Tunis said, not wanting to be left out.

The four slowed to a halt a few feet from the writhing, moaning man lying in the sand. "Get your hands in sight!" Carr demanded, his rifle pointed down at the wounded man, whose hands clasped his chest tightly.

"I—I can't," the man gasped and sobbed. "I'm . . . shot through."

Something about the man's voice gave them pause. "Who are you?" Carr demanded.

"I'm, I'm . . ." The man's voice fell away with a labored breath.

"Strike a match, Carr," Tunis said, easing forward, Dawson and Caldwell closing in around the dying man in a half circle.

Carr fished a long sulfur match from his vest pocket, struck it on his rifle hammer and leaned down over the drawn face, seeing the open eyes, the curl of blood down one side of the parted lips. "Oh, no, my God, it's Randall Wynn! One of the posse men," Carr said.

Dawson stooped down beside the wounded man and felt Wynn grasp him by his forearm with a bloody hand. "Marshal . . . thank God," Wynn gasped. "I thought I was . . . a goner." He coughed up blood from his shattered lungs.

"Try to lie still, Wynn," said Dawson, although he could see the man was dying; it made no difference if he lay still or not.

"I . . . I have been wandering around . . . out here, hiding, scared to come in. Thank God . . . I found you men . . . instead of Deacon Lucas'. . . ."

Dawson saw the light go out in the man's eyes. He sighed, shook his head slowly and loosened the grip of Wynn's bloody hand on his forearm. "The only man who lived through the gun battle in Julimez." He stared down at the flicker of firelight on the dead face. Then he stood up and stepped back, his rifle hanging in his hand. "We killed him."

"Not *we*," Tunis pointed out quickly, suddenly distancing himself from Carr in the shooting. "You heard Carr. He's the one who shot him, not me."

"But everybody heard you say *we both* shot him," Carr cut in sharply.

"No, Carr," Tunis said flatly, wanting to get himself off the hook, "we all heard *you* say that *you* are the one who shot the poor fellow. Don't think you're going to implicate me in this ugly mess."

"What was I supposed to do?" Carr simpered. "You told me to shoot him. I told him to stop." He turned a remorseful look to Dawson and asked, "Why did he keep running toward us like that?"

"You heard," said Dawson. "He's been out in the desert, scared and alone. He must've thought he'd found a place where he'd be safe."

"For God's sake," Tunis said, "and for all his effort, all the poor man got was two rifle slugs in his chest." He also shook his head. "I don't know how I can report this without making us all look bad."

Dawson and Caldwell just stared at him.

"I don't think I should admit it was me *alone* who shot him," Carr cut in, realizing how it was going to sound on Tunis' report.

"Be quiet, both of you," Dawson said firmly. "A man is dead, one of the posse men who was here to help us. His death was an accident. Let's not make it worse by denying it or covering it up." He looked first at Carr, then shifted his gaze to Tunis. "When you report it, just tell the truth. We owe Randall Wynn and his family that much."

"The truth you say?" Tunis' tone hardened. "I know how to report on matters of this sort. Believe me, the truth is important only if it serves our purpose. Success in cleaning up this border depends on how things are reported."

"Tell the truth," Dawson said more firmly. "Surely even Washington respects honesty."

"Ha! I can see that you know very little about how things work in Washington, Marshal Dawson," said Tunis.

"You're right, Tunis," said Dawson, looking him up and down with disdain, "but I get the feeling I still know more than I care to." He turned, Caldwell right beside him, and walked toward the wagon bed where they had laid the shovels.

"I've been fooling myself," Dawson said quietly to Caldwell on their way. "I had started thinking Tunis showed some promise, that maybe he's more than just some Washington lackey doing Messenger's paperwork to suit him."

"Why'd you think it?" Caldwell asked. "Just because he'd started to agree with you on things?" He gave a bitter grin as he tugged on his fingerless gloves. "That's the oldest Washington trick in the book—take control of things by agreeing with everybody. I should have warned you."

"Anything else you need to warn me about?" Dawson asked wryly, realizing that Caldwell was right. That was all Tunis had been doing, watching, agreeing, looking for a chance to take control.

"Not that I can think of offhand," Caldwell said in the same wry tone. "But I'll keep my eyes open."

"Good," said Dawson, "and if you see me allowing him to agree with me, flatter me or make me think that what I've said is important, be sure and crack me over the head with your pistol barrel."

"My pleasure," Caldwell said as they walked on.

*   *   *

In the first silver hour of dawn, Morgan Hatch and Sonny Engles looked back on the flatlands below them from a narrow trail meandering up into a long stretch of rocky hills. "What do you think?" Engles asked. "It's near daylight. Shouldn't we have heard some gunfire by now?"

"Yeah, we would have heard something if they'd rode in during the night," said Hatch, crossing his wrists on his saddle horn for a moment. He looked disappointed. Beside him stood one of the mules on a lead rope, filled water gourds tied down securely to the animal's knobby back.

"Maybe Wild Dick fell back asleep?" Engles asked.

"He would have woke right up when the law got there," Hatch said, " 'less he was dead."

"Maybe the whore cut his throat while he was asleep and gave him over without a fight?" Engles asked.

Hatch shook his head. "I don't think she's that kind of whore, unless there was some reward money on him she might've figured she could get. Something about that whore tells me she'll stick."

"Me too," said Engles. "Besides, there's no reward money on Wild Dick that I ever heard of." He grinned. "He was too slick to ever get blamed outright for anything. Far as I know, he was never even shot other than a scratch or two until all this happened."

"The lawdogs didn't show up last night," Hatch said with resolve, turning his horse back on the steep trail. "Marshal Dawson was wise enough not to ride into a dark town. It's that simple."

"Yeah, that lawdog son of a bitch." Engles spat as

if to get a bitter taste from his mouth. "It looks like
we'll still have him and his deputy to deal with."
The two nudged their horses forward and rode on.

In Arajo, Juanita Rey sat on the dirt floor wrapped
in a ragged blanket, beside the straw-filled pallet
where Wild Dick lay sleeping with his shoulders
propped against the bare wall.

When two young men slipped silently into the
adobe, she opened her eyes without lifting her face.
Beneath the blanket came the muffled sound of a gun
cocking. The sound caused Wild Dick to stir groggily
for a moment, then drop his head. One of the men
whispered to the woman, "Do not shoot, senora! We
come to warn you, the way the *americano* paid us
to do."

"Warn me, then," the woman said impatiently.

"Four more *americanos* ride into Arajo, from the
east. They will be here in a short time."

She looked at Wild Dick in contemplation, then
asked without taking her eyes off his pale sleeping
face, "Will I be able to see them from the window?"

The men looked at each other. "*Sí*, you will see
them when they ride in onto the street." He
shrugged. "But by then it might be too late to get
away."

Broodingly, she said in Spanish, without facing
them, "It is never too late to get away."

Chapter 12

Just inside Arajo, Dawson and the other three slowed to a halt and sat looking all around warily as the village leader stepped out into the dusty street. He stood flanked by two men on either side. One man carried a flintlock rifle; another carried a short-barreled Spanish shotgun. The town leader hooked his thumb in his belt behind the handle of a large revolver that rested in a brown waist sash.

"The men you are looking for have come and gone in the night," he called out, lying, earning the gold coins Hatch had paid him.

Dawson sat quietly for a moment, seeing whether the man would offer anything else on the matter.

"I know they are desperados running from your *americano* law," the leader said. "But they have done no wrong here in *Mejico*. They only came to Arajo long enough to water their animals and themselves. They eat, they drink and they are gone onto the hill trails before midnight." He gestured a nod toward the distant hill line. "If you hurrying you can catch them, I think."

"Yep, he's lying. He should have shut up sooner," Dawson said under his breath to Caldwell, seated beside him in his saddle, his rifle propped up, the butt resting on his thigh.

"I say we go down the street, kick some doors in," said Carr, not making much of an effort to keep his voice down. "Somebody will give them up."

"Shut up and sit still," Dawson warned him over his shoulder. "See how empty the streets are. Before we go into these narrow streets let's try to find out what else is being aimed at us."

Carr fell silent, looking nervously along the low rooflines as the village leader and the four townsmen began to walk closer. "We want no trouble," Dawson said firmly, his right hand resting on his thigh near the handle of his Colt.

The leader and the four men stopped a few feet away as if Dawson's words had been a warning to come no closer. "Neither do we, senor," the leader said. "I tell you the truth, they are not here."

"They have broken the law in Mexico," Dawson said, disregarding his words. He knew there had to be a reason why this man didn't want the four of them riding into Arajo. "We found three bodies and a deserted mine supply wagon yesterday evening. I figure they killed them for their water."

The news caused the village leader to swallow a sudden knot in his throat. "A mine supply wagon, you say?"

"That's right," said Dawson, keeping his eyes on the man, knowing Caldwell was beside him, looking all around, searching into shadowed doorways, alleyways. "One of the men was a Mexican. The other two looked like Swedes, maybe Germans."

The look among the four faces told Dawson that he had struck a nerve. He saw an ill and troubled look come over the village leader's face. "Tell them," one of the townsmen whispered harshly, his short-barreled shotgun lowering, to Dawson's relief. "We owe them nothing now, even if they did give you money. They have destroyed our future."

"*Santa Madre*," said the town leader. With a deep sigh he let his hands fall limply away from his revolver as he stepped to one side and gestured them toward the street. "There is one here, he is badly wounded. You will find him in the adobe there." Again he gestured.

"*Gracias*. Was there a woman with them?" Dawson asked, gazing down along the empty dirt street.

"Sí, a woman rode in with them, and she is still here. She tended their wounds. They leave her here to tend to the wounded man who is not doing so good."

Dawson gave Caldwell a curious look. Over his shoulder he said as he nudged his horse forward, "Let's go, spread out some when you can. We don't know what we've got here."

From the open window, the woman watched the four men ride into sight along the dusty street, knowing they were coming straight to her doorstep. She looked at the bed where Wild Dick lay sleeping. She knew she could easily slip out through the open door, go to the lawmen and end things right here and now. Couldn't she . . . ? Of course she could, she told herself.

Backing away from the window, she looked across the narrow street, where a skinny peasant woman her age stood in a darkened doorway with a baby on her hip. Three more young children clung to her thin legs, as if holding her to the earth. On the pallet, dark blood had already spread wide on the fresh bandages she'd placed on Wild Dick's chest.

Quietly, carefully, she untied the cloth strips holding the bandage and peeled it to one side, seeing the terrible wound, the empty blackness. Her eyes probed for a moment, knowing that at the end of that black hole lay a bullet, buried into flesh and bone. Then she pulled her eyes away from the wound and looked at the big Colt in its holster lying on the floor, the gun belt wrapped around it.

Wild Dick stirred slightly as she slipped the gun from the holster and weighed it in her hands. "*Aqua* . . . ," he whispered in a dry rasp. But instead of raising the small gourd of water to his mouth, she dipped her fingertips into it and touched them to his parted lips. "They are coming for you," she whispered, placing her free hand on his clammy forehead.

Wild Dick had barely the strength to open his eyes slightly and study her eyes as if through a veil. "My gun . . . ," he rasped, his hands too weak to reach for the weapon.

"I have it," she whispered with reassurance. She pulled back from his ear and examined the wounds on his chest again while she used both hands to cock the gun hammer. "Do you want it now?"

"Yes, give it . . . ," he managed to say brokenly, but with resolve.

With the barrel resting in her left hand, she raised the gun and held the tip of the barrel to the open wound at the center of his chest. Wild Dick felt the cool metal against his fevered wounded flesh. "No . . . Whore," he whispered, as if giving her instructions.

She moved the barrel two inches to her right, where his heart lay struggling to find its next beat. "Yeah . . . ," Wild Dick said in a weak tone, a look of peace coming to his tortured face as she found the right spot. Holding her head back to one side, the woman squinted her eyes and pulled the trigger. Wild Dick's body bucked and stiffened with the impact, then slumped limply onto the pallet.

On the street, at the sound of the single gunshot Dawson and the others stopped their horses instinctively and stepped down from their saddles, weapons in hand. They found cover quickly and centered their aim on the adobe. But after a silent pause when it appeared no other shot was coming, Dawson raised a cautious hand, keeping the others from firing on the small adobe.

"What are we waiting for, Marshal?" Carr asked, sounding impatient. "We know we have him outnumbered. Let's roust him out of there."

"Keep quiet, Grady," Tunis said to Carr. "We've seen what your haste causes us." To Dawson he said, "Say the word, Marshal, and I'll go around and secure any means of escape from the rear."

But before Dawson could give a reply to either of

them, they saw the woman running out of the open doorway toward them, her arms outspread, her face covered with the back-spray of Wild Dick's blood. "He is dead! He is dead!" she cried out. "It is over! I have killed him!"

Dawson caught her at a full run as she leaped into his arms, sobbing and clinging to him. Holding her to one side, he kept an eye on the adobe and motioned Caldwell forward. "Easy, ma'am, you're going to be all right," he said, trying to settle her.

"I'll go look things over," Caldwell said, checking his gun as he moved forward.

"Wait," said Dawson, "I'm going with you." To the woman he said as he watched her eyes for any sign of deception, "Is there anyone else in there besides Dick Bernie? Are there any others waiting to surprise us?"

"No, the others are gone," she said, shaking her head, gasping for breath. "There is only him, and he is dead." She began sobbing, looking greatly relieved. "At last I am free of them."

Tunis and Carr had ventured forward, seeing the gun smoke from the single shot find its way out of the open window and rise in a slow gray curl. "So, you nailed him, eh?" Carr said, turning to the trembling woman with a look of admiration.

"*Sí*, I—I had to," she offered, stepping away from Dawson, wiping her eyes with her palms. "It was the thing I could do in order to save myself. He told me if I did not take care of him he would kill me."

Dawson gave her a dubious look.

Replying to his questioning gaze, she said, "I saw the four of you men riding in, and knew it was then that I had to do something. He would have killed each of you from the window. He told me so."

Dawson only stared at her.

"Do you not believe me?" she asked, with a hurt, wide-eyed expression. "Do you think I—"

"Now, now, little lady," said Carr, cutting her off with a paternal grin. "You did good for yourself—real good." Seeing Caldwell and Tunis approaching the adobe with caution, he said to Dawson, "Go with them if you want to. I'll stay back and look after her."

Dawson looked them both up and down. Leaning in close to Carr, he said privately, "Don't turn your back on her until we get a chance to talk some more."

"Don't worry, Marshal, I believe I know how to handle a frightened woman," Carr replied under his breath with a trace of sarcasm.

As the marshal turned and hurried forward to catch up with Caldwell and Tunis, the woman said to Carr with a hurt look on her face, "Does he think I was with these murderers by my own choice? Does he not know that they forced me to come with them?"

"You pay the marshal no mind, little lady, you're safe now. That's the main thing." Carr reached out to her; she willingly placed herself in his arms. "The marshal sometimes takes himself a little too seriously."

Standing in Carr's arms, the woman looked back across his broad shoulder at the four horses standing in the street where the lawmen had left them. "You are kind," she said. As she spoke she slipped her hand in between them and eased the knife she had taken from Wild Dick's boot from inside her dress.

Inside the adobe, Dawson and the other two lowered their weapons as they looked around the empty room. Gun smoke still loomed in the air. The big Colt lay on the floor where it had fallen. Wild Dick's dead eyes lay half open, staring blankly at them like a man dozing in the morning heat.

But upon seeing the body lying stretched on the pallet, Dawson commented, "Uh-oh, she said he was at the window getting ready to ambush us when she shot him."

"So?" Tunis asked with a curious expression, "What difference does that make? She killed him. She got away from him."

"Big difference," said Caldwell, he and Dawson both hurrying out the door.

Carr stood in the street where Dawson had left him, but the woman wasn't there. Dawson caught a glimpse of her bare thigh and her long hair whipping back behind her as she raced out of sight around the corner of a building, on Tunis' horse, the other three horses' reins in her hands.

"She's getting away!" he shouted, running toward Carr.

But Carr stood with his back to him, rocking back and forth as if dumbfounded, his hands spread at his sides. "Damn it, man!" shouted Tunis, running out behind Caldwell. "She's stealing our horses!"

Only yards away, villagers stood looking on in horror as Carr turned around slowly, facing the other three as they drew closer. "Oh, no," said Tunis, slowing to a halt, seeing the shower of blood spewing from the long gaping wound across Carr's throat.

"Help him!" Dawson shouted over his shoulder to

Tunis and Caldwell as he ran past Carr and stopped at a place where he could see the woman and the horses racing away in a cloud of dust. He threw the rifle butt to his shoulder quickly. But then he slowed himself down, took a deep breath and steadied himself. He took careful aim out through the thickening dust, knowing he would get only one shot before the dust hid his target completely.

Not allowing his sight to be distracted by the rise and fall of the horses running behind her, Dawson squeezed off the shot and managed to see the woman jerk sideways in the saddle as the bullet struck her. Then the dust closed in like a thick curtain, blocking out everything. *Got her*, he told himself flatly, not at all pleased with the prospect of shooting a woman in the back. He levered another round into his rifle chamber and walked forward, his eyes searching the billowing dust, waiting for it to settle.

Out on the flats ahead of the rising dust, the woman lay low, struggling with one hand to keep from flying from her saddle. Dawson's shot had struck her high in her right shoulder, the impact of it rendering her right arm limp and useless. The reins to the other three horses had flown from her hand, but she'd managed to right herself enough to keep riding.

As the powdery trail dust settled, Dawson breathed a sigh of relief at the sight of his horse slowly galloping down in his direction. Caldwell's and Carr's horses were doing the same a few yards away. A second later he saw the woman crest a low rise and disappear out of sight.

"Did you get her?" Caldwell asked, hurrying up to him, a streak of Carr's spewing blood on his hand and shirtsleeve.

"Yeah," said Dawson, "I *wounded* her." He gestured toward the swirling dust lifting above the flats. "We've got our horses back." As he spoke, he looked back toward Carr, who lay on the ground in a wide pool of blood. Tunis sat in the dirt close by, hatless, his gun dangling from one hand. On the ground beside Tunis' hat lay his brown leather-backed journal, its small pages turning back and forth in the hot breeze.

"Yeah, Carr's dead," Caldwell said, anticipating Dawson's next words before he spoke them.

"The poor fool," Dawson said. "She must've cut his throat before he knew what hit him."

"Yep, I'd say she had it all planned down pretty good," said Caldwell. He looked at Dawson's grim expression.

"Carr's holster is empty. So if she's lying wounded out there, she's armed."

"Obliged," said Dawson. He studied Tunis for a moment, then said to Caldwell, "Let him wait here while we go get the horses."

PART 3

Chapter 13

Shaw watched the small twisted Spaniard swing the heavy iron door open and gesture for him to step inside. "You first," Shaw said firmly, not about to turn his back on the man, lest the iron door swing shut and lock behind him.

"Ah, you are the cautious one," the twisted man said with a sneaky grin, looking up at Shaw as he limped forward, the candle held high into the black darkness. To a shadowy corner of the room he said, "Gomez, get up, you sick, broken-lung *bastardo*. You're leaving."

A lethal-sounding cough erupted in the dark corner, followed by a rattling gasp for air. "Leaving?" said a weak and broken voice.

"Yes, leaving, *salir, poner ausente*," said the man. "Mr. Madsen has sent this man for you. Although I don't know why. You are more dead than alive. Perhaps he wants to kill you himself." As he spoke he gave a distrustful glance up at Shaw and added, "This piece of sick putrid flesh is no good for anything."

"It's none of your business *why* Madsen wants him," said Shaw. "He told me to come get him, and here I am. If you want to ride back to Zarco with me, you can question Madsen's reason in person. I'll escort you there."

"No," the twisted Spaniard said quickly, catching the threat in Shaw's words, "I would never question Mr. Madsen's reason! Who am I to wonder *why* about anything? I am just a stupid old cripple, eh?"

Shaw ignored him and said to a muffled cough in the darkness, "Come on, Gomez, I brought you a horse, let's get riding."

"Did he . . . ?" A rattling cough erupted, then settled in the darkness.

"Did he what?" Shaw asked. He took the candle from the Spaniard and gave him a slight shove forward, keeping him in front of him.

"Send you . . . to kill me?" Gomez said, choking and gasping with every word.

"If he wanted me to kill you'd already be dead," said Shaw, careful of what he said here. There would be time to explain things to the man once they were out of this place and on their way to Zarco. "Now get up, let's go." Shaw took a step forward and looked down in the flicker of candlelight at the emaciated face, streaked with countless days of grime, eyes blurred by searing pain from too many days without sunlight.

"I—I need help," Gomez said, struggling weakly to swing himself up from a pile of ragged blankets on the dirt floor.

"Help him up. Take him outside," Shaw commanded the Spaniard. "How long since you've fed him anything?"

The man shrugged. "I don't remember. I used to have to keep him chained of a night. But I stopped feeding him so much, to keep him from gaining his strength and trying to escape." He gave a sly, ugly grin. "To tell you the truth I thought he was dead. He does nothing but cough and choke on his own bloody spit, this sick, lazy fool."

Helping Gomez to his feet, the Spaniard led him out to the main mine shaft and into the bright light of day, where Shaw took over, looped the man's thin, limp arm over his shoulder and led him to the waiting horses. Gomez squinted his eyes shut in pain. "God . . . help me," he managed to say between coughing. "I thought I'd never—"

"Shut up," Shaw demanded in a harsh whisper, watching the Spaniard hobble off toward the dusty mine shack. "We'll talk once we're away from here." Above the mine shack stood a rifleman who stared down at Shaw as Shaw shoved the thin, brittle man up into a saddle.

But Gomez persisted, saying through his cough, "You did . . . come to kill me."

"No," said Shaw, "I didn't."

Holding the reins to Gomez's horse, Shaw mounted his own horse and led the frail, sickly man away. Once outside the perimeter of the Luzzo mining compound and on their way down the trail that would take them back to Zarco, Shaw handed the weak man a canteen of tepid water and said, "Here, sip some of this. We'll stop farther down the trail, long enough to get some food in your belly."

"*Gracias*, mister," Gomez said, his cough settling a little in the warmer air. "If you are not here . . . to kill me, what is it . . . that Madsen wants from me?"

"Madsen didn't send me, Nito," said Shaw, sidling his horse close to him. "Your daughter, Francisca, sent me."

"Francisca sent you?" Gomez looked frightened. "No, please . . . take me back to the mines! Madsen will . . . kill my family when he hears what you have done." His words ended in a violent fit of coughing. Shaw had to reach over and keep the man from falling from the saddle.

"No, he won't," Shaw said. "You have to trust me, he's not going to harm your family, not if you'll do like I tell you." Even as he spoke, Shaw questioned whether or not this man would have the strength to flee Zarco, to take his wife and child and disappear into the hill country until Madsen was gone from their lives.

Gomez seemed to summon up strength from inside himself and said in a ragged but stronger voice, "I— I will do . . . whatever you tell me to do, mister. Only, please . . . let my family come to no harm."

"You have my word on it," Shaw said to him; then to himself in an almost taunting inner voice he added, *The word of a desert angel . . .*

Two miles farther down the rocky hill trail, Shaw veered his horse over into the thin shade of some scrub cedar and stopped. Beside him, Nito Gomez gave him a questioning look, but stopped and stepped down beside him. Shaw had to catch the man by his bony elbow to keep him from falling.

Helping him over to a large rock, Shaw seated him and said, "Wait right here, I've got some food in my saddlebags."

When Shaw returned, he gave Gomez a handful of jerked meat and some dried *pan del maíz*, a thin flat corn bread he'd carried for a long time.

While the man ate, Shaw told him his name, and how he had come to know his daughter. He told him it was Francisca who had sent him to bring her father back to her. He didn't tell him that the girl had asked him to kill Quinn Madsen. Some things were better left unsaid, he reasoned.

"I don't know . . . how I will ever repay . . . what you have done for me, Senor Shaw," Gomez said, still watery eyed from adapting to the sunlight. He paused for a moment, then said with a bit of apprehension, "And, forgive me, but I . . . do not understand *why* you do it."

Shaw stared at him, wishing the man had not asked him that question. "Because it needed doing," he said finally.

"But I have no . . . money with which to—" Gomez's words stopped short beneath a renewed round of coughing.

"It's not for money," Shaw said. To change the subject he gestured in the direction of Zarco. "If we ride till dark, rest a couple of hours and ride all night, you'll be home by morning. Are you up to that?"

"I am up to . . . whatever it takes, Mr. Shaw," Gomez said through a mouthful of food.

"Good," said Shaw, reaching out and patting his bony shoulder. "Eat as much as you can stand. Get your strength up as fast as you can. You'll need it once we get you and your family back together." As he saw another round of coughing swelling up in Gomez's thin chest, he wondered if help had come too late for Nito Gomez. Had he ridden here to save a man whose life was long past saving? *God, he hoped not.*

Francisca stood in the window of the small room that faced out onto the desert floor. Before he had slipped out of Zarco, Shaw had managed to come to her window and tell her of his plans. He had sworn her to secrecy. Not even her mother should know, he had told her, not until he brought her father home and the three of them were safely under way. She would keep her word to him, she told herself.

In the heat of the afternoon, her mother came into the room, her eyes still bruised but healing from the beating Madsen had given her. "All day you have been at the window, child," her mother said. "What is it you are expecting?" She stood beside her daughter and looked out herself, squinting against the glare of afternoon sunlight.

"Nothing, *Mamá*," Francisca replied quickly. "I am only watching the sun go down." She knew Shaw hadn't been gone long enough to ride to the mines and back. It would be morning before he arrived. But she could not keep herself from going to the window and watching in anticipation.

"Yes," her mother said, "and this morning you were at the same spot when the sun came up. Now go away from the window. Looking into the sun is not good for you."

Francisca sighed; she grudgingly stepped back from the window and turned toward the door to the other room. But as she stepped through the doorway, Madsen appeared as if out of nowhere and placed a hand on her chest, stopping her. "Hold up, nit," he said. Looking past her to her mother, he said, "I have something to say to both of yas."

Protectively, the woman hurried forward and put an arm around Francisca. "What has this foolish girl done this time? I promise whatever it is, I will correct her for it—"

"Shut up, fool," said Madsen. "I didn't say she's done anything. It's just time we all three had a good talk about things here."

"What do you mean? A talk about *things here*?" Ramona asked, fear showing in her dark eyes.

Madsen smiled reassuringly. "Now, Ramona, it's nothing to get upset about. In fact, I've got some good news for you and Francisca."

"Oh, you do?" Ramona gave him a wary look.

"Yes," said Madsen. "Remember what I told you about forgiving what Nito owes me? About calling it even and bringing him home?"

Ramona held her breath awaiting his next words; so did Francisca, wondering what this would mean, with Shaw already gone to free her father.

"I'm going to do it," said Madsen. He spread his arms as if expecting both the mother and child to throw themselves into them. Ramona saw what he expected and gave it to him, going into his arms sounding grateful but not overly grateful, not enough to indicate how much more she cared for her husband than she did for him. "*Gracias*, Quinn," she said, "for being a man of your word." She looked at Francisca. "Do you hear, Francisca? Your *papá* is coming home. Do you not wish to thank Mr. Madsen for bringing him home to you?"

"*Gracias*, Mr. Madsen," Francisca said sullenly, without stepping any closer to him.

Turning back to Ramona, Madsen said, "There are a couple of things you and I need to talk about in private." He gestured a nod toward Francisca.

"*Sí*, I understand," Ramona said quietly. To her daughter she said, "Francisca, you must leave us alone. There are things Mr. Madsen wants to—"

"I heard him," said Francisca in a polite but smoldering tone. With a look at Madsen that did little to hide her hatred of him, she walked out the door onto the dirt street, her attention going immediately in the direction from which she knew Shaw and her father would be riding.

As soon as the child was out of hearing distance, Madsen held Ramona at arm's length and said to her, "Are you happy that I'm bringing Nito home?"

"Yes, I am happy," Ramona said, careful not to appear too happy and make him jealous of her husband.

"Good," said Madsen, "then I'll be bringing him home to you in a few days." He paused, then said, "There's something you're going to have to do for me in return."

"*Sí*, I will do whatever you ask," Ramona said. She swallowed a tight knot in her throat, realizing the kinds of demands a man like this could make.

Madsen gave a thin smile. "I'm giving Francisca to Deacon Lucas until he gets here."

"Oh, no, Quinn, I beg of you," Ramona said. "She is only a child. Please do not send her to—"

"Enough!" Madsen said, his grip on her shoulders tightening as his temper began to flare. "She's turning fourteen. It's time she became a woman. I've already given Lucas my word on the matter. I didn't even have to tell you. I was just being kind."

She knew that to press him on the matter would be futile. It would bring her a beating without having any influence on his decision one way or the other. Still, she ventured, asking as passively as she could, "But why, Quinn, why do you do this? She is not your daughter, she is mine . . . mine and Nito's."

"You want Nito to come home, don't you?" Madsen said, his face growing red with anger.

"Yes, I do," said Ramona. "But it will kill him to know that our child is the reason he was released."

"Oh?" Madsen seemed to settle down. He took a deep breath and decided to lie to her. "It so happens that Nito already knows about the arrangement. He sends his blessing."

Ramona only stared at him.

"Yes, it's true," said Madsen. "I sent a man to the mines. He told your Nito. It turns out your *good husband*, Nito, agreed to it."

"My Nito would never agree—" She stopped herself, knowing what she would get if she said what was really on her mind. She wanted her husband home. She wanted this man out of her bed and out of her life. Could Nito have given his blessing? In this country Francisca was not too young to become a wife. But to one of these outlaws, these killers?

Madsen gave a cruel grin, seeing the shock and

disappointment his words had caused her. "Maybe
your Nito ain't such a righteous soul after all. Maybe
it's time you looked at this the same way he does.
These young girls are like kids and yearlings. They
reach an age, it's better to trade them off and be done
with them."

She held her words. It was important to get her
husband home. Once he was here with her, the three
of them could flee Zarco in the dark of night if need
be. *All right. . . .* She calmed herself down. Just the
fact that there had been some word from Nito was
a relief. At least her husband was still alive. "*Sí*, you
are right," she said quietly. "If Nito has given his
blessing, what right have I to question it?"

"That's what I say." Madsen grinned. He stepped
past her, and sat down in a wooden chair and raised
a boot. "Now then, get these off me. I want you to
show me just how grateful you are."

As she turned around, straddled his foreleg and
took his dirty boot in hand, she asked carefully,
"Why do you promise Francisca to Deacon Lucas?
She is a skinny, foolish girl who knows very little
about anything, especially about men."

"For some men that's the best traits to look for in
a woman," Madsen said, lowering his stockinged
foot and raising his other boot. He wasn't about to
explain himself to this peasant woman. Why he'd
promised her daughter to Deacon Lucas was strictly
between him and Lucas.

But it was a good business move on his part, he
reminded himself with a guarded smile. Lucas had
wanted the girl ever since they'd been in Zarco.
Handing her over to him as a present would have the

gunman eating out of his hand. With Lucas' undying support came the support of his gang—something Madsen needed if he wanted to continue raiding both sides of the border. There would also be some gold changing hands between himself and Deacon Lucas, he thought, smiling, standing up in his stockinged feet and spreading his arms out, but that was just a little something extra for himself.

Chapter 14

In the grainy darkness, Paco saw the girl walking along the dirt street. She moved quietly in the dark shadows, trying to remain unseen. "Crazy *muchacha*," Paco said to himself. He ducked out of sight behind a mule cart and waited until she passed in front of him. "Ah, there you are," he said, jumping out quickly and grabbing her before she could bolt away from him. "Now what do you do for yourself?" he said under his breath, holding her firmly, yet not too firmly, by her arm. "What if this was not me? What if it was one of the drunken hombres from the cantina?"

Speaking just above a whisper, Francisca said, "I would do this." As quick as a whip she spun free of him, took a step back and kicked him solidly in his groin. "Then I would turn and run away, as quick as a rabbit," she added. "I would kick like a rabbit and run like a rabbit."

Caught completely by surprise, Paco had jack-knifed at the waist and grabbed himself with both hands. *"Oh Dios mio,"* he groaned in a strained and injured voice.

"Are you all right?" Francisca asked in a concerned tone, bending down and looking into his tortured face.

"Sí, I am . . . just fine," Paco said, struggling to catch his breath. He tried without success to hide the deep throbbing pain in his lower belly.

"Did I do wrong, Senor Ruiz?" Francisca asked, looking worried.

"Call me Paco," he managed to say. Struggling, he began to regain his breath and straighten upright. "No, little one . . . you did good," he said. He breathed deep and collected himself. "But the point is . . ." He stopped, took another deep breath and continued. "You have been told to stay off these dark streets." He raised a gloved finger for emphasis, his other hand still pressed to his aching groin.

"I am sorry I hurt you, Paco," she said.

"If I were one of those hombres, a kick down there would not have stopped me." He paused and considered it. "But it is good that you know how to defend yourself."

"Gracias," said Francisca. "I will be careful, as I always am."

Looking at her, Paco wondered if Shaw had told her where he was going. "Why are you out here tonight?" he asked, probing to see what she knew.

"Because Madsen is with my mother," she said, a bitterness coming to her voice.

"That is the only reason you are out here tonight, *of all nights*?" Paco asked, eying her closely in the dark, grainy light.

"*Sí*, why else would I be out here?" she asked, giving a shrug, she herself watching *his* face for any sign that he might know what Shaw was up to.

"Never mind," Paco said, deciding that even if she did know, it was still not a good idea for him to confide in her. Shaw would be back any time now. He would wait and keep his mouth shut. He'd already stuck his neck out too far by agreeing to cover for Shaw. He hoped he wasn't about to get himself killed over this girl and her dirty peasant family.

The girl started to speak, but at the quiet sound of horses' walking hooves, Paco held up a hand and quieted her.

"Horses, near the church!" Francisca whispered with nervous anticipation.

"*Shhh*, yes," said Paco, "be quiet." The two looked in the direction of the small adobe church and saw the silhouettes of two riders, their horses outlined against the purple night sky.

"It is *Papá!*" Francisca said, having a hard time keeping herself from crying out loud.

"Wait!" said Paco. But his words went unheard; the girl raced off along the darkened street. *"Muchacha loca!"* Paco whispered under his breath, hurrying along with a slight limp from the kick in his groin.

At the rear door of the church, Shaw had helped Nito down from the horse and looped his arm around his shoulder when Francisca ran up and threw her arms around her father. *"Papá! Papá!"* she said, tears streaming from her eyes. "You are home! Thank God! Mr. Angel has brought you home to me!"

"Easy, little lady," Shaw said, seeing that Nito was

so exhausted and sick he didn't seem to recognize the girl. "Your father is awfully sick. Let's get him inside, see what the priest can do for him." As Shaw spoke to the girl, his eyes went to Paco and conveyed a look of hopelessness.

"Here, you stay with me, little one," Paco said gently, putting his arm around the girl's shoulder as the old priest came out and helped Shaw take the sick man inside.

"What is wrong with him?" Francisca asked, the two of them following Shaw and her father inside the church, then stopping as the priest closed a heavy curtain.

"I don't know," said Paco, "but the padre is wise in these matters. He will know what to do." He patted the child's shoulder and kept her close beside him. On the other side of the curtain they heard Nito's weak cough and his shallow gasping for breath. "*Papá!* It is me," Francisca said to the curtain drawn between them. "Can you hear me?"

Leaning down over Nito, Shaw and the old priest saw a glimmer of recognition come to the man's eyes. This time, hearing his daughter's voice, Nito struggled to raise himself up on the cot where they had laid him. "Francisca, *mi hija*. Is it possible?" His weak hand gripped Shaw's wrist.

"Yes, it's Francisca," said Shaw. He started to ask the priest if it would be all right for the girl to come inside the curtain. But before he could, Francisca was beside him, leaning down over her father, sobbing and holding his head cradled in her arms.

Shaw stepped back. The old priest leaned in between the daughter and father long enough to lay a hot, wet herbal poultice on the man's emaciated chest. Then he stood up, stepped back beside Shaw and whispered to him, "Perhaps someone should go bring Ramona here."

"Oh?" Shaw gave him a questioning look.

"Yes," said the old priest, reading Shaw's question correctly. "And quickly," he added.

Shaw slipped back through the curtain and over to where Paco stood near the rear door, keeping watch on the darkness through the open slit of the door. Casting a glance at Shaw over his shoulder, Paco said, "Three times today, Madsen asked me where you were. I told him you were asleep. Then I told him you were with a woman. Then I said you were drunk and in a foul mood."

"*Gracias*, Paco," Shaw said. "The priest says we need to get the woman here fast."

"He is dying?" Paco whispered.

Shaw only nodded.

"Madsen is with the woman, but by now he is probably passed out," Paco said. "I will go to the back window and tell her to get here quickly." He paused, then said, "But she knows I am one of Madsen's men. How will I get her to—"

"Show her this," Shaw said. He held out a strip of rawhide that held a small tarnished silver ring. "Nito gave it to me, in case he didn't make it back here. He'd lost so much weight it wouldn't stay on his finger." He dropped the ring and its rawhide strip into Paco's hand.

"*Santa Madre*," Paco whispered. "Madsen has starved this poor man to death in order to rut with his wife." He gave Shaw a look, then said, "I used to think of myself as an evil man."

"What do you think now?" Shaw asked.

"I think it would not be evil if I killed Madsen before this night is through," he said as he slipped out the door and half closed it behind himself.

"You might have to beat me to it," Shaw said to himself under his breath, watching the Mexican disappear in the darkness toward the Gomezes' small adobe.

Ramona sat at the table with her head in her hands. When the door opened, she turned toward it expecting to see Francisca. But she rose half out of her chair when she saw Paco step inside with his Colt drawn and pointed at her. "Do not make a sound," he whispered. Raising a finger to his lips, he allowed her to see the string of rawhide hanging from his hand, the small silver ring hanging on it.

She gasped wide eyed, then said, "Where did you get that? What are you doing here?"

"I got it from your husband, Nito," Paco whispered.

"You have seen Nito?" Ramona asked breathlessly. She cut a guarded glance toward the bedroom where Madsen lay sleeping, an open bottle of tequila at his side.

"Don't worry, he is asleep," said Paco. "I looked in through the window." He lowered his gun a little. "Your husband is at the church. The padre said to bring you quickly." He hoped to convey the urgency without coming out and telling her the man was dying.

But she read the look in his eyes. "Is he . . . ?" Her words went unfinished. She stepped forward, grasped the ring and held it to her bosom.

" 'Come quickly,' is what he told me to say," Paco replied with a flat expression.

Grabbing a frayed shawl from a wall peg, the woman hurried out, giving only a short wary glance back toward the bedroom doorway. On their way through the darkness, she said, "You are one of his men. Why are you doing this? If he knew, he would kill you."

"I am one of his men, *sí*," Paco replied, "but that does not mean I like what I have seen Madsen doing to you and your family."

"Then why do you do something now? Where were you when he sent my husband away and began to shame me and my daughter? Were you so afraid of him?"

"I fear no man," Paco said. They hurried along in silence for a moment. Finally Paco said as if confiding in her, "I don't know why I am doing this now. But I am glad that I'm doing it."

"You do not even know when it was that you changed your mind," Ramona said.

"*Sí*, I know *when*," said Paco. "It was when the gunman, Shaw, rode into Zarco."

The two looked at each other as they turned the dark corner toward the rear door of the church. "The one my daughter calls Mr. Angel? The one she says is the answer to our many prayers?"

"*Sí*, that one," said Paco, sounding a little embarrassed to discuss such a matter as prayers and angels.

"She is such a foolish child," Ramona said almost to herself, hurrying along beside him.

Watching through the narrowly opened door, Shaw stepped to the side and let the two in. Ramona looked at Shaw, but only in passing as she hurried through the thick dark curtain to her husband's side.

"Look, *Papá*," said Francisca, "*Mamá* is here."

"Nito, oh, my Nito, what has he done to you?" Ramona wept, seeing the thin, frail shell of what had been her husband.

"He—he has killed me," Nito managed to say in a waning voice.

"He lied to me," said Ramona, caressing her husband's forehead, holding his cold skeletonlike fingers in her warm hands. "He told me he was feeding you good, taking extra good care of you! I—I believed him." She sobbed openly. "He said only today that you gave your permission for Francisca to stay with one of his men."

Francisca's eyes widened in terror.

"No . . . it is not so," said Nito. "I have not . . . seen him or any of his men . . . until Senor Shaw came for me."

Outside the curtain, Shaw and Paco looked at each other, realizing how terribly Madsen had treated these people. "Let's go out back," Shaw whispered, gesturing toward the door.

Outside in the darkness, Paco gripped his Colt handle tightly. "I have never wanted to kill a man so badly as I want to kill Madsen. No man does another man this way. He got what he wanted—to use the woman until he was through with her. Why was that not enough? Damn him to hell."

"Using her wasn't enough," Shaw said. "He had to keep coming up with more ways to use her. *De-*

ceiving her was one more way of satisfying himself. He liked making her think that sleeping with him was gaining better treatment for her husband, when all the while Madsen was killing him slowly."

"And giving the girl to Deacon Lucas was just one more way of using these poor people," said Paco, shaking his head slowly in dark speculation.

"Yeah, and all the while telling the woman that her husband had given him permission to do so," Shaw said. "That takes one truly cold-blooded son of a bitch." As he spoke he gazed toward the Gomezes' adobe, where Madsen lay sleeping in Nito's bed while Nito gasped for his dying breath.

"I am going to kill Quinn Madsen," Paco said with quiet resolve.

"That's twice you've said it tonight, my friend," Shaw said quietly.

Paco flared. "What? Do you think I am all talk? That I won't kill this pig?"

"No, I believe you'll kill him if that's what you make up your mind to do," said Shaw. "But right now, I still don't think you've made up your mind to do it."

Paco raised a finger toward him and wagged it. "Do not think that you know my mind so well, *mi amigo*. Because you do *not* know what it is I am thinking."

"Not word for word, I don't," Shaw said. "But I know it's got something to do with what you are going to do after you kill him. I'm betting you're wondering where you are going to make the kind of money you make riding with Madsen and these border raiders."

Paco stood in silence. Finally he said, "All right, maybe that is true. But now that the husband is here, there is nothing more holding the woman and the girl to Madsen. Perhaps I will wait and watch for the right opportunity, then kill him when the time comes."

"Did you get some horses lined up for the three of them to leave on?" Shaw asked.

"Yes," said Paco, "I took the horses of Bo Phelps, Cero Stewart and Tommy Layton, the three men you killed. So no one will notice them missing right away."

"Good thinking," said Shaw.

"They are hidden in the stable behind the church, only now they will only need two, eh?" Paco said with regret.

"Yes, I'm afraid so," said Shaw with a sigh.

As they stood in the dark, the old priest slipped his bald head out the door and said in a lowered voice, "Nito is dead, may his soul rest in peace." He made the sign of the cross on his chest. Behind him came the sound of quiet weeping. "Please take them both away from Zarco. I will see to it Nito is buried properly."

"*Gracias*, Padre, for all your help," said Shaw. He turned, facing Paco, saying, "Let's go get their horses for them while Madsen's asleep. They can slip out of here and get a lot of ground behind them before sunup."

"*Sí*," said Paco, "let's go."

Chapter 15

Quinn Madsen awakened slowly, feeling a wetness all around him—down his side, on his chest, his hair, his face. "Son of a bitch," he growled, raising the empty tequila bottle. "It's all over everything." He looked through the darkness toward the other room. "Ramona! Get in here! Clean this mess up, pronto!" he barked.

But when he heard the woman reply she was not in the other room at all, but rather standing beside the bed, unseen in the darkness until she raised the flame on an oil lantern and held it above her head. "Oh, there you are," Madsen said. "I'm all wet. Help me out here. I've spilled my tequila." He let out a short, gruff laugh.

"Here," Ramona said in a tense, quiet tone, "this will dry you off." She raised the lantern higher, then hurled it down, crashing it onto his bare chest. "*Quemadura para*, you pig from hell!" she hissed.

The fresh kerosene she had poured all over him ignited in a whooshing gust of flame, so quickly that she had to leap back to keep from catching herself on fire. She felt the heat singe her brows before she turned with deliberation and walked out the door.

Madsen's gut-ripping screams resounded throughout the town and out across the sand flats.

"What the hades was that?" Paco said, startled by the sudden terrible sound. He and Shaw had just stepped around the side of the church, having brought the three horses back with them from the stable. The old priest and Francisca stood staring stunned toward the Gomezes' small adobe, seeing Ramona walking briskly back toward them across the street. Behind her a ball of fire careened around madly inside the otherwise dark house.

"Uh-oh," said Shaw, also looking toward the sound of the scream, immediately realizing what had happened. "Get them out of here!" he said to Paco, handing him the reins to one of the horses they'd brought from the stable. "She lit him up." The two saw the screaming ball of flame bounce out onto the dirt and run zigzagging like some misguided comet.

Paco winced at the sight, but he got busy. As the woman walked across the street, she looked at the priest trancelike and said, "Forgive me, Padre, for I have—"

"Not tonight," said Paco, cutting her off, grabbing her by the arm and shoving her to the waiting horses. "You, get mounted," he said to Francisca, who had stood staring in stunned disbelief, as if frozen in place. Paco shook her by her forearm, saying, "Hey! Let's go, little one! You must both get out of here, pronto!"

"That goes for you too, Paco," Shaw said as Madsen's men ran from the cantina toward the burning adobe. The entire earth and plank structure now stood broiling in licking flames. "You've got to get them both out of here and to safety."

Paco didn't argue. He leaped into the saddle of the horse Nito had ridden. Looking down at Shaw, he said, "What about you? What will happen to you?"

"Nothing," said Shaw. "They have no idea what happened here. I can handle any questions they ask."

"But if you are wrong they will—" Paco tried to say more, but Shaw cut him short, reaching out and slapping his horse soundly on its rump.

"*Hyiii!* Get out of here," Shaw said to both the horse and its rider.

Paco and the mother and daughter raced away around the corner of the church. As they disappeared from sight, outside the burning adobe, the large ball of fire screamed, bounced, rolled, raced and flew from one point to another, still screaming wildly until it finally straightened and ran, falling and rolling and blazing its way out onto the sand flats.

"What was that, a devil? Some sound kind of *banshee*?" Drop the Dog Jones asked, staring after the long streak of fire. In its wake lay bits of burning dried brush that it had plowed its way through and left aflame.

"It wasn't nothing human, that's for sure!" Lying Earl replied. "I saw its eyes! It was some terrible thing, some fiend right out of the pits of hell!"

"It *was* human!" shouted Roscoe Turner. "It was Quinn Madsen, you damned fools. That's the Gomez woman's adobe. Her and her kid probably burned up too."

Out on the flats the fiery tail streaked and licked back and forth until it finally disappeared from sight, its screams having already ceased. On the dirt street the smell of roasting flesh and burned hair lingered heavy in the air.

Villagers had ventured forth out of the darkness and began running back and forth from the well carrying buckets of water to douse on structures standing near the Gomezes' home, seeing the futility of trying to save the burning earth and plank adobe. Through the villagers' midst, Shaw walked up to Roscoe Turner and the others, looked at the raging fire and said, "Those poor bastards never had a chance."

"What poor bastards?" Turner spun toward him. "Who are you talking about? Was somebody else in there besides Madsen, the Gomez woman and the *nit*?"

Shaw shrugged as if he had no interest. "I walked by the open door a while ago. Madsen and Paco Ruiz were sitting at the table drinking. The woman and girl were in there too. Madsen waved me over, but I didn't go." He shook his head. "Looks like I made the right decision."

Turner studied his eyes in the flickering firelight, not knowing what to say.

"Huh," said Lying Earl, "I don't believe that. Shaw's been missing all day. I heard Madsen ask Paco about him earlier."

Shaw gave him a flat, hard stare. "And what did Paco tell him . . . ?" he asked.

Lying Earl's face made a strange grimace. "He said you was asleep. That's what."

Turner and the others gave Lying Earl a confused look.

"So what are you saying?" Shaw asked. "That I'm lying, that Paco was lying?"

"I don't know," said Lying Earl, "but there's something suspicious about this."

"Shut the hell up, Lying Earl," said Turner, trying to get a grip on things, being Madsen's second in charge. He turned to Shaw and asked, "Where have you been all day? I heard Paco say that you was with a woman, that dope-snorting whore who lives behind the cantina." He stared at Shaw closely.

"No," Shaw said, on the chance that Turner was only baiting him. "I've had a belly sickness from too much mescal. I spent most of the day searching for a fresh spot in the sand out back of the stables. That's why I didn't have a drink with Paco and Madsen."

Turner nodded with a trace of a wry grin. "God help you, I've had that mescal sickness myself."

"Hold on, Roscoe," Drop the Dog said to Turner, seeing Turner was believing what Shaw had to say. "I have never seen Paco and Madsen drink together."

"That's right," Lying Earl cut in. "I happen to know that Madsen would never drink with a Mex."

"Oh?" Turner and the men looked at him.

Lying Earl's eyes darted back and forth. "No, he wouldn't," he added quickly as if the thought had just struck him. "All the years I've known him, he always said it was bad luck drinking with a Mex."

"I expect this didn't do much to change his mind," said Shaw, giving a nod toward the burning adobe and the trail of smoldering brush and weeds in Madsen's wake.

The men all nodded as if in agreement. Shaw looked at Lying Earl, then Turner. "I don't see what my whereabouts have to do with any of this, do you?"

"No, I don't," said Turner, still having a problem with it, but not even knowing what to ask. Madsen was dead, Deacon Lucas and some more of his men were on their way. He was in charge until Lucas got here, maybe even afterward, depending on how Lucas felt about it. He didn't want trouble with Fast Larry Shaw, especially over something like this. Still, he felt he needed to make a show of some sort. "Did you ever let Quinn know if you was going to ride with us?" he asked in a firm tone.

"Not yet, I hadn't," said Shaw.

"Understand me, Shaw," said Turner. "If you're with us, you're welcome here. But if you're not with us, I believe it's time you rolled your blanket and go."

"You're running me out of Zarco?" Shaw asked bluntly.

The men standing near Turner stepped away a few feet, their hands near their guns, their expressions tense in the flickering firelight. Turner cut a quick glance at them. "Stand easy, all of yas." Then he said to Shaw, "I'm not running you nowhere. I'm no fool, Shaw. I've seen how fast you are. But this is our bunch, this is our town—leastwise until we're through with it. If you're not a part of us, what *is* your business here?"

"Same as before," said Shaw. "I came to water my horse and get supplies. Madsen asked the Mexican to show me around some, see if I wanted to join you men."

"You've had time to decide, Shaw," said Turner. "So, what's it going to be?"

"Madsen gave me until this Deacon Lucas Leeman fellow gets here," Shaw said.

Turner considered it. Not wanting to look weak in front of the men, he said, "Well, as you can see, Quinn Madsen has no more say. He's dead, so's the Mexican. You've worn out your welcome."

Shaw looked all around, and nodded, not wanting any of them to see that leaving was exactly what he'd had in mind after setting the Gomezes free. "All right," he said grudgingly, as if having to give it some careful consideration, "come morning I'm in the saddle and gone. Does that clear with you?"

Turner hid the flood of relief he felt at hearing Shaw's words. "Yep, come morning, be out of here," he said in a rigid voice. He felt even more relieved when Shaw nodded, turned and walked away. To the rest of the men, Turner said, "All right, a few of yas get mounted. We're riding out and finding where Madsen landed. The poor sumbitch." He shook his head with a grim expression.

Deacon Lucas Leeman, Charlie Bone and Blackie Waite had been riding along a high ridge trail when they heard the faint distant screams reach out across the flats from the direction of Zarco. "Hot damn," said Bone, "sounds like somebody's night's been ruined."

"I'd say he must've sat down on a barrel cactus," Blackie Waite mused.

The three veered their horses off the trail and sat looking out across the flats at the fiery ball as it made its way out of Zarco and eventually burned itself out in the purple night. "I bet ole Quinn has been up to some mischief," said Lucas Leeman with a grim smile.

"Maybe he got tired of that woman of his and this is his way of tying a can to her tail," Waite remarked.

"Whatever it was, it's all over now," said Leeman. He turned his horse back to the rocky trail and nudged it forward at a walk. "Speaking of women, I've got myself a little gift waiting for me in Zarco."

Waite and Bone gave each other a knowing look as they turned their horses behind him. Bone grinned and said, "I was wondering how much longer you was going to let Madsen put you off over taking that young woman home and showing her what a man wants."

Leeman replied, "Whatever *wondering* you've done, you can put it to rest now, Charlie. I've waited as long as I'm going to. Either Madsen offers her as a token of friendship, or I'll take her."

"What if he's saving her for himself?" Waite asked, nudging his horse along behind him.

"Then he's about to come face-to-face with bitter disappointment," said Leeman. He paused, then said, "He knows I'm going to take her. I made my intentions boldy known to him before we rode out of Zarco. He's just had to find himself a way to make it look like it was *him* offering her, instead of *me* taking her from him."

They rode on through the grainy moonlit night, down from the hills and across the sand flats. Near dawn they stopped less than a mile from Zarco and looked all around. Waite sniffed the air and said, "What's that smell?"

"Smells like somebody overroasted a goat," said Bone, fanning his hat in front of his face.

"Yeah, and forgot to skin it first," Waite added, with a sour expression.

Suddenly a voice called out to them from a few yards across the flats. "Deacon, is that you?" asked Filo Hewes, from the cover of a sandy rise.

"Who's asking?" Deacon replied, he and his two riding companions spreading out, their hands on their guns.

"It's me, Filo," said Hewes.

"And me, Sandy Kerns," said another voice, from a few yards away. "Hold your fire, we're coming out."

"Come on out, then," said Leeman. He gave the other two a look. They all three kept their hands resting on their weapons.

"Damn, Deacon, I'm glad that's you boys," said Hewes as the two walked in from the darkness.

"Just who were you boys expecting it to be, Filo?" Leeman asked, looking the thin Kansan outlaw up and down. Beside Hewes, Sandy Kerns walked in closer, a Winchester rifle hanging from his hand.

"This has been one of the strangest damn nights I ever seen," Hewes said, stopping and shaking his head. "We saw a firelight flare up, out yonder in the hills—one of yas lighting yourself a smoke, no doubt," he said, gesturing in the purple dark toward the hills they'd ridden down from. "So Turner left a couple of us out here, to see who come riding in. Lucky for all of us it's you."

"We didn't light any smokes," Leeman said. "We've all three got better sense, out in the dark like that." He glanced back toward the hills. "How long ago was this you seen it?"

"Must've been three hours," said Hewes, looking to Kerns for support.

"Yeah," said Kerns, "we all saw it clearly."

"We were already halfway across these flats by then," said Leeman. He stopped, then said, "Wait a minute. What do you mean, Turner *left* you out here? What were you doing out here to begin with?" Without giving either of them time to answer, he went on to ask, "Why is Turner giving the orders? Where the hell is Madsen?"

"That's Quinn Madsen you're smelling," said Hewes. "He's dead."

"What? Madsen's dead?" Leeman looked back and forth between the two men.

"Yep, burned all to hell," said Kerns. "The Gomez adobe burned up, killed Madsen, Paco and the woman and her girl. Turner and some of the boys roped Madsen's burned carcass and dragged it to town. It looked like they'd jerked up a tree stump and pulled it along behind them."

"Ah, hell," Leeman said with a tone of remorse, not seeming to hear about dragging Madsen's body back to town. "I wanted that little girl so bad."

"Not now you wouldn't," said Hewes, " 'less you wanted to keep her in a snuff box."

"You think that's funny, you son of a bitch?" Leeman shouted, his Colt coming up, cocked and ready to fire.

"No, I surely don't, Deacon!" Hewes said quickly. "I never meant to say it. I don't know what come over me! I must've lost my mind!"

"Deacon," Bone said quietly, "don't shoot him out here before daylight. We've got them lawdogs on our tails, don't forget."

Leeman cooled down, uncocked his Colt and held it loosely in his gloved hand. "Don't you say another word to me about nothing, Hewes," he warned. To Kerns he said, "I expect Turner is somewhere in hog heaven, being left in charge?"

"Well, I haven't paid close attention, but I 'spect he rightly is," said Kerns, picking his words carefully after seeing what almost happened to Hewes.

"Well, amigos, that's all about to change real quick-like," said Leeman. He gave a grin. "I was only a hair away from taking this bunch over. Now is as good a time as any."

"There's been a gunman name of Lawrence Shaw ride into Zarco, Deacon," said Kerns. "I thought you ought to know."

"Fast Larry Shaw?" said Leeman with surprise.

"Yep, that's him," said Kerns.

"Hell, I thought he was dead," Leeman said with a short chuckle. "Got himself et by a bear up in Montana Territory."

"They call him the fastest gun alive," Kerns said, carefully, watching Leeman's face to see his reaction.

"Yeah, I know," said Leeman. "I remember hearing him called that. But that was all hot air and horse droppings. He never was near as fast as everybody used to think he was." He turned in his saddle and said, "Let's get into Zarco. I can use some tequila, take my mind off losing my little darling." He batted his boot heels to his horse's sides and raced away in the silver gray of morning.

As soon as the three had ridden away, Kerns looked at Hewes and scratched his head. "I didn't want to dispute him, but Shaw looked awfully damn fast to me."

"Me too," said Hewes, "but I wasn't going to get my head shot off for saying so." He spat on the ground and watched the three riders raise a cloud of dust in the morning light.

PART 4

PART 3

Chapter 16

Paco, the woman and Francisca had ridden across the sand flats and up onto one of the many hill trails north of Zarco. Once in the shelter of the high rocky terrain, as they kept the horses moving along at a walk, the woman sidled up closer to Paco and said, "Now that we are safely away from Zarco, you can leave us on our own. We will be all right."

He looked at her in the thin moonlight for a moment, then said, "Do not judge me to be like Quinn Madsen and the others. I ask nothing from you or the child." Francisca rode along a few feet behind them, listening.

"Oh, I see," she said, returning his scrutinizing gaze. "You come with us out of the goodness of your heart, eh, Paco Ruiz?"

"I come with you because my friend Shaw asked me to," he replied. "This is dangerous country, especially after what happened in Zarco. He wants me to stay with the two of you until you are far away from the border raiders."

"And where is this safer place you speak of?" she asked.

Paco considered it for a moment, then said, "Mexico City, perhaps?"

"No, that is too far," said Ramona. "Francisca and I will be fine if you turn and leave right now. We know our way through the hill trails."

"Why are you afraid of me?" Paco asked, knowing the woman was uneasy traveling with him. "I am only along to make sure you get away from Madsen's border raiders. I am here to protect you. I ask nothing from you in return."

"Protect me? Madsen was only trying to *protect me*," she said with a bitter tone. "When he had sent my Nito off to be starved to death, he told me it was not safe for me and Francisca to live alone, with so many men in Zarco. Then he moved into my home, took over my life and beat me when I tried to resist in any way."

"I told you, I am not like Madsen," said Paco. "I am sorry for what happened to you, but it is over now. You and the child must put this part of your life behind you."

Ramona stopped her horse on the rocky trail, as if she would refuse to ride any farther with him. "Do not tell me what my daughter and I must do. It is because of men like you that I am fleeing my ho—"

"Quiet," Paco hissed, cutting her off by jerking the reins from her hands and pulling her horse along behind him.

Francisca had heard him and started to pull her horse back away from him. But Paco snatched her reins from her as well and dragged both of them off the trail into the sparse shadows of brush, rock and tall slender saplings. "Let me go!" said Ramona, struggling against his hold on her horse.

"Shut up!" Pace growled, his Colt coming out of his holster, cocked and ready.

Seeing the dull glint of gunmetal, Ramona froze in her saddle for a moment. So did Francisca.

"Listen," Paco whispered, his Colt gesturing higher up the trail. "Horses coming." He paused, then added in an even lower whisper, "Two . . . no, three horses coming."

The woman and the girl sat stone silent as the sound of slowly moving hooves drew closer and more audible on the rocky trail.

Watching the trail closely from only a few feet away, Paco saw Morgan Hatch and Sonny Engles move past him like ghosts. Behind them rode Juanita, the whore, who had caught up with them on the way up the other side of the hill lines. She looked back and forth warily, a soiled and bloodstained bandage on the bullet wound in her shoulder. At one point her attention seemed to fix on Paco, who sat aimed and ready to fire.

"I'm telling you I heard a woman's voice, Morgan," Sonny Engles said to Hatch, both of them also looking around in the shadowy moonlit darkness.

"I think you've been riding too long," Hatch replied, searching along the trail all the same. "What the blazes would a woman be doing out on these high trails at this late hour?"

"I don't know," Sonny whispered. Then he gestured a nod back toward Juanita. "Ask the whore, she's out here, ain't she?"

Hatch gave a thin smile in the darkness. "She's an exception. She's out here 'cause she craves the company of bold, adventurous men like us."

"Is that right, Whore?" Sonny asked over his shoulder with a chuckle. "Do you crave the company of men like us? Is that why you stuck with ole Wild Dick to the end? Is that why you took a bullet for us?"

The woman didn't answer. She rode along in silence, both Wild Dick and Grady Carr's blood dried dark and mixed with her own on the bosom of her dress. She carried Carr's big revolver stuck down behind a wide leather belt that Hatch had given her to wear. "Don't pick at her, Sonny," Hatch said, half joking yet half-serious. "She's armed with both gun and knife. She would chop you down quicker than a Chinaman can chop a duck."

"I'm not picking at her, am I, *hon?*" Sonny said, glancing back, his eyes going to the gun at her waist.

The woman didn't reply.

"Don't ignore me, Whore," Sonny warned her, cocking a gloved hand threateningly. "I'll wear you out without batting an eye."

"Leave her alone, Sonny," said Hatch. "She did what we needed done. She earned her place at the table—she's one of us now. She's got a bullet through her shoulder to prove it."

"Yeah?" said Sonny, still turned in his saddle facing the silent woman. "Just because you did what we expected of you doesn't mean I'll tolerate any of your guff. Bullet or no bullet, I'm primed to backhand the cold piss out of you if I take a notion."

The woman only stared at him until he finally gave

a short laugh and said, "Damn, she don't spook easily, I'll give her that."

"Good for her," Hatch said.

Sonny turned forward in his saddle and gazed ahead along the shadowy trail. "I can't wait to see Deacon Lucas' face once we get down from here and across the sand flats," he said, finished with taunting the woman. "He's bound to think we're lying dead back in Julimez."

"Yeah," Hatch replied grimly. "I just wish ole Wild Dick was along to dabble his fingers in Deacon's warm brains when we open his head up." ·

Sonny took a bag of fixings from his shirt pocket, rolled a smoke, lit it and shook out the match.

"Damn it, Sonny," said Hatch, "you've both been striking matches all night."

"So?" Sonny said, letting go of a stream of smoke and handing the fixings back to Juanita.

"So anybody can see us coming from miles off," Hatch said in a harsh tone.

"*Tornillo ellos todo,*" Sonny said. With a laugh he looked back at the woman and said, "Did I say it right, Whore, *screw them all*?"

The woman only shook her bowed head slowly without answering yes or no. She busily rolled herself a smoke. Running the thin cigarette in and out of her mouth to firm it up, she lit it and blew out a thin silvery stream into the moonlit darkness. Ignoring Engles, she looked back again toward the spot where she thought that she too had heard the sound of a woman's voice. They rode on.

When the three had ridden a safer distance farther down the trail, Ramona breathed a sigh of relief.

"Let's keep silent," Paco whispered, leading both Ramona's and Francisca's horses back onto the trail and giving them back their reins.

Francisca rode along, glancing back over her shoulder, until they had reached a fork in the high, narrow hill trail.

When she felt safe enough to talk, Ramona asked Paco in a hushed voice, "Did you recognize those three?"

"*Sí*, I recognized the men and their voices," Paco replied. "They are Morgan Hatch and Sonny Engles. Both of them are border raiders—two very dangerous killers. The woman I have never seen before."

"Then it is a good thing that you heard them when you did and guided us off the trail," Ramona remarked.

Paco only shrugged. "I have ridden this country for a long time. Like a fox, I have learned when to be *brave* enough to prowl or *wise* enough to lie low."

After a pause Ramona said apologetically, "I was wrong to resist when you tired to lead me off the trail."

"I caught you by surprise. It is understandable that you questioned what I was doing," Paco said. "You do not know me, and I ride with the same men who have caused you such misery."

"I am grateful to you for leading us away from Zarco," she said in a gentler tone than she had been speaking in.

"You are both very welcome," he said with another slight shrug. "I wish none of those bad things had ever happened to you." He paused, then said, "And now I leave it up to you. If you do not want me to ride any farther with you, tell me so. I will go one direction, you can go the other." He nodded at the two trails lying before them. "I will not lead you against your will."

Ramona looked at both trails as she considered how close they had come to riding right into the two border raiders in the darkness. She hadn't heard a sound; but Paco had heard, and he'd known exactly what to do. "Where will you go?" she asked. "Will you follow this trail around and go to the border raiders?"

Paco thought about it. "That is what I had intended to do. I make lots of money stealing from the *americanos* and racing back across the border." He gave a trace of a devilish grin.

"Money is all that is important to you, then?" she asked, searching his eyes.

"*Sí*, it is," said Paco. He shook his head as if catching himself in a change of heart, then said, "That is, it *was* all that is important to me." He looked at her. "I have seen how bravely you, your daughter and your husband have tried to stay together. It makes me think maybe there are things more important than money."

They sat in silence for a moment, Francisca moving her horse a few feet away from them and gazing off up the meandering hill trail. Finally Ramona asked, "What is it you want, Paco Ruiz?"

"I want . . ." He paused, then continued. "I want whatever it is that you and Nito Gomez had."

"That is what Madsen wanted," Ramona said. "He killed my husband for it . . . still he did not get it. I don't think he even knew what it was."

"Neither do I," said Paco. "I do not know what it is, and I do not want to kill to get it, the way Madsen did. Yet I have seen it, and I want it . . . even more than I want money."

"I will be mourning my husband's death for a long time to come," she said.

Paco nodded. "I understand."

"I do not know if my heart will ever heal after all that has happened here," she said.

"This I understand too," Paco said. "Perhaps all that happens is that I lead you and Francisca to a new place, where you will be able to live in peace. I ask for no promise and I make none myself. If there is no place for me when we get there, then so be it . . . I will go."

"A new place . . ." She nodded slowly. "My Nito would want that for us." She looked off along the high trail and said, "All right, Paco Ruiz, lead my daughter and me away from this terrible place . . . *por favor*."

Without another word on the matter, Paco turned his horse toward the high trail. Ramona nudged her horse forward, following him.

Francisca looked longingly back into the moonlit night and across the distant sand flats. She crossed herself silently, wondering where Shaw might be at that very moment, and if he'd known all along, as she was certain any angel must, all the dark and painful ways in which the things she had prayed for would have to be answered.

She wiped a warm tear from her eye with the back of her hand. "*Gracias*, Senor Angel. *Adios*," she whis-

pered under her breath. Then she followed her
mother and Paco away into the high desert night.

In the morning light Shaw had grained the big
buckskin and led it from the livery stables to the
water trough beside the town well. While the animal
drew water, he sank four canteens at the edge of the
well, filled them, capped them and hung them by
their straps from his saddle horn. He looked all
around at footprints back and forth from the well to
the pile of simmering, smoking rubble that had been
the Gomezes' home. Villagers stood staring at the
charred heap.

He thought about the woman and her daughter for
a moment, knowing the two were in good hands
with Paco Ruiz. The Mexican was a good man in
spite of how he made his living. Shaw had known
when he'd sent him off last night there was a good
chance he'd never see him again. Shaw gazed off
toward the distant hills. Who knew where Paco and
the women's paths might lead them by the time they
got where they were going?

As an angel, his work here was done, Shaw
thought wryly, tightening the straps holding his bedroll. He looked at the buckskin, and the horse raised
its dripping muzzle and stared back at him. "All
right, I'm ready," he said, as if the animal had told
him it was time to go.

But before he could gather his reins and swing up
into his saddle, Shaw heard a voice call his name
from the street out in front of the cantina. Upon hearing the voice resound along the dirt street, the villag-

ers standing by the burned rubble seemed to vanish without a sound. Taking his time, Shaw turned slowly toward the voice as it called out again.

"Yeah, you, Fast Larry," said Deacon Lucas Leeman as he walked forward. Six gunmen followed close behind him, three on either side, spread out with a few feet between them.

Shaw patted the buckskin's side and said quietly to the animal, "Why is it you get in trouble every time you drink here?"

"I'm Lucas Leeman. I know you've heard of me," said the tall, broad-shouldered gunman. As he spoke he made a show of drawing the lapel of his dark swallow-tailed suit coat back behind the handle of his tied-down Colt. "I want to talk to you." Dust and sand from the desert trail still lined his hat, his shoulders and covered his boots.

Shaw looked him up and down, making no reply as to ever having heard of him. "Talk," he said flatly, making no move to pull up the corner of his poncho and reveal his own tied-down weapon.

Leeman caught the deliberate slight on Shaw's part. "Well, I've heard of you, *Fast Larry*—all that *fastest gun alive* malarkey. I never believed a word of it. To tell the truth, I thought you died long ago. I even heard once that a bear ate you." He gave a thin, mirthless grin. A tense hush fell over the street.

"Was that your *talk*?" Shaw said, unmoved.

"Hell no." Leeman's face reddened with rage. His demeanor and voice changed. "Let's get down to matters," he said. "These men told me what happened here last night. Now I want to hear what you've got to say about it."

"I've got nothing further to add," Shaw said in the same flat tone.

"Nothing further to add?" Leeman gave a short bemused chuckle. "You haven't even heard what they told me."

"I know," said Shaw.

Leeman creased his brow. "Are you giving me a hard time here?"

"Not yet," said Shaw.

The men flanking Leeman took heed to Shaw's thinly veiled threat. They tensed, having seen his merciless handiwork on Bo Phelps, Cero Stewart and Tommy Layton.

Leeman caught the threat as well. His hand wrapped around the butt of his Colt and tightened there, his thumb over the hammer. "This gang lost three good men to you, *Fast Larry* Shaw," he said with a note of contempt. "Not to mention Madsen and the Mexican dying in that fire last night. You've got to convince me you had no hand in things, if you plan on living out the day."

"I have got no plans made. Do you?" Shaw said in the same flat tone.

Shaw looked from face to face at the men flanking Leeman. Among the six men, Charlie Bone and Blackie Waite stood nearest to the big gunman. Off to the side Shaw saw Bert Sibott standing away from any upcoming fight. Siboott shook his head slightly, as if advising Shaw not to let things get out of hand. The big bare-knuckle brawler's face still carried the scars, bruises and red scorch marks from their previous encounter. Then Shaw riveted his eyes on Leeman, letting him know he'd be the first to fall.

But Leeman wouldn't be stopped. He started to make his move; Shaw saw it in his eyes. Yet before he begin to snatch his gun up from his holster, a voice called out from the rooftop of the cantina where a gunman named Towan Bartley stood with a long telescope in his hand, "Deacon! Riders coming! It's Morgan Hatch and Sonny Engles. They're alive! There's a woman with them!"

Leeman froze. His face went blank. "I'll be damned," he whispered loud enough for Shaw to hear him. In his stunned surprise, he straightened, eased his hand up from his gun butt and stood staring at Shaw as if uncertain what to do or say next. Finally he raised a hand and pointed at Shaw. "I'm not through with you. Don't try leaving town."

Something in the look on Leeman's face struck a curious chord in Shaw. He looked past Leeman and saw the same stunned look on the faces of Waite and Charlie Bone. Farther out he saw the rise of dust from the approaching riders. Then he looked back at Deacon Lucas Leeman and said in the same flat, unrevealing tone, "I wouldn't think of it."

Chapter 17

Seeing Filo Hewes ride out toward them across the sand, Morgan Hatch said, "Keep your bark off until we get Leeman and those other two snakes right in our gun sights. Then we'll chop them off at their boot tops."

"Don't worry about me," said Sonny, "I've been practicing killing them in my mind so long I know it by heart." Behind them the woman rode in silence.

Over his shoulder, Hatch said to the woman, "You keep quiet, just like you have been. As soon as we've done our killing, we'll see to it Madsen lets you in with us."

"Yeah," said Sonny, "we'll tell him what a crazy, killing, cutthroat whore you are. How could he say no?" Looking back, he gave her a grin and a wink.

"*Hola*, Morgan. *Hola*, Sonny," said Hewes, racing in close, then sliding his horse sideways to a halt a few yards away. He looked surprised to see them. "We heard you fellows got yourselves shot to pieces."

"*Hola* yourself, Filo," Hatch called out. "As you can see, your information was wrong." Beside him, Sonny just touched the brim of his battered Stetson and nodded courteously.

"I'm damn glad to see you both still aboveground. Who's the woman?" Hewes asked, looking Juanita up and down, noting the dried blood on her bosom.

"Just call her Whore," said Engles before Hatch could answer.

"*Hola, Whore*, ma'am," Hewes said hesitantly, uncertain how to address the woman.

"Her real name is Juanita," Hatch said to Hewes, "if you'd prefer calling her something a little more civil." He gave Engles a cross look.

"Begging your pardon, ma'am," said Hewes. "Juanita it is, then."

Engles only chuckled.

"Where's ole Wild Dick Bernie?" Hewes asked, looking all around as if Wild Dick might pop up out of the sand. "You three always stick together."

"Wild Dick *is* dead," Engles said flatly. "That much of what you heard is true. We shot it out with a border law posse back in Julimez. Wild Dick took on some bad wounds and didn't make it."

"Damn, I hate to hear it," said Hewes. "We've lost some good men here too."

"Is Deacon, Bone and Blackie still in town, or did they just pass through last night?" Hatch asked, as if not hearing what Hewes said about losing some men. He gazed ahead toward the streets of Zarco.

"Yep, they're all three still here," said Hewes. "Why would they ride on?"

"No reason, Filo," Hatch said, dismissing the question out of hand.

"Fact is, it looks like Deacon's going to be running this bunch from now on," Hewes added.

Sonny and Hatch glanced at each other. "Oh yeah, why's that?" Sonny asked.

"One of the men we've lost here is Madsen himself," said Hewes.

"Quinn Madsen is *dead*?" Sonny asked in surprise.

"He's deader than hell," said Hewes. "He caught himself on fire and ran off into the desert before anybody could put him out. Turner and the boys dragged his remains back to town. I'll tell you it was a terrible sight, a man roasted alive like that."

Staring toward Zarco, Hatch said, "But Deacon was more than willing to take over and start running things before Madsen even stopped sizzling?"

"Deacon wasn't here when it happened. Turner was second in command," said Hewes. "But as soon as Deacon rode in he commenced telling us all how things are going to be from now on."

"I just damn well bet he did," said Sonny, also staring toward Zarco.

"Tell us, Filo," said Hatch, "did Deacon know you were riding out to meet us?"

"I never asked," said Filo. "I always ride out any time I see more of our men showing up." He shrugged. "I never thought to ask, now that he's taking over." He looked back and forth between them. "I hope I haven't gone and done the wrong thing, riding out here. I already got off wrong with Deacon last night over something I said in fun."

"Naw, you did the right thing. Why wouldn't it be all right with Deacon?" Hatch said, nudging his horse forward at a walk, Sonny right beside him, the woman following in silence.

"Here's something else," said Hewes, seeming to feel as though it was his duty to catch the two gunmen up on things. "Fast Larry Shaw rode into Zarco the other day. I expect you've heard of him?"

"Man, I'll say!" said Engles. "He's the one who killed Barton Talbert, Blue Snake Terril . . ." He stopped as his mind came up with too many names to mention. "Hell, he's killed more men than the *plague!*"

"Well, you can add three more to that long list," said Hewes. "He shot Bo Phelps no sooner than he rode in, before he'd even finished watering his horse!"

"Damn!" said Engles, looking impressed. Bedside him Hatch just shook his head, unable to tell whether Sonny was serious or mocking Hewes.

"That ain't all," said Hewes. "He hadn't been here an hour, he killed Cero Stewart and Tommy Layton!"

"Nobody held him to account for it?" Hatch asked. "Quinn Madsen just let it happen, never said a word?"

"Madsen said they all three *started* the fight," Hewes explained. "All Shaw did was *stop* it. Madsen called it all self-defense."

"If he called it self-defense, there was no more to say on the matter." Hatch spat and gazed ahead.

"Besides," said Hewes, "Madsen was trying to get Shaw to ride with us. Seems a big gun like Shaw gets job offers the rest of us has to bow and scrape for."

"Did you see us bow or scrape?" asked Engles, his voice turning cold all of a sudden.

"I didn't mean you, Sonny," said Hewes. "I was just using all the rest of us as an example—"

"What about Deacon Lucas?" Hatch asked, cutting off Engles and Hewes. "Is he trying to get Shaw to ride with us?" As he asked he gave Engles a look.

"They were talking in the street when I rode out here," said Hewes, "but I can't say what about."

Hatch nodded. Then, to get rid of Hewes for a few minutes, he said, "Why don't you do us all a favor and ride back and check our back trail for a mile or so? We've had four lawdogs on our trail since Julimez. Can't shake them loose in this blasted sand. We'd be obliged."

"Sure thing, Morgan," said Hewes. Before turning his horse and riding away, he cautioned them both. "Walk easy around Deacon. He's had some bark on all morning. He's tight as a fox squirrel for some reason or another."

"Thanks for the warning, Filo," said Hatch. "We'll be on our best game."

As Hewes rode off on the trail behind them, the two stared toward Zarco with bitter expressions. "How about these jackpotting sons a' bitches?" Hatch said. "We come to kill them, and damned if Deacon hasn't managed to take charge of all the border raiders."

"He can still die," said Sonny. "Can't he?" he asked as if having to make certain.

"Oh yeah, we came to kill him, and we'll get it done," said Hatch. "But we're going to be a couple of cool, calm hombres about everything, until we find ourselves the right time and place to do it."

"You hearing all this, Whore?" Sonny asked, tossing a glance over his shoulder.

"*Sí*, I hear it," the woman said, speaking to Sonny for the first time after a long period of silence.

"Don't get any ideas about putting yourself in good with Deacon Leeman by telling him what we've got in mind. We're the ones who brought you here. We're the ones who can stop you. Don't forget where your loyalty lies."

"My loyalty will lie with the one who crosses my hand with the most gold," she said calmly.

"Damn, Whore." Sonny chuckled aloud. "It sounds like you've been studying our ways for a long time."

She only smiled thinly and fell silent, riding along behind them.

When Towan Bartley had announced the three riders coming in off the sand flats, Deacon Leeman had quickly gathered Charlie Bone and Blackie Waite to one side and given them both a nod, letting them know to be ready for anything.

Shaw had been watching ever since he'd seen the strange look come over Deacon's face when he'd heard the two men were riding into Zarco. It wasn't hard to see that something was at work here, he thought, watching Deacon from a spot he'd taken in the shade out in front of the cantina.

As the three riders approached Zarco, Bert Sibott

sidled up to Shaw and said between the two of them, "I want you to know I wasn't taking Deacon's side a while ago."

"I'm obliged, Sibott," Shaw said, looking the big fighter up and down. "How's the burns and bruises coming along?"

"I'm still sore as hell," said Sibott. He managed a stiff grin. "But it's nothing a few slugs of tequila and smoking some strong Mexican dope can't handle." He patted his bulging shirt pocket. "If you want some for any pains you might have, just let me know." He gave a wide, crooked grin. "You don't even have to *have* any pain, you might want some just to keep any pain away."

"No, thanks, but it's most kind of you to offer," said Shaw, keeping an eye toward the coming riders as he spoke to the big Frenchman.

"Don't mention it, Shaw. I owe it to you," said Sibott. "I'm not forgetting what you did for me." He rounded his big shoulders and added, "I know if you hadn't got me out of that chimney and poured water on me, I'd be looking the same as Madsen over there."

He nodded across the dirt at the twisted, lumpy pile of charred substance that had been Quinn Madsen. A skinny dog had ventured forward, stuck its nose close to the brittle, blackened remains, then sneezed and gagged and backed away, as if in disgust.

"I'm glad that didn't have to happen to you," Shaw remarked, seeing Deacon, Bone and Waite talking quietly among themselves, every now and then casting a glance toward him. "Who are these riders coming? Why is Deacon Leeman so concerned about them?" he asked as if just out of curiosity.

"I can't say why he's so concerned about them," Sibott said, gazing toward Hatch and Engles. "But Morgan Hatch, Sonny Engles, and Wild Dick Bernie have ridden with some of the toughest gangs in the frontier territories. They are not men I would want to cross and have them looking to kill me." He paused. "I'm surprised you haven't heard of them."

"I've been away from the territories for a while," Shaw said, watching the three riders draw closer.

When Deacon stepped away from Bone and Waite and walked toward Shaw, Sibott said, "I best make myself scarce. It looks like Deacon is wanting to have a word with you." As he turned to walk away he added in a whisper, "Keep an eye on him. Don't turn your back."

"Obliged, I'll remember that," Shaw replied.

Hurrying his pace a little, Deacon Leeman walked up to Shaw, this time without his swallow-tailed coat pulled back behind his Colt—this time by himself. Bone and Waite walked closer and lingered a few yards away, watching the three riders enter the far end of the dirt street.

"Fast Larry Shaw," said Leeman, his voice still a little harsh, but trying to sound more sociable than before, "you and I got off on the wrong foot a while ago. I was just tired and edgy from too long on the trail."

Here it comes. . . . The voice inside Shaw's head spoke quietly to him. "I understand," he said, making no attempt at offering an apology in return.

"I just learned that Quinn Madsen and you had been talking some about you riding with us. Is that right?"

"Yep," said Shaw, offering nothing more, watching out the corner of his eye as the three riders drew closer down the dirt street.

"Well, I don't know what he offered you, but whatever it was, that offer still stands," said Leeman. "I trust Quinn Madsen's judgment enough to know that he was right in wanting a big-name gunman like yourself riding at his side." He paused, expecting Shaw to say something. When Shaw didn't, he cleared his throat and said, "So what say you? Can you ride with a bunch like the border raiders? I have to warn you these men are tough, bold and dangerous."

"I know," Shaw said flatly, "I've killed three of these tough, dangerous men."

Deacon didn't pursue the matter of Shaw having killed three of the raiders. He gave a sidelong glance toward the three riders, then said, "What's it going to be? I need to hear something from you. We've got posse men and U.S. Marshals on our trail. I don't have time to fool around."

U.S. Marshals . . . ? Shaw's interest was piqued.

Leeman saw the slight change in Shaw's expression and seized upon it. "I know you rode as a deputy marshal. The men told me about it last night. Said you still carry the badge as a keepsake. But that don't bother me. Clell Butterfield rides with us. He used to be a Montana lawman. I say a man's past is his own business." He took another nervous glance at the three riders as they drew nearer.

"Who are these U.S. Marshals hounding you?" Shaw asked, taking his time, knowing that Leeman was feeling pressured by his putting him off. A bead of sweat broke free on Leeman's forehead and rolled down into the thick beard stubble on his cheek.

"Marshal Crayton Dawson," said Leeman. "Him and his deputy, a fellow named Caldwell, used to be an undertaker, I heard."

"Yeah, that's right, he did," said Shaw.

Leeman eyed him closely. "So you know Dawson and his deputy?" he asked, getting more and more edgy as the three riders reined their horses down to a slow deliberate walk down the middle of the dirt street.

"Yeah, I know them," Shaw said, not looking at Leeman now, but rather staring toward the approaching riders.

"Well, like I said, I don't hold that against you," Leeman said. "I know you've had plenty of time to think it over, so what do you say? Are you going to ride with us?"

Shaw shrugged and said, "I'm not doing anything. Sure, why not?"

Leeman looked relieved.

"But give me a couple days before I start," Shaw said, still staring at the riders. "I've got something I need to do first." He wasn't about to ride with Deacon Lucas Leeman and this bunch of thieves and murderers. But this wasn't the time to turn him down. First chance he got, Shaw's plan was to ride out and not look back on Zarco. Now that Paco had taken the woman and her child safely away, there was nothing to keep him here. *Now that my angel work is done,* Shaw told himself, thinking fondly of Francisca and the wide-eyed innocent way she'd adored him.

Chapter 18

Shaw and Deacon Leeman watched the three riders enter Zarco and stop ten yards away in the middle of the dirt street. Charlie Bone and Blackie Waite stood a few feet apart. They made an attempt at hiding the fact that they were expecting a fight. In a narrow alleyway Sandy Kerns stood out of sight with a rifle ready and poised, its barrel resting on a pile of building planks.

"*Hola*, Deacon Leeman!" Morgan Hatch called out from his saddle.

Leeman stepped sidelong into the street facing him. "Here I am, Hatch," he said. "You two step down and make whatever move suits you." He had shoved his coat back behind his Colt again, and stood ready.

"Whatever suits us?" Hatch looked all around with a thin, bemused smile. "Hell, Deacon, you don't seem at all happy to see us."

Deacon paused for a second, then said, "I know your blood's up over what happened in Julimez. I'm not going to deny we left the four of you in a bad spot. If you've got something to settle, let's get to it.''

Hatch shrugged. "You and Bone and Waite managed to get out. Me and my pards didn't. That's the bad breaks of this business. I've got nothing to settle, have you, Sonny?" He looked sidelong at Engles.

"Naw, not me," Sonny said. "All in a day's work, far as I'm concerned." As he spoke to Deacon Leeman, he looked Shaw up and down.

Leeman didn't trust them, but he went on to ask, "Where's Wild Dick and Orville, both dead, I suppose?"

"Yep, you suppose right," said Hatch. "The posse killed Orville before he got his trousers up. Dick took some bullets in his lungs and wasn't able to ride past Arajo. We left him there with this woman." He nodded at Juanita, who sat listening in silence.

"And the posse stuck on your tails?" Deacon asked, wanting to know as much as he could.

"Naw, we killed off that posse," Hatch replied matter-of-factly.

"You killed the *whole* posse?" Leeman asked in stunned disbelief.

"Killed them dead, and got away," said Hatch. "So you see, we've got ill feelings. We made out all right. Found some water canteens the posse had with them," he lied. "We cut straight for Arajo, took on fresh water and come all the way here."

"The lawmen who's been dogging us all the way here is Dawson and Caldwell," said Sonny. "There was two more with them, but the whore here cut one's throat and left him bleeding to death."

"She's the meanest whore ever thrown out of hell,"

Hatch cut in. "We left her to take care of Wild Dick. When he died, she killed the lawman and got clean out of there—took a bullet but never slowed down."

Leeman looked the woman up and down. "Well, well, you three have had a hell of a ride," he said, feeling more at ease now. They hadn't mentioned seeing where he'd shot holes in the water bags at the supply wagon and left them stuck with no water to cross the desert to Zarco. "Hell, get down out of them saddles, get something to drink, get the woman looked after."

"Obliged," said Hatch. The three stepped down and walked their horses to a hitch rail near the spot where Shaw stood watching.

"I bet you're Fast Larry Shaw," Sonny said, appraising Shaw, his frayed poncho, his broad, battered sombrero, his overall demeanor.

"I am," was Shaw's only reply.

"Shaw's one of *many* good new men who'll be riding with us," said Leeman, cutting in. He spoke not only to Hatch and Sonny, but to the entire gang— some twenty-odd men, Shaw had estimated, spread out all around the dirt street.

"Is that a fact?" Engles replied. He kept his eyes on Shaw, sizing him up.

Shaw knew that look. He'd seen it in the eyes of many gunmen who upon meeting him for the first time began to question whether or not they could kill him. Shaw returned the look, answering the gunman's question with a single stare—it would cost no less than his life to find out.

"Why so many new men?" Hatch asked Leeman as Sonny stood wondering whether or not he should push Shaw a little, just enough to see how Shaw would handle it.

"We're going to need a lot of men," said Leeman. "Now that I'm in charge, we're taking on some bigger jobs."

"Oh, what sort of jobs?" Hatch asked.

Shaw listened to the two men talk. At the same time he kept an eye on Sonny Engles.

"I always figured the tales I heard about you was more wind than muscle, Shaw," Engles said, keeping it civil, but at the same time testing Shaw's temperament. He stepped in closer, a move that told Shaw he didn't intend on turning this into a gunfight, not right now. Had he wanted a gunfight he would have stayed back a ways. This was something else. But it was nothing Shaw hadn't seen before.

"How about the Mexican government's gold station at Durango for starters?" Leeman replied to Hatch, keeping his voice private between the two of them, Shaw hearing it all the same.

"That sounds good to me," said Hatch. Shaw caught every word of it. *The government gold station at Durango . . .*

Standing in Shaw's face, Sonny Engles said in a threatening tone, "See, I'm awfully dang fast myself, Shaw. I figure it ain't likely anybody could be as—"

Hatch, the woman and Leeman all three turned quickly at the sound of gunmetal against jawbone. The rest of the men in the street tensed. Engles had already crumbled to the ground, not knowing what had hit him. Morgan Hatch grabbed for his gun instinctively, uncertain whether this was something between Sonny and Shaw or something Leeman had set up. But before his gun barrel cleared the holster, Shaw's Colt was pointed at him, cocked. The woman stood with her hand on the gun at her waist.

"When your *monkey* wakes up, tell him I could have killed him if I had a mind to," Shaw said to Hatch, knowing his words were also meant for Hatch himself to consider.

Hatch uncoiled, knowing Shaw was right. He let his Colt slip back down into the holster. He'd run a glance across Deacon Leeman and seen that Leeman had been as surprised as he was by Shaw's move. "I'll tell him," Hatch said calmly, raising his hand away from his gun. The men in the street relaxed; so did the woman.

"Tell him next time, I'll kill him," Shaw said with resolve. Keeping a cold gaze on Morgan Hatch, he uncocked the hammer on his Colt and holstered it with a slick flick of his wrist.

Leeman chuckled. "Well now, I have to say, that was as slick and skillful as anything I've seen for a while." He wanted to appear as if he maintained some say-so over Shaw. "Next time, don't be jerking iron without letting me know beforehand." He looked down at Engles, shook his head and laughed for the other men to hear. "It looks like you put Sonny on soup and water for the next week or two."

"That was the *best* thing I had for him," Shaw said, again giving Hatch a look. He took up his horse's reins and led the animal away toward the stables. But when he had turned a corner out of sight, he stepped up into his saddle and nudged the big buck-skin toward a long trail leading out of town.

On the street, Hatch reached down with the woman's help and raised Engles to a slumped sitting position. "Was Sonny crowding him?" Leeman asked.

"More than likely," said Hatch. "He crowds everybody, especially somebody he thinks is good with a gun."

"So Shaw saw trouble coming with him and didn't even give it a chance to start," Leeman said in contemplation. "I expect it's that kind of forethought that's kept him alive all this time."

"Yeah," said Hatch. "Trouble is, Sonny is not the kind to let something like this go. He'll be down Shaw's neck first time he's able."

"I expect Shaw allows for that possibility too," Leeman said, looking off toward the stables where he thought Shaw had taken his horse.

From a high trail, Dawson, Caldwell and Tunis stood looking down at the flyblown carcass of the water mule that Hatch, Engles and the woman had left behind. The animal's throat had been cleanly cut. Only a portion of its hind leg had been carved off and roasted over a low fire at the edge of the trail. Caldwell stooped down, held his hand close to the ashes, then pressed his gloved palm down in the brittle embers, finding not the faintest warmth.

Standing, he brushed his hands together, shook his head and said, "The fire's cold . . . four hours or more."

Dawson nodded. Looking up from the mule and fire ashes and down the trail, he said, "At least we know they're getting close to where they're headed."

"Oh, why's that?" Tunis asked.

"They took what was left of the water from the

mule and killed the animal," said Dawson. "That means they won't be needing another load of water. They'll get by with what's hanging on their saddle horns."

"We should have questioned the Mexican family we saw ride past us on the lower trail yesterday," Tunis said. "They might have seen them."

"It would have cost us a half hour riding down and around to them," Caldwell said.

"Besides," said Dawson, "if the family had passed close by them, these three would have killed them for their guns and horses." He spat and thought about it. "The Mexican was wearing a big modern Colt. Him, his wife and the young girl were all three riding good horses."

Caldwell said, "These raiders couldn't have resisted robbing and killing them, had they come upon one another."

"Lucky those folks took the trail they're on," Dawson said. "This one would have gotten them killed." He turned and stepped back up into his saddle. "Let's go. I've got a feeling we'll find them holed up out on the flats once we get down there."

"Where's the nearest water stop out there?" Tunis asked, he and Caldwell also stepping up into their saddles.

"Zarco," said Caldwell. "It used to be used as a *federale* outpost, a resting place for soldiers hunting down the Apache. Last I heard there's few people living there now. But there *is* water there. The government sunk a deep well for the soldiers. So folks have come and gone ever since."

"Sounds like a dandy place for a gang like the

border raiders to hide out," Tunis said, nudging his horse along beside Caldwell, Dawson in the lead down the high meandering trail. "I don't mind telling you both, this desert has worn me down. If Messenger wants an official report when we get through out here, he'll have to write one himself."

Dawson gave a thin, wry smile, realizing he hadn't seen a pencil or paper in Tunis' hand since the day they had buried Grady Carr. Once they had gathered their scattered horses from the desert floor and ridden away from Carr's shallow grave, Tunis had held his writing paper above his head and let the hot wind sweep it away.

They rode downward along thin natural switchbacks carved into the rocky ground by hundreds of years of wild hooves and claws. In the afternoon as shadows drew long across the flats below, Dawson spotted the single rider moving in and out of sight before he had the opportunity to see that it was Shaw riding up onto the hill trail toward them.

"We've got a rider coming up," Dawson said quietly. "We'll be meeting him at just about dark," he estimated, gazing toward the low red sun on the western edge of the jagged earth.

The three rode on, Tunis reaching down and drawing his rifle from its boot and laying it across his lap.

"Take it easy, Tunis," said Dawson. "We don't want any more innocent blood on our hands."

Tunis caught the reference to his and Carr mistakenly shooting Randall Wynn. His chin tightened in. "I'm not a complete idiot, Marshal," he said. "At the same time, I plan to be prepared if this is not some innocent pilgrim." He looked around as if questioning what innocent pilgrim would be caught in such a godforsaken place.

"I understand," said Dawson. "But think long and hard before you bring your Winchester into play. We don't need to reveal our position, especially this close to dark."

Tunis understood. With no more said on the matter, he left his Winchester on his lap, but he took his hand away from the stock near the trigger guard.

They rode on.

Below, as darkness closed in along the high shadowy trail, Shaw heard the first sound of hooves click slowly on the rocky trail coming down toward him. Veering his buckskin over along the trail's edge into the cover of a pile of fallen rock, he waited and listened closely until the sound of the hooves drew nearer. Moments later, when he was certain of what he was hearing, Shaw slipped down from his saddle, drew his rifle, wrapped his reins around his saddle horn and gave the buckskin a nudge out onto the trail.

Twenty minutes later, on a shadowed ledge above the trail, Caldwell and Tunis moved along in a crouch, the reins to their horses in hand. They looked down, keeping close watch on Dawson as he rode his horse along at a walk, the sound of the buckskin's hooves drawing nearer.

Dawson held his rifle ready across his lap. As the sound of hooves came around a turn in the trail, he started to raise the rifle and tell the rider to halt. But at the sight of the empty saddle on the big horse, he looked all around quickly, knowing he'd been tricked.

From the ledge above the trail Caldwell and Tunis

saw it too. "Uh-oh," said Caldwell, "we've got trouble!" He stood and started to turn and lead his horse down to the trail. But the voice in the darkness behind him said, "I'll say you've got trouble, Deputy."

Tunis started to swing his rifle toward the darkness, but Caldwell, having recognized Shaw's voice, said, "Don't shoot, Tunis. It's Lawrence Shaw."

On the trail below, Dawson recognized the buckskin and Shaw's saddle and tack and called up to Caldwell, "Jedson, watch where you shoot. Shaw's out here somewhere."

"No, he's not," Caldwell called down. "He's up here. He's managed to slip around and get the drop on us."

"Hold my horse for me, Cray," Shaw called out. "We're coming down. I've been riding all day looking for you."

Chapter 19

In the shelter of a cliff overhang, the four men had coffee and rested their horses while Dawson and Caldwell told Shaw about their mission to break up the border raiders by any means necessary. When they were finished telling him about the posse, Grady Carr and Randall Wynn, Shaw shook his head and gazed for a moment into the low flames of the fire.

"I suppose Messenger still doesn't realize that you need more men if you really plan on cleaning up the border," he said quietly.

Tunis cut in, saying in Messenger's defense, "I believe he does realize it. That's why he sent Agent Carr and myself along on this matter."

"No offense, Agent Tunis," said Shaw, "but it's a waste of time and lives, sending two men who don't know this terrain, and who haven't dealt with these kinds of men before."

"No offense taken," said Tunis, a bit grudgingly. He didn't attempt to argue the point. Instead he sipped his coffee and fell silent.

"I'm afraid Messenger got himself overly impressed by what the three of us did at Hell's Gate," said Dawson. "Now he thinks we can do the impossible."

Shaw nodded. "You two did do a hell of a job taking down Sepreano and the Barrows Gang."

"We had some good fortune," said Dawson.

Caldwell cut in. "We had you riding with us. You managed to get on the inside."

Shaw just looked at Caldwell.

"Jedson's right," said Dawson. "You softened them up for us before we even got there. We had some lucky breaks at Hell's Gate. We've had nothing but a hard ride and a lot of casualties this trip."

"If you don't mind me asking," Caldwell said warily to Shaw, "what happened to you after Hell's Gate? You just rode off, didn't say when you *was* coming back, didn't even say *if* you was coming back."

Shaw studied the short blue flames dancing beneath the battered coffeepot for a moment. "I didn't know *when*, and I wasn't sure *if*," he finally replied. "I had my own reasons for being on the Barrowses' trail. I was out for blood. I got it. It was time to go." He sipped his coffee.

"You never turned your badge in," Dawson said. "Far as that goes you never told anybody you quit. You're still a deputy, if you want to be."

Shaw gave a thin, tired smile and said, "After all this time? Messenger would still take me back?" He shook his head. "He must be hard up for good help." He cast a glance at Tunis and added, "Again, no offense intended."

"Again, none taken," said Tunis, studying Shaw's face in the flicker of low firelight. Like everyone else,

Tunis, the government agent, found himself curious about *Fast Larry* Shaw, the man known as the *fastest gun alive.* "So, are you ever going to pin that badge on?" he asked.

Shaw looked at him.

"Agent Tunis will be reporting to Messenger what he learns out here," said Dawson.

"I see," said Shaw, "so the folks in Washington will know whose side to take when it's time to call this venture either a success or a failure."

"Well spoken," Tunis said, having to give a short grin at Shaw's political insight. He looked at Dawson and Caldwell. "The fact it, I'm not concerned with giving Messenger a report. I haven't been since the day Grady got his throat cut. I simply want to bring this hunt to an end and go home. If there's a report called for at that time, I'll come up with something. I doubt if it will be completely accurate, but it won't be anything like it was living out here." He paused, then added, "Messenger probably knows that already."

"You're starting to sound like us," said Dawson, with a pleased look on his face.

"No matter what you think of me, of my savvy or my lack of savvy, I came out here to fight. When the time comes I plan on fighting gamely. Live or die, I will do my best."

"Hear, hear," Caldwell said sincerely. He reached out, picked up the battered coffeepot and topped off Tunis' cup.

Shaw studied their faces, seeing men act the way men act toward one another when they know they're about to face death together. "That brings me to why

I'm here," he said. "I came to tell you that Zarco is crawling with border raiders, and there's more showing up every day."

"But Madsen is there, and by now so is Deacon Lucas, and the ones we chased from Arajo," said Dawson, "the ones who killed all the posse men."

"Madsen is dead," said Shaw. "A Mexican woman he'd been bullying set fire to him."

"Good, that's one less . . . ," Dawson said, slightly raising his coffee cup as if in a toast.

"But, yes, the rest are there," said Shaw. "There's over twenty gunmen gathered there." He looked from face to face to see whether the numbers made any impression on these two lawmen and the government agent. They didn't seem to. He paused, then asked quietly, "Did everybody hear me?"

"We heard you, Shaw," said Dawson, "but the number of guns doesn't change anything. We're doing our jobs. I think you can understand that."

"I can," said Shaw. "I can also understand if you decided to wait a few days until they ride out of Zarco, then take the gang apart a little at a time up along these hill trails."

"What makes you so sure they'll be leaving Zarco in a few days?" Dawson asked.

"I heard Leeman telling Morgan Hatch they're going to hit the gold station in Durango," Shaw said. He checked their faces for a response.

"The government gold station," Caldwell said, contemplating the news.

"That sounds awfully ambitious," said Tunis, taking an interest in Shaw's information.

"Too *ambitious*," said Dawson, considering it. "Any chance Leeman was just feeding that to you, knowing you might bring the information to us?"

"No," said Shaw. "I was talking to Sonny Engles at the time. Leeman didn't think I heard him. He has no fear of the law. Why should he? The border raiders have been playing both sides of the border so long, they don't think either side will hold them to account."

"Does he know you wore a badge and took down Sepreano and the Barrowses with us?" Dawson asked.

"Yes, he does," said Shaw. "Drop the Dog Jones and Lying Earl Sunday have been riding with him ever since they got away from you two at Hell's Gate. They told him everything they could think of about me. He knows I was a deputy, but he still wanted me to ride with him."

"We can't put this off any longer," Dawson said, after considering things. "We've got to strike while they're gathered in one spot. Maybe they'll head to Durango, maybe they won't. But if they break away three and four at a time the way they're known to do, we'll be chasing them all over this desert again."

"You won't kill all of them if you hit them in Zarco," said Shaw. "You three against over twenty men?" He shook his head slowly. "You'll still end up chasing them on to the next village, the next water hole—that's provided they don't kill all three of you first thing."

Dawson eyed him. "So, you rode all this way just to cheer us up?"

Shaw sipped his remaining coffee. Seeing nothing was going to stop these three, he gave up and said, "Yeah, I suppose so."

As Shaw was about to stand up to leave, Caldwell asked quickly, "Why don't you ride with us, Shaw? You know that's what we want to ask you to do." He looked at Dawson. "We're just too stubborn to come out and say so."

"I worked for the law because I had accounts to settle with Titus Boland for killing Anna Bengreen," said Shaw. "All I want now is to be left alone." He set his empty cup aside, stood up and dusted the seat of his trousers. "I've warned you what's waiting in Zarco. Now I'll take my leave."

"Obliged," said Dawson, not about to pursue the matter of Shaw riding with them. "Where are you headed now?"

"Durango," said Shaw.

"What's there?" Tunis asked, not knowing better than to ask a man like Shaw what his purpose might be.

Shaw only gave him a slight nod without answering.

Caldwell still hadn't given up. "Think about it, Shaw. It would be like Hell's Gate all over if you were there, waiting inside for us when we make our move."

Instead of answering, Shaw touched the brim of his battered sombrero, looked from one to the other and said, "Take care of yourselves, amigos."

"Adios, Shaw," said Dawson, staring into the fire, lying leaned against his saddle on the ground.

When Shaw had taken the buckskin's reins and

walked out of sight, Caldwell sighed and said, "Well, there went our best chance of putting an end to all the border raiders in Zarco for once and for all."

"I don't think so," Dawson said quietly without looking up from the fire.

Caldwell and Tunis looked at each other. Clearing his throat, Tunis said, "Did you or did you not say yourself that having Fast Larry Shaw with us would tip the scales greatly in our favor?"

"I *did* say it," Dawson replied quietly, still gazing into the low fire. "I still do."

Caldwell shook his head and stared down at the ground in front of him. "Three of us against the border raiders isn't good odds, far as I'm concerned."

"Not three," said Dawson, *"four."*

"Four?" said Tunis. Again he and Caldwell looked at each other.

Caldwell started to speak, but his and Tunis' attention went to the sound of Shaw walking his buckskin back under the cliff overhang. "All right, here's the deal," Shaw said as if he'd never left. "There's dirt between Leeman and his two close pals and Morgan Hatch and his partner Engles. Seems Leeman ran out on them in Julimez. Hatch and Sonny said it didn't matter, but I didn't believe it."

"There's dirt between them, and rightly so," Dawson replied, looking up from the fire at Shaw with the same look of surprise that had come upon Caldwell's and Tunis' faces. "We saw where Leeman shot holes in some water bags instead of leaving them behind for Hatch and Engles and Wild Dick. He figured on feeding those three to us while he and Bone and Waite made their getaway."

Shaw gave a slight grin and said, "Hatch didn't even mention it. He said they took canteens off the dead posse and rode straight to Arajo." Shaw considered it, then said, "But just because Hatch didn't mention it doesn't mean he's forgotten about it. No man jackpots his pards that way and they let it go without a fight."

"Yeah, so?" Dawson said, trying to reason along with him to their advantage.

"So give me two days in Zarco," said Shaw. "Let me see if I can stir things up before you come charging in."

In Zarco, Filos Hewes stood watch from the roof of the cantina. But he saw nothing when Shaw circled wide of the trail and rode in through a dark alleyway two hours before dawn. At the stables behind the cantina, Shaw stepped down and walked the buckskin quietly past Sonny and the woman, who lay passed out and naked on blankets in the sand. In the pale moonlight he looked down and noted Sonny's bruised and swollen jaw.

Beside the passed-out gunman lay three empty mescal bottles. A snuff container of refined opium powder lay opened and half-empty on the edge of the blanket. The woman slept with a hand resting on the handle of the Colt lying near her face. Shaw heard Sonny mumble gruffly in his sleep. But then the mumbling turned into a whine as pain shot through the gunman's cracked jawbone.

Silently, Shaw led the buckskin into the stables, wiped him down in the dark with a handful of clean straw, grained him and watered him from a clay pot of tepid water sitting inside the sables. Finishing with his horse, Shaw wet his face and head and dried himself on his loosened shirttails. He took off his gun belt and draped it over his shoulder. Then he left the stables on foot and walked to the cantina where a dim light glowed through the open door.

Inside the cantina, Morgan Hatch stood drinking alone at the bar. Looking around, Shaw saw men lying passed out on the dirt floor and draped over battered wooden tables where they had fallen. Shaw stood at the far end of the bar and motioned for a bleary-eyed bartender to serve him coffee from a large blackened coffeepot. The coffee had been boiled on a *chemnea* out back and now sat steaming behind the bar.

While the man poured the coffee into a cup, Shaw looked down the bar at Hatch, who looked away from him and puffed on a slim green cigar. In front of Hatch sat a steaming cup of coffee, next to a half-full bottle of tequila. On the floor lay a pile of green cigar butts. "There'll be no trouble between you and me, Morgan Hatch, unless it's of your making," Shaw said quietly.

Hatch didn't answer.

Shaw continued. "Sonny Engles got in my face. I saw what he was leading up to, so I stopped it before it got out of hand. Would you have done any different?"

After a silent moment, Hatch said in a harsh tone, "Like as not he'll kill you, Shaw."

"Like as not he'll try," Shaw replied.

"Sonny's fast, Shaw, faster than anything you've ever seen." Hatch took a sip of tequila and chased it with a sip of coffee. *"Fastest gun alive?* Ha! He'll take that name right away from you." There was bitterness to Hatch's voice that Shaw knew he hadn't caused. Whatever dark mood Hatch was in had been there long before Shaw arrived.

"If he's that fast, he's welcome to it," Shaw replied calmly. He sipped his coffee with a sigh. "Did you tell him what I said," he asked, "that I could have killed him if I'd wanted to?"

"I told him," said Hatch. "He didn't listen."

"Too bad," Shaw said.

"Too bad?" Hatch turned, looked him up and down, then looked away. "Why? Are you starting to have second thoughts about it?"

"No," Shaw said. He shrugged. "I'll kill him when the time comes, if that's what it's going to take." He sipped the coffee and asked, "Are you going to stand with him?"

"No, it's between the two of yas," said Hatch. "He's my pard, but this is his fight. Every man has to shovel his own dirt."

"Good," said Shaw. "I wasn't looking forward to having to kill you too."

"Kill me too . . ." Hatch chuckled under his breath. "You're awfully cocksure of yourself, Shaw," he said. "I'll give you that."

"I better be," Shaw said. He turned, facing Hatch along the bar, and said, "But enough about Sonny. What changed your mind out there? Leeman and I were both certain you'd ride in looking for blood."

"Yeah?" Hatch said guardedly, taking a quick glance around at the sleeping drunks. "What're you talking about?"

"Come on, Hatch," Shaw said, "we all knew you and Sonny intended to ride in and kill Deacon Leeman, Waite and Bone. That's why Leeman had me in the street with him, to back his play." He checked Hatch's expression, seeing the rage rise in his eyes. "I don't blame you, after him shooting holes in the water bags, leaving you stuck that way."

"How'd you know about the water bags?" Hatch asked, his voice lowering into a tight growl.

Shaw said calmly, "How do you think I knew?" He stared at Hatch closely.

"That son of a bitch *told* you about it?" Hatch said, his voice going even lower, even more enraged.

Shaw didn't answer; he didn't have to.

"He must've thought it was a joke, leaving me and Sonny stranded . . . poor Wild Dick lying dead." He swallowed a tight bitter knot in his throat. "He told everybody, didn't he?" Hatch said in dark speculation.

Shaw only gazed coolly at him. "Like you said, *How did I know about it?*"

Hatch thought about things, then said, "Shaw, are you going to run straight to Deacon Leeman, tell him what you and I talked about here?"

Shaw gave him a flat stare and said, "I don't run to *anybody* about *anything*. You stay out of any trouble I have with Sonny Engles, I'll stay out of any trouble you have with Deacon Leeman."

"Deal," Hatch said bitterly. He pushed his coffee cup aside and took a long drink from the bottle of tequila.

Chapter 20

As first light pushed its way onto the eastern horizon, Hatch walked out of the cantina with the tequila bottle hanging from his fingertips. Shaw stifled a yawn and turned back to his coffee, hearing a rooster begin to crow near the stables behind the cantina. The bartender stepped forward and shook his head as he wiped drops of spilled tequila from the bar top.

"He is boiling mad inside, that one," the bartender said, nodding in the direction of Morgan Hatch. "I hope he does not go somewhere and start trouble—"

His words stopped as a single shot exploded out back by the stables and the rooster's crowing ceased abruptly.

Shaw only nodded and sipped his coffee.

Before he'd finished his coffee, Deacon Leeman and Charlie Bone walked into the cantina. "Well, well, Charlie," said Leeman, with a wide but unpleasant grin, "it looks like I'm not the only early riser around here." He looked Shaw up and down, seeing his gun belt hanging from his shoulder, his shirttails out.

"Couldn't sleep," said Shaw. "I must've slept too much yesterday evening."

"I expect that's why I didn't see you around much after you gun-barreled Sonny's head for him." Leeman rapped his knuckles on the bar top and nodded toward the coffeepot.

"Sí, café, en seguida!" said the bartender. "I mean 'coffee right away,' " he translated, quickly correcting himself as Leeman gave him a cold stare.

"What's wrong, Shaw, does pistol-whipping an idiot wear you out?" Bone chuckled as the bartender hurriedly produced two coffee mugs and began pouring them full.

Shaw just looked at Bone without replying.

Leeman sipped his coffee. Lifting his Colt from its holster, he dropped a spent cartridge from its cylinder, replaced it and slid the Colt back into its holster. To the bartender he said, "Luis, run out back. There's a dead rooster lying along the corral fence. Dress it out and cook it for breakfast."

"Along the corral fence, senor?" Luis the bartender looked confused.

Leeman sighed. "Go with him, Bone, find that bird and get some fire under it."

"Hunt for a dead rooster?" Bone looked shocked. "What am I, a fool?"

"You are if you open your mouth again!" Leeman raged at him with no attempt at civility.

Bone and the bartender hurried away, out the back door, as Leeman turned back to Shaw. "Everybody must wake up with a little bark on, eh, Shaw?" he said. "I know I do."

Shaw only nodded.

"The truth is, I've been wanting to talk to you, just the two of us." He stopped and looked toward the rear door and shook his head. "See how I had to put my foot on ole Bone's neck? It's not easy being a leader of men like us. Bold, willful men like Charlie, Blacky Waite and yourself don't like being told what to do." He sipped his coffee and gave a sigh. "But when a man takes charge, he has to rule with an iron hand, else things start going bad for everybody."

Shaw stood staring.

"I know it doesn't sit well with some of the men, taking orders from me, when I started out as just one more gun under Quinn Madsen. But the mantle was laid upon me. I've got to keep this gang tight and ready."

Shaw could see that being in charge had Deacon Leeman feeling full of himself. Sliding his empty coffee cup away, Shaw said flatly, "Is that what you've been wanting to talk to me about, just the two of us?"

"No," Leeman said, looking a little red faced. "Now that you're riding with me, I've been wanting to talk in private about what you stand to gain for yourself."

"I've been wanting to talk about that myself," Shaw said with a thin smile, hoping he sounded interested in where he stood with the border raiders. "I'd like to know what my share of the booty will come to."

Leeman cocked his head a little to one side and raised a finger as he spoke. "You and I both know that you're no *seasoned* thief, Shaw, leastwisc I never heard it said about you."

"That's right, I'm not," Shaw said honestly. He

patted his gun. "I've always had a skill that's in high demand. So high that I've never had to worry about money. If I want money, I've always known where to find it."

"I understand that, and I admire it," said Leeman. "To be honest that widow maker on your hip is what's got you into the raiders. Without your gun skills I've got nothing for you."

Shaw gave him a bristly stare.

"Hold on, now," said Leeman, knowing he had no backup in the cantina. "I meant no offense. I'm just talking straight with you. You still get a full share, same as if you came here from riding with the James Gang. But I want you to stick close to me, and leave the robbing up to the others. Is that a good deal for you or not?" He smiled, knowing Shaw couldn't possibly have a problem with such a deal.

But Shaw didn't answer right away. Instead he said, "What you're offering is a full share for me, just for being your own personal bodyguard."

Leeman grinned, and this time it looked more real. "Damn right, that's what I want. Thieves and gun tramps come cheap out here. I want the *fastest gun alive* at my side, at all times."

"I got the impression that you didn't believe all that *fastest gun alive* talk," Shaw said.

"I know you're faster than most I've ever seen, Shaw," said Leeman. "As for you being the *fastest gun alive* . . ." He hesitated, then said, "If it's something everybody wants to think, who am I to argue?" He gave a sly wink, as if he and Shaw shared a secret.

"I see," Shaw said, not interested in trying to convince Leeman of anything.

"So, there's the deal, Shaw," Leeman said. "Have you had any better offers lately?" He looked Shaw up and down, his frayed shirt collar, his down-at-the-heels boots.

"What about Morgan Hatch and Sonny Engles?" Shaw said flatly.

"What about them?" Leeman said.

"I suppose you'll be wanting me to kill them both first chance I get?"

Leeman took on a concerned expression. "What made you think a thing like that? Those two are a couple of the best men I've got."

Shaw said in a lowered tone as if the passed-out gunmen lying around might hear them, "I figure with them knowing you jackpotted them and shot holes in the water bags they needed, you couldn't afford to leave them alive."

Leeman looked stunned. Leaning in closer, he asked, "Where the hell did you hear that?"

"Where the hell do you think I heard it?" Shaw came back sharply, without mentioning either Hatch or Engles.

Leeman took a deep breath and let it out, looking troubled by his thoughts. "So they didn't take the canteens from the dead posse men after all. . . ."

"So," Shaw said, "do you want them both dead?"

Leeman considered it, then said in frustration, "Damn it, no, not right now. We're shorthanded and I've got a big job coming up."

"This is all of the border raiders?" Shaw asked, gathering what information he could for Dawson.

"No, I've got more men coming. But I can't afford

to lose any right now," said Leeman. "Keep a close eye on those two, but don't make a move on them until I tell you to."

"I understand." Shaw nodded; that was good enough for now, he thought. He'd given each side plenty to think about. Now he needed to make certain Dawson, Caldwell and Tunis would be able to ride in without being spotted from atop the cantina. It had been easy enough for him—one rider in the dark of night. But it might not be as easy for the three lawmen.

Clell Butterfield watched the four young *federale* soldiers ride downward in and out of sight on the low hill trail. "They're falling right into our laps," he whispered to the two men lying beside him along the meandering sandbank.

"These boys are just an advance party, scouting the trail for a whole damned column of soldiers!" said Wallace Pearl, lying five feet to his right, holding his rifle tight in his gloved hands.

Butterfield said with a note of sarcasm, "Well, thank you, Wallace. But I believe we already had a damned good notion that they're just forward scouts."

"Clell, we've got no business fooling with these boys," Pearl said. "I've got a bad feeling about this."

"Keep your bad feelings to yourself, Wallace," Butterfield warned him. "We're going to take a couple of these troopers to Madsen, just to show him we can."

"Wallace is right, Clell," said Andy Mertz, an Arizona gunman and stage robber who'd been out of

Yuma Territorial Prison for only a few months. "This is messing with dynamite. Let them pass and let's get on into Zarco."

Butterfield spat in contempt. "Chickenshits," he whispered to himself, staring out at the bottom of the trail the four *federales* would be riding down toward them. "Get ready, here they come," he added, seeing the riders appear into sight.

"Damn it to hell," Wallace Pearl whispered. But he levered a round into his rifle chamber and lay tense and poised.

Feeling the hooves of the four horses rumble in the sand beneath them, the three men stayed down behind the cover of the sandbank until Butterfield jumped up and shouted, "Let them have it!"

Leaping to their feet, firing repeatedly, the three gunmen watched two of the *federales* fall to the ground, one of their horses also falling under the hail of rifle fire.

Butterfield jumped forward, rifle raised, and pointed and shouted, *"Manos arriba! Manos arriba!"*

The two soldiers' rifles fell from their hands. Their hands went up above their heads. "Please, don't shoot us! Don't shoot us!" one of them shouted in awkward English.

"Down off the horses," Butterfield commanded. As the two slid from their saddles, one of them bleeding from his side, Butterfield said to the others with a grin, "Now, wasn't that as slick as grease on a stove handle?"

"We need to get away from here, *pronto*," said Pearl, casting a wary glance toward the hill trail the four soldiers had ridden down on. "We've got no idea how far behind the rest of their column is following them."

"Relax, Wallace, before you soil yourself," Butterfield laughed. He walked forward, gesturing the two soldiers away from their horses. He looked down at one of the other two soldiers lying writhing and moaning on the ground.

"*Agua, agua,*" the dying young soldier pleaded.

"He asks you for water, senor," the soldier without the wound said.

"Hell, I know that," said Butterfield. He tipped his rifle barrel down and shot the dying soldier. Then he turned his rifle toward the two standing and levered another round into the chamber. "Anybody else need *agua*?" he asked with a cruel grin.

The two young soldiers fell silent, looking helpless and frightened.

"All right, then," Butterfield said, walking over to the whimpering horse lying in a wide patch of red wet sand. "*Adios, caballo,*" he said. He shot the wounded animal in its thrashing head, and watched its life melt and leave it lying limp and still on the ground. "Pity." He shook his head in mock regret and said in a solemn tone, "This desert country eats horses up."

Pearl and Mertz walked up onto the sand quietly, their rifles cocked and aimed at the two remaining soldiers. "Don't neither one of you try anything," Mertz warned.

"Oh, hell, Andy," Butterfield laughed, "what are they going to try?" He gestured both men forward.

"Get their sidearms and let's get on into Zarco. If we fool around out here long enough, there really will be a swarm of *federales* coming down the trail."

"This was a mistake," said Mertz, looking at the dead horse, the dead soldiers and all the tracks in the sand. "They'll be on our backs like boils."

"You don't get it, do you, Andy?" said Butterfield. "They were headed down on us anyway. There's never any *federales* this part of the desert. Somebody has told them we're here."

"Then we've sure as hell cinched it for them," Mertz grumbled.

Ignoring him, Butterfield turned to the soldier who spoke English and asked, "How many others soldiers are riding down here?"

The young soldier had nothing to hide. "Over fifty," he said with no hesitation.

"See?" said Butterfield to Mertz and Pearl. "What do you think, that fifty soldiers were just out romping around in the sun and then they all decided to ride across the hills into the desert?"

"Where is it you're headed?" Andy Mertz asked the young soldier. "Don't lie to us or I'll nail a bullet in your forehead."

"To Zarco," the young soldier said.

"What's so damned important in Zarco?" Butterfield asked sharply, getting into the soldier's face, keeping him off balance and too afraid to lie.

"We met a man and his family on the north hill trail. He said the border raiders are in Zarco. Him and his wife and daughter fled the village when they saw all the outlaws gathering there." The soldier pointed northeast. "We were at the bottom of the hill trail when we met them, so we took a shortcut and saved a day and a half of riding by crossing this lower hill line."

"Well, wasn't you boys just as smart as circus baboons?" said Butterfield. He looked at Mertz and Pearl. "Now, pards. Do you see why it was important to find out what the hell is going on out here?"

The two outlaws looked at each other, a little embarrassed by having doubted Butterfield to begin with. "All right, Clell," said Mertz. "You're right, we're wrong. What are we going to do now? I don't cotton to riding into Zarco knowing soldiers are going to be waiting to jump down my shirt."

"We're going to warn Madsen, that's what we're going to do," said Butterfield. "Then we either split the gang up and fade into the desert, or we stand and fight until one side gives up and crawls away. Does that make sense?"

"Makes sense to us, Clell," Pearl said, speaking for him and Mertz.

"Good," said Butterfield with a taunting grin. He turned to the bleeding soldier. "Are you able to ride?" As he asked, he cocked his rifle.

"*Sí*, he is able to ride," the other soldier cut in, before the wounded man could answer for himself. "He will not hold us back. I will look after him and keep him moving."

"See that you do, amigo," said Butterfield. "Ain't nothing pleases me more than shooting *soldados*, *comprende?*"

"*Sí*, I understand," the young *federale* said somberly, hooking an arm around the wounded soldier's side and helping him up into his saddle.

Chapter 21

———

"What the hell do we have coming here?" Leeman shouted up to Drop the Dog Jones, who stood watch atop the cantina. Jones quickly wiped dust off the lens of the telescope and held it up to his eye. Out across the sand flats to the southeast, he saw the rising dust of five horses boring down on Zarco at a hard run.

"Hot damn, Deacon," Jones called down to him from the flat roof, "it's Clell Butterfield, Pearl and Mertz, riding like the devil's on their tails!"

"Little doubt he is," Deacon commented to the men gathered around him on the dirt street. He grinned, glad to know Butterfield and the other two had made it across the border and all the way to Zarco. "Once they get here we'll be able to head to Durango and take care of business."

"Uh-oh! Looks like they've got a couple of *federales* with them, Deacon," Jones called down. "One of them is wounded sure as hell. He's barely hanging on in his saddle."

"Aw, hell," said Deacon, "it sounds like Clell has taken on some prisoners. I hope he hasn't led the whole damn Mexican army down on us!"

Looking all around, seeing Hatch and Engles walking toward him from a block away, he turned to Sibott, who stood nearby, staring out across the rolling flats. "Sibott. Go find Shaw, tell him to get out here pronto. Tell him I might need his help. He'll know what I'm talking about."

"Sure thing, Deacon," said Sibott, turning and bounding away on foot toward the stables where he'd seen Shaw earlier in the day.

In a stall next to his buckskin, Shaw stood with one jaw cleanly shaved, the other still covered with soap lather. When he caught a glimpse of Sibott in the shaving mirror, he lowered the razor into a pan of water and turned around, a cloth stuck down in the front of his shirt.

"Shaw, Deacon wants you, out in front of the cantina," Sibott said, in a rushed voice. "He said to tell you to get over there *pronto*, and you'd know why."

Shaw jerked the cloth from his shirt collar and wiped the shaving lather off his face. "First shave in a week," he said, tossing the cloth aside, grabbing his poncho from over a stall rail and slipping it down over his head. "What's going on out there?" he asked.

"Three more of our men are riding in. It looks like they've taken two *federales* captive."

"*Federales*, eh?" Shaw rubbed his cleanly shaved jaw and took his battered sombrero from the stall rail and placed it on his head. "I haven't seen soldiers on this side of the desert in months."

"Well, you're going to see them now," said Sibott. The two turned and left, the big Frenchman leading the way.

On the street, Deacon, Bone and Waite stood watching the five riders drawing closer across the sand flats. When Shaw walked up, Deacon turned his gaze to him and said in a lowered tone, "What took you so long? What were you doing?"

Shaw wasn't about to explain where he'd been or what he'd been doing. "Take a guess," he said with a flat stare, letting Deacon see his half-shaved face.

"You can finish later," said Deacon. He gestured toward Hatch and Engles, who stood only ten yards away, the woman right behind them. "I want you keeping an eye on these three at all times."

"I've got you covered," Shaw said, cutting a glance at the gunmen and the woman. Then he looked out at the approaching riders and asked Deacon, "What's this about?"

"Beats me," said Deacon, seeing the riders slow their horses down as the animals rode onto the dirt street at the far end of town. "But there better be a damn good reason for Butterfield and his boys to be dragging soldiers into our midst."

When the riders had stopped in the middle of the dirt street fifteen feet away, Butterfield slipped down from his saddle and said to Deacon, "Look what we found riding down off the low hills trail." He grabbed the English-speaking Mexican by his trousers leg and yanked him down out of his saddle. Andy Mertz raised a foot and booted the wounded soldier. The young soldier fell to the ground and struggled to get to his feet. The other soldier reached down and helped him up.

Shaw stepped in closer, watching intently.

"Is this all of them?" Deacon asked Butterfield.

"No," said Butterfield with a grin. "We left two more lying dead in the sand."

"You didn't bury them, cover them up, or something?" Deacon asked, getting irritated.

"No," said Butterfield mockingly, "I couldn't find my shovel or my prayer book."

"Damn it to hell!" said Deacon. "What if there's more, what if they come along and find the bodies? What if they're coming here?"

"Don't get nervous on me, Deacon," said Butterfield. "There *are* more coming. They *are* coming here. What the hell do you suppose they were doing out there, sunning themselves?" He looked all around as if searching for someone.

"How far behind are they?" Leeman asked, turning a quick gaze out across the sand flats.

"Three hours, four hours at the most," said Butterfield, still looking around for someone. "But since I figured they were headed here anyway, I decided we ought to snatch them, just to make sure. Then I thought we'd best bring them here, let them tell everybody in person." He gave a shrug with the same grin on his dust-streaked face. "But hell, there's no need to thank me for it."

"How did you know they were headed here?" Deacon asked, on the verge of losing his temper with Butterfield.

Looking tired of answering questions, Butterfield

grabbed the English-speaking soldier by his shirt-front and jerked him forward. "Tell him, Jose," he said. Once again he looked all around.

"My—my name is not Jose, it is Private Martene," the young soldier said to Leeman. "It is true our column was already coming here to Zarco—"

"Tell him why, Jose!" Butterfield said, cutting the young soldier off.

The soldier related the same story to Deacon Leeman about the Mexican and his wife and daughter fleeing Zarco, which he'd earlier told Butterfield. Shaw listened and thought to himself, *Way to go, Paco, you made it.* He watched Leeman's face take on a dark expression.

When the soldier had finished, Leeman scowled in the direction of the burned rubble of the adobe that had been the Gomezes' home. "Paco Ruiz . . . ," he said bitterly. "The girl, Francisca. My girl . . ."

"No, senor," said the soldier. "His name is not Paco Ruiz. He said his name is Poncho Vesti, or Vilsta." He paused, then gave up and said, "I cannot remember his last name."

Leeman's rage exploded. "His name is Paco Ruiz! You stupid son of a bitch! He's one of us! He's nothing but a damned outlaw himself!" Leeman struck the soldier, knocking him to the ground. He stepped in close and kicked the soldier in his stomach. Then he snatched his Colt from his holster and cocked it. But Shaw moved fast. He grabbed Leeman's gun from his hand, pulled him back and held him for a moment from behind.

"Take it easy, Deacon," Shaw said. "Think about it. A gunshot is only going to speed up the *federales*, especially with two of their men dead and two more missing." In an even lower tone he added, "Besides, we've got hard eyes on us right now. Save your bullets, you'll be needing them for *federales* before long."

Leeman settled down.

Noting the way Leeman acted, and the way Shaw jumped in and stopped him from killing the soldier, Butterfield looked all around once again and this time said, "Where the hell is Quinn Madsen? Who's in charge of this *hoedown* anyway?"

"Madsen is dead!" Leeman growled at him, his gun back in his hand after Shaw handed it to him butt first. "I'm in charge, you idiot!" he said, his knuckles turning white around his gun butt.

Shaw cut in, seeing the stunned look on Butterfield's dust-streaked face. "Madsen burned up in a fire." He gestured a nod toward the pile of charred rubble and fallen adobe walls. "We thought Paco Ruiz burned up with him."

"Damn," said Butterfield, rubbing his chin, trying to take in everything Shaw told him. "There's an awful lot goes on with this bunch between jobs."

"You're damned lucky these soldiers were headed this way anyway," Leeman said, settling down more, easing his grip on the big Colt and shoving it back into its holster. He turned to the soldier who had struggled back onto his feet and said, "How well armed is your column?"

"Each trooper carries a French breechloading rifle," the young private replied. "The officers also carry a sidearm."

Shaw could tell from the look in the young soldier's eyes that he was lying.

"No light field cannon?" Leman asked, not seeming to see what Shaw could see. "No Gatling gun?"

"Our column is only a light cavalry force on patrol, senor," said Private Martene.

Leeman looked back and forth, not seeming too concerned over the *federales* headed toward Zarco. "Butterfield, you brought these two here, you take them to the stables and tie them to a post."

"Ain't we going to go ahead and kill them, Deacon," Butterfield asked, "then everybody split up and hightail it away from here for the time being?"

"I'm not play that game anymore," said Deacon. "We've got better guns, ammunition, more experience. To hell with them. Let them do the hightailing." He looked around and said to all the men, "It'll be dark by the time they get across the flats. I figure they won't hit tonight. But tomorrow morning all hell is going to break loose. Everybody get set for the fight of your life. We're not running!"

The men whooped, whistled and cheered. Shaw only watched and shook his head.

"Damn it, come on," Butterfield said to the two bedraggled soldiers, motioning them toward the stables out behind the cantina. "Give me any reason at all, I'll bend a rifle barrel over your backs."

Leeman looked at the wounded soldier, then turned to the woman standing behind Hatch and Engles. "You, Whore, go with them. See to it this one's side wound gets cleaned and bandaged."

The woman looked first at Morgan Hatch before stepping forward. Hatch said to Leeman, "Sounds like you're already playing the angles, treating these two good in case you end up in the hands of the *federales*."

"I've got over twenty good crack-shot riflemen," Leeman replied. "Fifty kids with French rifles don't scare me. I don't plan on ending up in the *federales'* hands." He paused and made it a point to look Hatch up and down with contempt. "Or anybody else's," he added.

"You mean not if there's anybody else around for you to jackpot!" Hatch growled, his hand poised near the Colt on his hip. "I expect you've had a good laugh or two telling about shooting holes in those water bags. Leaving us dry, with the law on our backs."

"That's it, Morgan," said Leeman. "I figured you knew about the water bags. So let's get it out in the open. If you've got to settle something with me, get it done right here, right now. I don't want to have to worry about getting a bullet in the back while I'm killing *federales*."

Shaw saw the dark, hate-filled look on Hatch's face as he'd spoken to Leeman. Bone and Waite took a step toward him. Shaw remained in the same spot and watched, knowing that Leeman thought he was there to protect him, when in fact Shaw thought he couldn't care less if they splattered Leeman all over the dirt street.

But instead of making their move, at the last minute Hatch seemed to take control of his temper. He cut a glance at Shaw, then back to Leeman. "Yeah, it's in the open now, Deacon. I'm going to kill you—all three of yas. You jackpotting sons a' bitches."

"Then do it now!" Charlie Bone shouted, stepping forward, his hand poised near his gun butt.

Hatch raised a hand to keep Sonny Engles from making a move for his Colt, knowing that once his and Sonny's guns left their holsters, there would be no stopping until the street lay strewn with dead people. "No, we're not doing it now. Sonny and I have all the time we need to kill the three of yas, and having a big gun like Shaw won't save you from what's coming to you, Deacon."

"Charlie's right, Morgan!" said Blackie Waite, also taking a step out beside Bone, the two of them goading Hatch for a fight. "Let's get it done!"

But Hatch took a step back; Sonny followed his lead, bristling at Bone and Waite. "All of yas see this," Hatch called out to the rest of the men gathered in the street, most of them checking their Winchester rifles, their Colts and Remingtons, in preparation for an ensuing battle with the Mexican army when the time came. "These snakes are wanting to throw down right now. But I say for the good of everybody, I'm holding off until the *federales* are all dead."

"That's right," Sonny Engles joined in, beginning to see what Hatch was getting at. "We're holding off for everybody's good," he said repeating Hatch's words.

Hatch stepped forward with his gun hand away from his Colt and pointed at Deacon Leeman. "Once the *federales* are dead, I'm putting Leeman and these other two snakes in the sand. Then you can each one decide whether or not I should be the leader of the border raiders."

"You hear him, men?" said Leeman. "This gun

tramp and his simpleminded sidekick think they can take over and lead the raiders." As he spoke he looked around at Shaw. "Anybody here want to tell these bummers how wrong they are? Shaw, what about you?"

Shaw didn't take the bait. He only stared back and forth between the two opposing sides.

"Shaw doesn't count for nothing in this bunch," Sonny Engles cut in, his swollen face turning red with rage at the mention of Shaw's name. "As soon as Hatch gives me a go-ahead, I'm killing Shaw, no matter which way the chips fall."

Shaw glared at Engles.

"Tell them where you stand, Shaw," Leeman said confidently, hoping the rest of the men would realize that he had Shaw backing his every move.

"Yeah, Shaw," said Hatch, "where do you stand once the fat's in the fire? Maybe you best tell everybody which side you're on here."

"I'm on *my own* side, like always," Shaw said. He looked all around, taking his time, letting his eyes go from man to man, then said, "There's dirt between these hombres. I say, once the *federales* are gone, may the best man win." He spat, turned and walked away toward the stables.

He had more to think about than which of these men would kill the others. He needed to figure a way to get word to Dawson and Caldwell that there would be *federales* closing in on Zarco real soon.

This changed everything, he thought. He wasn't sure how much good he had done coming back here, provoking the bad blood that ran between these men. But Dawson didn't need him here in Zarco now. The

Mexican army would keep the border raiders busy from one side, Dawson, Caldwell and Tunis from the other. All he had to do was find a way to slip the soldiers out of town, he told himself. Once they were safely headed south toward their column, he could ride north and warn Dawson what was about to happen.

But as Shaw considered things, he looked away toward the stables where Butterfield and the woman had taken the two soldiers. What would happen to the soldiers when the *federales* charged the town? He knew the answer: These men would kill them. But he couldn't let that happen. Not if he wanted to keep his stature as an angel, he told himself wryly, picturing the face of Francisca, her dark innocent eyes, the way she looked up to him to do the right thing.

Shaw sighed to himself. Being an angel was the toughest work he'd ever done.

Chapter 22

Inside the stables, the woman kneeled over the wounded soldier, holding a wet cloth on the wound in his side. The other soldier, Martene, stood nearby, watching, his wrists behind his back, tied together around a support post. Butterfield turned to Shaw with his gun in hand. Mertz and Pearl had led the horses over to the livery. They'd followed Shaw inside as he entered. Shaw looked at the gun in Butterfield's hand, then at his face.

"Point it away from me, Butterfield," Shaw said quietly, but with a threatening stare.

"Clell, do you know who this is?" Pearl asked, he and Mertz standing inside the open doorway behind Shaw.

Butterfield looked at Shaw closely, then said in a mocking voice, "No, I don't know *who this is*. Am I supposed to know every half-shaved peckerwood in Mexico?"

"It's Fast Larry Shaw," Mertz added, hoping to stop Butterfield before he got any more insulting.

Butterfield's face went blank for a moment. "*The Fast Larry Shaw?*" he asked, staring at Shaw, this time with a whole new attitude and demeanor.

"Yep," said Mertz, "it's *the* Fast Larry Shaw."

"Well, I'll be whupped blind," Clell Butterfield said, still staring at Shaw. "I had no idea that you're Fast Larry Shaw. Man, I have heard a lot about you, all over Texas." He added quickly, "I meant no offense about your face being only half-shaved."

"Forget it, Butterfield," Shaw said. He idly rubbed the smooth side of his face. "I've heard a lot about you too."

"You've heard of me?" Butterfield smiled and gave Mertz and Pearl a smug look.

"Yes," said Shaw. "You shot Whispering Tommy Lazlor in Benton Springs. You tracked down three jailbreakers and hung them by hand, up in Montana Territory."

Butterfield pointed out to Mertz and Pearl quickly, "That was back when I worked on the other side of the law." He looked back at Shaw and changed the subject, saying, "So, you're riding with us now? That's a damn good thing to hear." His voice took on a formal tone. "Allow me to introduce you to Andrew Mertz and Wallace Pearl."

"Friends call me Andy," said Mertz, giving Butterfield a look.

"Pleased to meet you, Shaw," said Pearl. "Glad to hear you're joining the raiders."

Shaw didn't answer. Instead he said, "I bet you could all three use some tequila, some mescal, to cut the dust from your gullets?"

"You bet we could," said Butterfield, "in the worst
kind of way."

"Go ahead, then," said Shaw, "I'll keep an eye on
these two while *la dama* takes care of them."

The lady . . . ? Juanita looked around at Shaw, then
went back to cleaning the soldier's wounded side.

"Obliged, Fast Larry," said Butterfield. "It's been
a long, hot ride across the flats, what with killing the
soldados and all." He gestured toward the soldier tied
to the post. "I expect we'll see you at the cantina
later?"

"You can count on it," Shaw said over his shoulder, stooping down beside the woman.

As soon as the men left, Shaw asked the woman,
"How is this one doing?"

"It is a clean wound," she replied in good but
seldom-spoken English. Shaw could tell by her wary
expression that she wasn't used to being spoken to
in a civil manner. She touched a skilled fingertip to
the bullet hole where a thin stream of blood ran
down. "Luckily for him, the bullet went all the way
through. He has lost blood but not so much that he
is in danger. He will be all right so long as he catches
no infection."

Shaw looked at her closely. "This is not the first
bullet wound you've ever cleaned and dressed, I can
see that."

"No, it is not." The woman appeared relieved by
Shaw's perception of her.

"Where did you get so good at it?" he asked, not
in a prying sort of way.

Her saw her defenses rise. Her dark eyes turned

caged, protecting things about herself she was not accustomed to revealing. "I am a *puta*, a whore, have you not heard?" she asked as if surprised. "Whores learn many things, including tending to gunshots."

Shaw studied her as she gently pressed the wet cloth to the bleeding wound, blotting it. "That's not what you started out as. That's not where you learned your nursing." He looked through the tough patina the Mexican desert, its sun, its sand, its life had woven over her. Beneath it he saw the fine features, her nose, her brow, the tilt of her chin. "You're not from this part of Mexico, are you?"

"No, I am not." She breathed deep, letting her defenses back down a little, knowing this man saw more to her than what she had presented to the world in a long time. "I come from far south of here, from Chepaz." As she spoke, she tore a strip of white cloth, folded it expertly and laid it over the wound.

"What brought you here?" Shaw asked, wanting to keep her talking as he decided whether or not he could trust her.

"Men, of course," she replied. "Men like those." She nudged her head toward the doorway. "Men like Sonny Engles and Morgan Hatch." She held the cloth in place with her fingertips, looked at him and added with a questioning gaze, "Men like you, perhaps?"

Shaw didn't reply. He watched and listened. She had more to say, he knew it.

"I am from Casa de Gutierrez. My father was the physician for the whole of Chepaz. I learned my skill from watching him attend people. But I foolishly fell in love and ran away with a man. He was not a good man. He brought me north and sold me to a brothel in Mexico City." She stopped and shrugged. "Much has happened after that. I threw my fate on the mercy of a bad world and became as bad as it is. Anyway, I have been here in this *purgatorio* for over a year now, waiting for a chance to escape it."

"You think riding with these men is the way out of purgatory?" Shaw asked, lowering his voice.

"Is this where you offer to show me a better way," she asked in a cynical tone, "if I will follow you?"

"I don't believe in purgatory, but maybe I should," Shaw said, considering it.

"It does not matter whether or not you believe in it," she said with resolve. "I find myself stuck in it. I do what I must to get out of it."

"I can think of a lot better ways out than riding with the border raiders," he added, looking into her dark eyes. "But I bet there's none you haven't already considered. Anyway, I've ruined my own life." He shook his head. "You would not want to follow me."

"*Gracias*," she said. A trace of a smile passed across her lips, then went away. "*Following* is what has doomed me to *purgatorio*."

Shaw had heard enough; he decided to take a chance and trust her. "Maybe *taking the lead* will get you out," he said as he took a quick glance around toward the open doorway.

"Oh . . . ?" She gave him a cool gaze.

"When the *federales* get here it will be too late to risk riding through the gunfire," Shaw said. "But tonight, as soon as the sun goes down, you could cut this man loose, let him and this man make a run for it."

Juanita looked up at the soldier tied to the post, then back at Shaw. "If the raiders caught me doing that they would kill me."

"Not if this one managed to get loose, caught you off guard and knocked you cold," Shaw said.

They both looked up at Private Martene. He swallowed a knot in his throat. "I want to live. We both do," he said, nodding toward the wounded soldier. "Tell us what to do and we will do it. When we reach our column I will tell my *capitan* what you have done for us."

"There's something else I want you to tell him," Shaw said. "Tell him there will be three American lawmen coming from the north. Tell him he needs to keep from killing them if they all run into one another."

"I will tell him, senor," said the young soldier. "But it will be hard to keep from killing them."

"I know it will," said Shaw, "but he can tell his men to keep watch for them coming out of the north and—"

"That is not what I mean, senor," said the soldier, cutting him off. He looked out the open doorway, then lowered his voice to almost a whisper. "I did not tell them, but I must trust you. My column has a pair of German field cannons that will level Zarco to the ground."

"There's still some villagers here," said Shaw.

The young soldier shook his head. "If they stay here they will be *dead* villagers." Then he said, "But they always know somehow when a battle like this is coming. They leave in the night."

"I hope so." Shaw took a deep breath. "Obliged to you for telling us about the cannons," he said. After considering it he said, "I'll just have to let the lawmen know what to expect." He turned to the woman and said, "This changes things, ma'am. You need to get out of here too. Cannons don't care who they kill."

"What about you?" she asked.

"I'll be back late in the night," Shaw replied. "I'm going too. I have to let those lawmen know what's going on."

At the southeastern end of Zarco, Shaw stopped Sibott as the big Frenchman hurried along, pulling a small mule cart by hand. Farther along the street lay a pile of other mule carts, buckboards, crates and heavy furniture that had been dragged out and stacked across in the dirt, forming a barricade. Seeing the look of puzzled concern on Shaw's face, Sibott said, "Can you believe this, Shaw?"

Shaw stared at him, thinking about the field cannon the young soldier had told him about. "No, I can't," he said. Up the street Lying Earl Sunday and Drop the Dog Jones carried a large wooden cabinet they'd pillaged from one of the abandoned adobes whose owners had fled only days after the border raiders' arrival.

"I've never seen being in charge go to anybody's head as fast as it has Deacon's," Sibott said, sweat running down his broad cheeks.

"Where is he, Bert?" Shaw asked, not seeing Leeman among the men on the street.

"Ha! He's in the cantina, out of the evening sun," said Sibott. "Where did you think he'd be, out here sweating with the rest of us?"

"Listen to me, Sibott, this is just between you and me," said Shaw. "The smartest thing you can do is leave that cart where it's sitting and get out of here tonight."

"Huh, get out, tonight?" Sibott saw that Shaw knew something he didn't.

"That's right, tonight," said Shaw. "You'll have all night to get across the flats and into the hills. By morning nobody here will come looking for you. Fact is, some of them will wish they'd gone with you."

"Look up there, Shaw," said Sibott, gesturing toward the rooflines. In addition to Filo Hewes standing guard atop the cantina, Leeman had posted two other riflemen on the town's taller roofs, one of those being the church, whose modest steeple stood thirty feet tall. "That's not just to keep him informed who's riding in, it's to shoot anybody in the back when they try to leave."

"Those extra riflemen wouldn't stop you if you really wanted to get out of here tonight, Bert," Shaw said, giving the big Frenchman a guarded but knowing look. "I've got a feeling things are going to get even worse than you think they are, come morning."

"I wouldn't be surprised," said Sibott, struggling to get the heavy mule cart started forward again. "But I see no way out of here for me."

"*Make* yourself a way out, Bert," Shaw warned as the man pulled the cart down along the dirt street.

From a block away, standing in the open doorway of the cantina, Leeman called out, "Shaw, over here."

Shaw walked quickly to the cantina, not about to tell Leeman what he'd just told Sibott. As soon as he'd stopped a few feet from Leeman, Bone stepped out of the cantina, Waite right behind him. "Tell me something, Shaw," said Leeman. "What was that all about, you acting the way you did, telling everybody you're on your *own side?* You're supposed to be my personal guard."

"That's right, I am your bodyguard," said Shaw. "I didn't think it was wise to announce it to Hatch and Engles, right then. I figured it best to keep them wondering what side I'm on when it comes down to it." He gave Leeman a cool, steady gaze. "If you want to play it different, we will. But I thought it best to keep them wondering."

"Yeah, maybe *you* think so, Shaw," said Charlie Bone. "But the fact is it ain't your call."

"Nor is it yours, Bone," said Shaw, not about to give an inch. "What else you got to say?" he added firmly.

"I'll tell you what else I've got to say." Bone took a step closer, his hand poised near his Colt. "It's one thing to keep everybody else wondering where you stand. But damned if you're going to treat us that way."

"Hold it, Bone, that's enough," said Leeman. "Shaw knows what he's doing. So do we. I don't need my top men shooting each other full of holes when we've got a battle coming our way."

Bone eased down, but kept a cold stare at Shaw. "Whatever you say, Deacon," he said calmly. To Shaw he said, "I'm watching you, Fast Larry."

"We both are," said Blackie Waite.

"That's good to know, I'll keep it in mind," Shaw said, not letting up, his gaze still fixed on them.

"Come morning I want the four of us sticking close together," Leeman cut in, changing the subject. "We can win this fight, but it's going to start getting bloody here on the streets."

Shaw thought about the cannons that would start most likely at dawn or shortly before. Leeman had no idea how bloody it was going to get. "What about the few people still staying here?" he asked.

"What about them?" Leeman asked, as if he hadn't given any thought to the villagers.

"I figure we'd want to run them out of here, just in case any of them might side with the army," said Shaw, hoping he could get the people out of the cannon fire. He knew the *federales* would be merciless toward the villagers when it came to killing a band of outlaws who'd ambushed two of their men and still held two captive.

"To hell with the villagers, don't worry about them," Leeman chuckled.

"We're not Quakers, we're gunmen," said Waite, having no regard for the people of Zarco.

Bone said, "If they stick their noses into a gunfight, they ought to expect to get them shot off."

Leeman looked all around, then said, "The main thing is, soon as we finish with these soldiers, I want us all four to turn our guns on Hatch and Sonny Engles. We're going to shoot them to pieces."

Bone looked at Shaw. "That is, provided you're not *worried* about them too."

"I'll try not to *worry* much about anything, Bone,"

Shaw said, "so long as I don't have you behind my back."

"That's enough out of you two," said Leeman. He turned to Shaw and said, "Tomorrow morning we all four stick together, but tonight I'm changing guards at midnight, putting Bone and Waite on the roofs just in case these soldiers feel scrappy enough to try anything in the dark. Take yourself a pot of coffee, some tequila, whatever you need. But find a good spot and stay there till daylight."

Shaw gave him a look of displeasure, but he thought this could work out well for the woman and the soldiers getting away. "All right," he said, "if that's where you need me."

"Hey, *Fast Larry*, we all have to do our part," Bone cut in, speaking harshly to him.

Shaw just stared at him.

Chapter 23

———

After dark, the men still drank at the cantina. But the atmosphere was not as rowdy, the drinking not as heavy. No music rang out from the open doors, Shaw noticed, watching the empty street from a battered wooden chair out front, his rifle lying across his lap. Hatch and Sonny had made themselves scarce, staying away from the cantina, separating themselves from Leeman, Bone and Waite.

Shaw was certain the two had been making contact among the rest of the men, seeing which of the gunmen might be on their sides after the fray with the Mexican army was over and it came time to settle the border raiders' internal dispute. He didn't care. Let them kill one another, he thought, if the army cannon left any of them standing. He had managed to saw as much division among the raiders as he could. Now it was up to him to get the soldiers, the woman and himself out of there.

The young soldier had been right about the few remaining villagers. They seemed to have vanished, the musicians, the cantina women who had stuck around to squeeze what money they could from the men, even the stable attendant. Zarco sat empty except for the gunmen who had ridden in and taken over. Now those same men waited, with eyes as wild and wary as wolves, to see whether they themselves would be displaced.

Just before midnight, as Bone and Waite appeared on the dirt street, headed for their respective guard positions on the rooftops, Shaw stood up and walked purposefully toward the south end of town, letting them both see him. But as soon as he had passed out of their sight, he ducked into the shadows beside an adobe and circled around off the main street and hurried along in a crouch.

When he reached the stables he slipped along the wall and entered through a rear door. In the dim light he saw the woman watching for him through the open front door, her Colt hanging from her hand. "Back here," he whispered, not wanting to startle her.

She turned, looking relieved, and said, "I saw a shadow move along the wall. I'm glad it was you instead of one of the others."

"All right," Shaw said, "let's cut them loose and get moving." He turned and saw the soldiers, both of them tied to posts now. The wounded one sat slumped, his arms tied behind him, his side neatly bandaged and showing only a slight bloodstain. He had a bandanna tied tightly around his mouth. At the next post, still standing, the other soldier struggled to talk, a bandanna tied tightly around his mouth as well.

"What's this?" Shaw said. As soon as he asked, he

realized what was going on. But it was too late. Before he could make a move, Sonny Engles stood up from behind a pile of hay and clubbed him from behind with the butt of a rifle barrel.

The woman stepped back and stared down at Shaw, lying knocked out on the floor. Engles slipped his arm around her waist and said, "Good work, Whore. Taking you captive was the smartest thing I ever done." He gave a crooked grin, his jaw still swollen from where Shaw had cracked him with his pistol barrel. "Every man needs a cutthroat whore he can ride *with* all day, and ride *on* all night."

Juanita shoved his hand away as it tried to crawl around under her arm and fondle her breast from behind.

"Brag about it later, Sonny," said Morgan Hatch, stepping out of the shadows of a dark stall. "Drag him over and tie him up."

"Can't I go on and kill him?" Sonny said, his fingers going instinctively to his cracked jaw. He held his hand around his rifle stock.

"No!" said Hatch with a frown. "Not with a gunshot you can't. You know better than that."

"Hell yes, I know better than that," Sonny said, a little peeved at Hatch's admonishment. "I'm not an idiot." He gave Hatch a cross look as he stooped and lifted Shaw's Colt from its holster and pitched it aside. "I'll stick him a few times, quiet-like." He looked at Juanita and grinned again. "Maybe let Whore slice his throat open good and wide."

Juanita shook her head. "It was you he pistol-whipped, not me," she said, looking down at Shaw. "All he did to me was try to fill my head with *goody-*

good talk." She made a sour face. "He called me a *lady*, like that would make me feel so important. I told him I am a whore, but *noooo* . . . that wouldn't do." She spat down at Shaw, who moaned and tried to raise his throbbing head.

"He couldn't fool you, could he?" said Engles, reaching out with his boot toe and gigging Shaw in his ribs.

"No," said the woman. "I gave him my sad story . . . the one I always give, when I see a man is feeling sorry for me."

"He's coming to," said Hatch. "Drag him to a post and tie him up like I told you to. We've got to get moving if we expect to get out of here and across these flats tonight."

"But I really want to kill him, Morgan," Engles said in a solemn voice, as if he wouldn't take no for an answer.

"Stick him before we leave, after he wakes up some," said Hatch. "Right now let's get our horses out and get ready to ride!"

"All right," said Sonny. "I'd like him to be awake and see his blood running out of him anyway."

The wounded soldier sat slumped, his head bowed, still sore and weak. But the standing soldier watched wide eyed as Sonny dragged Shaw to his feet. "Over we go with you, Fast Larry, ole pard," Sonny said with a dark chuckle. He shoved and guided the half-conscious Shaw over to the next post in the row of posts, and tied him to it.

Juanita joined Hatch, leading their saddled horses out of their stalls and closer to the rear doors. "Sonny, come check your horse," Hatch called out in a harsh whisper. "What the hell is wrong with you tonight?"

"Nothing," Sonny snapped back at him. He stood searching his boot well and the back of his trousers. "I can't find my knife!"

His knife . . . ? Against the post, Shaw heard their voices. In the faint glow of a candle lantern, he caught a glimpse of their shadows on the straw-covered floor. As a fog lifted from his mind, he realized what had happened, and he struggled hard to regain his strength and his senses.

"Damn it, Sonny! Get the hell over here and check your horse," Hatch demanded.

Sonny walked over to the horse, checked its cinch, looked the animal over and walked away. "There, I checked it! Satisfied?" he fumed, still searching himself, going over and over the same places.

Hatch shook his head and said to the woman, "Bring his horse. He's going into one of his crazy spells." The two swung up into their saddles, Juanita pulling Sonny's horse along by its reins.

Sonny stood in front of Shaw.

"Let's clear out of here and head to Metagore," said Hatch. As he spoke he loosened a bandanna from around his neck and held it down to Sonny. "Here. If you're not going to stick him, gag him with this, keep him from hollering out when he wakes up."

"I'm going to stick him!" Sonny said, his voice growing louder. "I just can't find my damned, *agggg*—" His words turned into a pain-filled grunt.

Shaw, holding on to the post behind him, lifted both feet and clamped his boots on either side of

Sonny's head. His single-point riding spurs clamped an inch deep into Sonny's bleeding ears. *"Hee-eelp!"* Sonny pleaded.

"Damn it, shut up!" said Hatch, wincing at the sight of Sonny's head spiked between the two boot heels.

Shaw held on tight and shook the hapless gunman hard, back and forth. As Sonny flayed wildly to get out of the steel-pointed clamp, Shaw turned one boot loose long enough to hook it behind the dazed gunman's head to hold it in place. He pounded his other boot heel rapidly, repeatedly into Sonny's face.

"Holy Joseph! He's beating him to death!" said Hatch, turning to slip down from his saddle and help Sonny. But before he could get there, he saw Shaw turn Sonny's head loose from his boot hold, cock both feet in close to his chest and release them in one powerful kick. Both boot heels launched Sonny into a backward flip. He landed facedown on the dirt floor, gasping and slinging his battered head like a stunned bull.

Hatch reached down and grabbed his own knife from his boot well, determined to bring this to an end without making any more noise.

But Sonny wasn't through. He struggled to his feet, sobbing in rage and pain, one ear dangling loose where Shaw's spur had ripped down on it. His face was a mass of bloody welts filled with straw and dirt. He snatched his Colt from his holster and cocked it quickly.

"No, Sonny!" Hatch shouted, seeing the gun extend arm's length toward Shaw.

Shaw clenched his teeth. This was it, he thought,

finally it was over. His life ended here, in a livery stable, in the glow of a candle lantern, in old Mexico. *So be it. . . .*

When the shot resounded, it was the loudest shot he'd ever heard. Instead of it hitting him in one spot on his chest, it hit him all over. His breath left him; he slammed backward, the post behind him not even stopping him. It was over; he was dead. Sweet death, he thought, feeling himself fall into a soft, harsh world of darkness.

Wait a minute! He wasn't dead. That was no gunshot, he thought, feeling his back still against the post, but both he and the post lying in a thick pile of straw. Dust showered down on him in the darkness. He heard the three horses neighing wildly. "Morgan!" he heard Sonny cry out.

"Hang on, I've got you," Hatch cried out in reply.

Shaw watched three silhouettes ride out through the open doors. *What the—?* Hooves thundered away along the street, headed north out of town. Then another explosion ripped through the air. The impact of it hitting the ground next to the stables caused everything to start making sense to him. He looked quickly to where the soldier had been standing tied to the post to his right. In the darkness he saw Private Martene struggle in the straw with the post still tied to his back. Past Martene the wounded soldier did the same.

Private Martene had managed to get the bandanna down from his mouth. He wallowed his way toward Shaw, saying, "Senor, quickly, we must get out of here, before they reload the cannons."

As Shaw worked the broken post from between

his back and his tied wrists, he said to the soldier, "I thought they would attack in the morning."

"So did I," said Martene, "but I'm only a private, and it looks like I was wrong." The two turned back to back, each finding the ropes and working quickly to loosen the other's wrists. "Now I think they are trying for the livery barn tonight, to kill all of the animals."

Shaw felt his wrists come free. He sat up and quickly began untying Martene. "They must have Zarco surrounded and are going to soften things up with cannon fire all night, then ride in and finish everybody off in the morning." He looked back through the darkness for the buckskin, hearing the other horses whinny in terror. "Get your pard untied," he said over his shoulder. "I'll get some horses."

He hurried back to where the buckskin stood waiting, scraping a nervous hoof in the dirt. As he opened the stall door, he looked at the next three stalls in the darkness, knowing these were the ones where Leeman, Bone and Waite kept their horses.

Even in the shadowy darkness he could tell the three stalls were empty.

Why hadn't he seen this coming?

This was why Leeman wanted his two best men standing guard tonight, Shaw told himself, and that's why Leeman wanted him watching the flats from the south end of town. So the three could slip away in the darkness, Shaw thought. That meant all the top men in the border raiders had cut out on the others.

Leeman, Bone and Waite . . . Hatch and Sonny Engles. They were all gone now. If the *federales* didn't catch them crossing the flats tonight, all they would find come morning would be the underlings, Drop the Dog, Lying Earl . . . He thought of the others, Kerns, Bartley, Butterfield, Mertz, Pearl. There were others he hadn't even met. He thought of Bert Sibott and shook his head.

But he'd warned Sibott; that was all he could do. Anybody left here would have to figure things out for themselves—which they would pretty quick, he reminded himself, grabbing a saddle and throwing it up onto the buckskin's back. So would Dawson and Caldwell, once they heard the cannon fire and started seeing gunmen flee Zarco like snakes from a burning bush.

Knowing the cannons were targeting the livery barn, Shaw gathered the two soldiers' already-saddled horses, then threw open the stall doors and sent the others running out onto the street. He led the three horses quickly over to where Martene had the wounded soldier standing up, his arm looped around his shoulders. "We've got to hurry," Shaw said, hearing voices shout back and forth, the men caught by surprise and scrambling to gather their guns and gear and grab their fleeing horses.

"Yes," said Martene, "and *gracias*, Senor Shaw, for all you have done for us."

"Don't thank me yet, Private," said Shaw, helping him shove the wounded soldier up onto the horse's back. "Wait until we're out of here alive." Shaw turned to the buckskin and swung up into his saddle.

"I thank you now in case we do not *make* it out of here alive," said Martene, leaping onto his horse.

Leading the wounded soldier's horse by its reins, Martene followed Shaw out of the half-fallen livery barn and off along the dirt street, headed north, gunfire blazing from the street behind them.

Four miles north of town, Dawson, Caldwell and Tunis jumped up from the ground and stared out across the sand flats from the shelter of a clump of brush the wind had gathered at the bottom of the draw. "That was cannon fire," Dawson said. They stood in silence for a moment longer, then looked at one another as the second round rumbled across the night. This time they saw a quick flash of fire on the horizon in the direction of Zarco.

"What's Shaw doing in there?" Caldwell asked, more to himself than the other two bewildered lawmen. "Has he found himself a cannon?"

"No," said Dawson, "I'm betting that's *federale* cannon fire."

"*Federales?*" said Tunis. "What the blazes are they doing out there? They never come this far! We don't need them sticking their noses into this game."

"This *is* their country," said Dawson, but he knew what the government agent meant. They didn't need more guns to worry about—especially *big* guns—in the dark of night.

A moment later, after a reload, another cannon shot resounded, then another. "They must be planning on pounding Zarco into the sand," Dawson said almost under his breath.

"What do we do now?" said Caldwell, picking up his gun belt and strapping it around his waist. "We gave Shaw *two days*."

"Right," said Dawson. "But it sounds like things haven't gone the way he had them planned."

"So we're going in?" Tunis asked, also picking up his gun belt.

"Not into the cannon fire," said Dawson, "but in close enough to get an idea what's going on in there. As soon as the cannon fire stops we want to be the first ones on the street."

The three turned and walked quickly to where their horses stood hitched to some of the heavier bundles of dried brush, their ears piqued, nervous from the exploding cannon fire and the rumble of it in the sand beneath their hooves.

In moments the animals stood saddled and ready. "If we get in any gunfire let's be careful we don't shoot Shaw," Dawson said, as they swung up into their saddles and rode away toward Zarco.

From the south, Morgan Hatch and the woman had looked back as the second round of cannon fire took a bite out of the earth and spat it high in the air only five feet from the livery barn.

"It looks like we got out just in time," Hatch said to the woman. When the first cannon shot had hit the livery barn, Hatch had grabbed Sonny by his collar and trousers and thrown him up into his saddle. Now he looked all around until he saw Sonny riding a few feet ahead of them, looking back and forth in the purple shadowy darkness as if he were lost.

"Sonny! Wait up!" Hatch called out, trying to keep his voice down, having figured out that *federales* would be scouring the flats, searching for anybody trying to escape from Zarco.

Seeing that Sonny wasn't going to stop, the two turned their horses and bolted forward. Grabbing Sonny's horse by its reins, Hatch said in a lowered voice, "Damn it, pay attention here, Sonny! We'll have soldiers all over us if we're not careful."

"Huh? What?" Sonny said, holding a bloody hand to his dangling ear. "Hatch, I can't hear nothing. Shaw's ruined my ears."

Hatch looked at Sonny's better ear, the one not ripped away from his head by Shaw's spurs. "Your hearing will come back, Sonny," he said. "But not if you wander into soldiers and get your head shot off."

Juanita also looked at Sonny's ears, unable to see clearly in the purple light. She shook her head and said to Hatch, "Yes, hearing will come back, some of it anyway. But it could take days."

"Damn Shaw," said Hatch, considering the long way they had to go across the flats, and the disadvantage he'd be in, traveling with a man who wouldn't be able to hear their enemies coming. "Damn him to hell." Hatch let his horse fall back a step as he reached down to his boot well and pulled up a double-edged dagger. Seeing what he was about to do, the woman veered her horse away a few yards into the darkness, as if to say she wanted no part in killing Sonny Engles.

"Time to go, Sonny," Hatch said, knowing Engles couldn't hear him. He gigged his horse forward a step in preparation. But before he could reach over, clasp a hand over Sonny's mouth and thrust the dagger into his back, he stopped at the sound of nearby voices speaking low, in Spanish.

Holy Joseph. . . . Hatch slid the dagger back into his boot. He sidled up to Engles, grabbed his horse by its bridle and clasped his hand over Sonny's mouth anyway.

Sonny's eyes widened, until he saw Hatch gesturing for him to keep quiet. Without a word, Hatch lowered his hand from Sonny's face, slipped Sonny's rifle from its boot, placed it into the deaf gunman's hands and cocked it.

Sonny nodded his head, getting the idea. He gave a wink, pulled his horse a step away, then gigged it hard and sent it racing straight ahead across the sand. Hatch had seen the woman veer away on his right. Instead of following her, he veered to the left and gave his horse a strong bat of his boot heels. He'd gone less than fifteen yards when he heard gunshots explode in the direction he'd sent Sonny Engles. "Damn Shaw," he said again, riding away in the purple darkness.

Chapter 24

By the time Shaw and the two soldiers stopped and looked back on the glow of firelight in Zarco, several more cannon rounds had bored through the livery barn. By now the barn would have been flattened, Shaw surmised, knowing some of the raiders had managed to catch their frightened horses and make a getaway.

"Now Palo and I can thank you, senor," said Martene, still holding the reins to the wounded soldier's horse, the three of them looking back on the glow of firelight and the sound of rifle and cannon fire.

"You've still got to get to your column without your own men shooting you," said Shaw. He thought about Dawson, Caldwell and Tunis being somewhere on the sand flats trail ahead and asked, "Can you both make it all right from here?" As he spoke a blast of gunshots resounded less than five hundred yards to their right, the place where Sonny Engles had ridden into a half dozen soldiers.

"*Sí*, we will be all right," said Private Martene,

"but what about you? Our soldiers will be looking everywhere on these flats for raiders."

"I'll be all right," Shaw said. He turned the buckskin and tapped his boot heels to its sides. The two soldiers watched him ride away into the darkness.

Three hundred yards beyond where the blasts of gunfire had erupted, Dawson, Caldwell and Tunis all three stopped and turned their horses toward the muzzle flashes and the sound of what sounded like a raging gun battle. "Sounds like it could be the men we're looking for," said Dawson.

"Or Shaw," said Caldwell.

"Or both," said Tunis.

"The Mexican soldiers have knocked a hornet's nest down on their heads," said Caldwell. Far to the east of Zarco another gun battle erupted. The three lawmen looked in that direction, then back at the gun battle nearest to them.

"Let's get closer, see what we've got," said Dawson. He gigged his horse up into a run, Caldwell right behind him, Tunis following Caldwell.

By the time they had arrived at the spot where the battle had raged only moments earlier, the firing had ceased. On the ground lay four Mexican soldiers, three dead and one wounded. When Dawson eased down from his horse and walked toward him in the purple moonlit night, the soldier groaned and said, *"No dispara! Por favor, no dispara!"*

"We're not going to shoot," Dawson replied. "We're not with the raiders. We're lawmen, on their trail." He pulled his U.S. Marshal's badge from his duster pocket and held it out for the man to see.

"Ah, thank God," the soldier said in a strained voice, holding his bloody upper right ribs.

"Which way did they go, Sergeant?" said Dawson, seeing the stripes on the man's sleeve as he stooped down for a closer look at the wound.

"He went west, toward Saltilo and Metagore," the sergeant said, letting Dawson take a look. "It is where anyone on the run goes from here, if they know the desert and do not want to die of thirst."

"He?" said Caldwell, stooping down beside Dawson.

"Yes, only one man did this," said the soldier. "But he was a wild man. He shot the four of us, and sent two more running." He looked into Dawson's eyes and said, "His ear is falling off! His face is cut and bruised. He will not be hard to recognize."

Dawson and Caldwell gave each other a curious look. While the two sat stooped over the wounded man, Tunis walked a few yards away and came back leading a horse. Seeing Tunis and the animal, Dawson asked the man as he untied his bandanna, folded it, laid it in the wound and pressed the man's hand on it, "Are you able to ride?"

"*Sí*, in a little while," the man replied.

"Are you going to be all right out here?" asked Caldwell. "These outlaws are everywhere."

"I am all right." The wounded man sat up some and gestured toward a canteen hanging from the horse's saddle horn. "Give me the canteen, please. I will rest here awhile and find my way back."

"When you see the soldiers, tell them we're out here," said Tunis.

"I will *tell* them," the man said, but with a look that asked what good it would do.

"*Gracias.*" Dawson patted the man's sweaty shoulder. Then the three mounted and turned their horses to ride on. But before they could, a voice called out in the darkness, "Stop where you are! Hold up your hands!"

"Soldiers," said Dawson, hearing the broken English.

Behind them, the three lawmen heard the wounded soldier call out in Spanish telling them not to shoot. "These men are not the border raiders. They are lawmen hunting them down, the same as we are."

"*Americano* lawmen?" said a thin, narrow-eyed lieutenant, as his horse carried him forward at a slow walk. Out of the greater darkness a circle of riflemen on foot closed in around the lawmen, their breechloading rifles up and pointed.

"*Sí, americanos,*" said the sergeant. "They helped me. Look, this one gave his bandanna for my gunshot wound. They are not border raiders. He showed me his marshal's badge."

"Ha! Any of the border raiders could have killed a marshal and taken his badge," the lieutenant said. "I will decide if they are lawmen or not." To the circled riflemen he said, "Take their guns and their horses. We will hold them until we know who they are."

The three lawmen looked at one another, knowing how long it could take and how hard it might be for them to prove they were lawmen. "Go!" shouted Dawson, nailing his spurs to his horse's sides, charging through the soldiers as they stepped forward to disarm them.

"No!" Tunis shouted, sitting still as Caldwell took Dawson's command and the two raced away into the darkness with bullets whistling past them. No sooner were the two out of sight than Tunis realized what a mistake his hesitancy had been. He watched the soldiers close around him again, this time jerking him from his saddle, jerking his Colt from his holster, his rifle from its boot.

Fifty yards out, Dawson and Caldwell slid to a halt and looked back. "Why didn't he come?" Dawson asked.

"I don't know," said Caldwell, "but it'll go hard on him, after us running away."

"I know," said Dawson, letting out a tight breath. "Circle around. We'll cut through from two directions, get him out before they get settled."

"Got you," said Caldwell, booting his horse around before Dawson had hardly gotten the words out of his mouth.

As some of the soldiers stood reloading their rifles, the others hurried Tunis over and stood him in front of the mounted lieutenant. "I will make you wish you never heard of the border raiders," he said.

"We're not raiders," said Tunis. "We are lawmen. But the fact is—"

Before he could finish his words a rumble of hooves converged from two directions, causing the men to look back and forth until both riders bolted in out of the darkness. Their paths crisscrossed right in front of the startled lieutenant, whose horse reared with him, causing him to have to wrestle with his reins and settle the spooked animal down. By then all that remained of Tunis were his guns and his horse.

"Find them! Kill them!" the enraged lieutenant shouted, looking all around in his humiliation.

"But they are not the raiders!" the wounded sergeant shouted. But the lieutenant didn't seem to hear him.

A hundred yards away, Caldwell slowed his horse to a stop and looked over at Dawson, who did the same. "Now we'll have the army on our backs," he said.

Behind Caldwell, Tunis said to both of them, "I'm sorry. I don't know why I stalled on you. I suppose I thought I could explain everything away and get us set free."

Dawson kept himself calm. "We all three got away, that's the main thing."

"I—I don't know what to say," Tunis stammered. "I didn't expect the two of you to come back for me." He looked at Dawson, then at Caldwell, who'd turned in his saddle and faced him. "I'm much obliged. I won't make a mistake like that again."

"You better not," said Dawson.

"What do we do now?" Caldwell asked. "He's got no horse, no guns."

"We've got to go on into Zarco, even if we're riding double," said Dawson.

"Wait," said Tunis, "I know you're in charge, but I have to say, we're crazy to not pull back and get out of here, let the *federales* have the raiders this time. We can't fight them if we're rotting in a Mexican prison while somebody in Washington decides whether or not to claim us."

The three sat in silence for a long moment; then Caldwell said, "What about Shaw, Tunis? How do we know he's not stuck in Zarco, waiting for us to come get him?"

"Right," Dawson said quietly, "the way we came back and got you?"

"Yes, of course, Shaw . . . I understand," Tunis said, looking off toward the sound of cannon fire.

Three miles away, as separate gun battles flared up randomly on the flats behind him, Shaw had ridden straight in the direction he knew the three lawmen would be coming from. When the flurry of hoofprints running in every direction turned into three sets riding toward him across an otherwise smooth white desert floor, he knew the three were already on the flats somewhere between himself and the cannon fire still pounding Zarco in the darkness behind him. *All right . . .*

He couldn't blame Dawson for not waiting as they had planned to do. The *federales* and their cannons had changed everything. But the fight wouldn't be in Zarco now. The leadership of the raiders had already scattered. All Dawson and his two lawmen were going to find if they made it through the soldiers there were underlings, the ones not fortunate enough to catch themselves a horse and get away when he'd fanned the animals out onto the street.

Shaw sat looking back and forth across the wide, seemingly endless stretch of flat and rolling sand, from one streak of gunshots to the next, the desert having turned into an even more dangerous place than it had been already. He was finished here, he thought, now that he'd gotten the two soldiers out without getting them killed.

He'd done what he'd told Dawson he'd do. He'd

kept Leeman and Hatch at each other's throat. Had
the army not shown up when it did, he was certain
he would have had them killing each other on the
street. He gave a thin, wry smile, thinking about it.
No, he reflected, flashes of gunfire glittering in his
eyes as he nudged the buckskin forward, back
toward Zarco, there was nothing holding him here,
but what the hell? Picturing Francisca, knowing what
high regard she held for him, he drew his Winchester
rifle out of its boot and levered a round up into the
chamber. *Angels don't always need a reason.*

Besides, he'd heard Hatch telling Sonny where
they were headed. If they were headed for Metagore,
he had a strong hunch Leeman and his two close
henchmen were headed the same direction. He
needed to find Dawson, Caldwell and Tunis and let
them know. With the flash of cannons casting a circling glow on the horizon, Shaw rode back toward
Zarco, keeping an eye on the three sets of tracks once
again until he saw the flurry of both boot prints and
hoofprints. Then he struck on again, this time following only two sets of tracks, but having a pretty good
idea they belonged to the same riders.

Dawson, Caldwell and Tunis had managed to
dodge stray bullets and avoid soldiers all the way
across the sand flats, to the safety of a low sandy
draw less than a thousand yards from Zarco. Cannon
fire still pounded the town; rifle fire resounded in
reply, but more sparingly now.

"The raiders still in Zarco must've figured out the
soldiers have found themselves cover out on the
flats," said Tunis, staring out at the random streak

of rifle fire as the cannons pounded steadily, shot after shot, one firing while the other reloaded.

Dawson looked at Caldwell and asked, "How long before daylight, Jedson?" He looked all around as he asked, knowing the desert would be crawling all night with fleeing gunmen and pursuing soldiers.

Caldwell took a railroad watch from his vest pocket. After squinting to make out the time in the grainy moonlight, he gave up, opened the front of the case and felt the watch's hands with his fingertips. "A couple more hours," he replied.

"Are we going in at first light?" Tunis asked.

"Before first light," said Dawson. "Come sunup, we'll never get through the soldiers. We're going in long enough to see if Shaw's there. If he is, he comes out with us. Otherwise we'll take down any raiders left alive, and get out as fast as we can, before the army rides in chopping off heads."

As the three spoke quietly among themselves, Shaw heard their whispered voices as he stepped down from his saddle and led the big buckskin forward. Finally he heard Dawson say to the other two, "Hold it, what's that?" A silence followed as Shaw stopped his horse for a second, then said quietly, "Dawson, it's me, Shaw."

"Shaw!" Dawson said in surprise. He looked at Caldwell and Tunis, then said, "Get in here. This place is crawling with soldiers."

"I know, I've been ducking them the past hour," said Shaw, stepping in over the edge of the low rise of sand in a crouch. He looked back and forth, and asked, "Who lost their horse back there?"

"It's a long story," said Dawson, covering for

Tunis. But the government agent would have none
of it. "That was me," he said quietly. "The soldiers
had us surrounded, Dawson told us to make a run
for it, I didn't do it."

Shaw gave Dawson a look. "That wasn't a long
story after all."

Dawson changed the subject. "What happened in
Zarco, Shaw? It sounded like the whole army came
down on the place."

"That's what the raiders must've thought too,"
Shaw replied. He took a breath and told them everything, including the fact that Leeman, his two main
men and Hatch and Sonny had cut out and left the
other men on their own. When he'd finished, he said,
"I figure the rest of them hightailed as soon as they
could, either riding or on foot. That's the gunfighting
we've been hearing all over these flats."

"We had a pretty good idea that's what it was,"
Dawson said flatly.

Shaw looked at Dawson closely and asked, "What
brought you here anyway? Anybody still alive has
cut out by now."

"Seeing how the plan got changed, we thought we
ought to come in and make sure you got out all
right," said Dawson.

"I'm much obliged," Shaw said, not admitting his
only reason for riding back was to find them. "But I
figure this waltz is over. The raiders are gone. The
cannons are only firing now to make sure none of
them come back. The *soldados* are running them
down."

"There it is now," said Caldwell, at the sound of
a sudden outburst of rifle fire in the distance.

"Yep," said Shaw, "the buzzards will have a fiesta for the next week." He looked at Dawson and said, "I heard Morgan Hatch tell Engles they were headed for Metagore. I figure if that's where they're headed, it's where we'll find Leeman too. They're both dead set on killing each other."

"Metagore sounds right," said Dawson. "We found a wounded soldier who said the man who shot him headed out in that direction. Said the fellow had an ear ripped off, hanging by a shred. I wonder what happened to him."

"That's Sonny," Shaw said. "I spiked him in the ears with my spurs."

"Spiked him?" Dawson and the other two looked at him curiously, then down at the one-inch blunt spike spurs on his boot heels.

Shaw shrugged. "I was tied to a post, it's the best I could do."

The three shrugged with him, in acknowledgment.

"You were out of here, Shaw?" Dawson asked. "What brought you back?"

Shaw didn't answer, which to Dawson was an answer in itself. He had come back looking for them. Dawson glanced at Caldwell with a slight nod.

Instead of an answer, Shaw sighed and said, "Now that the raiders are headed for Metagore, the army will be right behind them come morning when they see there's hoofprints headed that way. Do you want to leave them to the Mexican army now that they're on their tails?"

"What do you think?" Dawson asked.

Shaw looked toward Zarco, then out across the dark purple sand flats toward the west. "I think we better travel quick and quiet. These soldiers have done enough shooting tonight. They're bound to be trigger-happy." He stood up and dusted the seat of his trousers.

Chapter 25

The four traveled in silence throughout the night, avoiding any sound of approaching hooves on their meandering journey across a sea of pale white sand and purple night. Tunis rode double, first with Caldwell, then with Dawson, until they finally came upon Filo Hewes lying mortally wounded on the ground, his horse's reins in hand. Next to Hewes lay Sandy Kerns' body, a ragged bullet hole above his left eye.

Shaw rode in closer and stepped down beside Hewes, the three lawmen lagging back a few feet, keeping an eye on the surrounding darkness. Looking up at him in the moonlight, Hewes said in a weak voice, "Shaw, hot damn . . . I see you made it out okay." He coughed up dark foamy blood and said, "Some wild night, eh?"

"Yeah, some wild night, Filo," Shaw replied, realizing this man had no idea what had gone on, with Leeman, with Hatch, with himself and the two soldiers making their getaway. "How bad are you hit?" he asked in a low whisper.

"Me? Oh, hell . . . I'm dead," said Filo, not sounding too concerned with the matter. "I'm just lying here . . . waiting for it."

"I see," said Shaw, not even bothering to stoop down and check his wounds. "You need anything?" The surrounding sand beneath Hewes was too darkly sated with his blood for him to live out the night.

"Not that I can . . . think of," Hewes whispered.

Shaw reached out, took the reins to Filo's horse and tugged them. "I could use this cayouse, if you're sure you're through with it."

Filo let the reins slide free of his hand.

"Obliged," said Shaw. "Who else made it out of there?"

"Anybody who had any sense . . . one way or the other," Hewes said. "Towan Bartley stayed, so did Sibott . . . a few others." He shook his head. "I don't know what they . . . were thinking."

"Neither do I," said Shaw. "You sure you don't need anything . . . ?" His words trailed at seeing Hewes slump down and let out a wet rasping breath.

Behind Shaw, the three lawmen had moved in closer. Tunis slipped down from the back of Dawson's horse and took the reins that Shaw held out to him. "Thank goodness," Tunis said, sliding Hewes' rifle from its boot and looking it over. He reached down into the pasty blood, picked up Hewes' Colt and shook dark, wet sand from it.

"Let's go," Shaw whispered, stepping back and picking up the reins to his buckskin. "This is no place to stay in one spot for long." He turned and swung up into his saddle.

They rode on.

An hour later, they come upon the bodies of two

soldiers, one's trousers down around his ankles, his throat cut from ear to ear. The other was lying in a ball, his hands grasping the handle of a dagger buried to its hilt in his bloody chest. To their far left rifle shots erupted suddenly. Someone screamed in a voice akin to a wounded panther. Another voice swore curses in English until a single bullet cut his voice short.

By the time they'd reached the black shadows of a hill line and started up a rock path, the first thin ray of sunlight was crawling along the eastern horizon. A half hour later, they stopped in a grainy silver light and looked back from the shelter of rock and brush. "Good Lord," said Tunis, looking out across the sand flats below. "I have never witnessed such a sight in my life." Hewes' Colt had been cleaned with a bandanna and was resting in the tied-down holster on the lawman's hip.

"Me neither," Dawson whispered as if in awe. Silver and brown gun smoke hung in patches on the still morning air.

Beneath the wispy patches of smoke lay the bodies of soldiers and outlaws alike, horses wandering among the dead like sentinels keeping watch over some blood-anointed holy land. Soldiers still patrolled here and there on horseback. As the four lawmen watched, two soldiers flushed a wounded outlaw from the cover of a draw, chased him down and shot him as he tried to limp away on foot.

"That's what we just rode through," Tunis whispered, more to himself than anyone else.

"It certainly looks different from here," Caldwell stated almost reverently. "I suppose when you're in it you don't notice, but looking down on it"—he shook his head slowly—"it looks like hell."

Shaw listened to each of them, looking back and forth at each of their faces as they commented. He looked down and farther out across the flats to where an officer stood waving men toward him to form a rank. Then he looked up at the wide endless sky and said, "I expect the higher you go, the worse this looks, until you get so high you don't see it."

The three turned facing him with curious looks on their dirty, dust-covered faces. Shaw spat and turned the buckskin back to the thin rocky trail. "They'll be heading this way as soon as they get formed up and accounted for. We best keep moving."

On the trail, fresh hoofprints overlapped, all headed in the same direction.

Four miles into the hilled terrain, they came upon a dead horse. Two miles farther, they passed another horse, this one alive, but too exhausted to even move out of their way as they approached it. Blood dripped from its nostrils. Its saddle had slipped all the way down and hung under its belly. Shaw stopped long enough to step down and drop the saddle from the worn-out animal's belly. Then he climbed back atop the buckskin, patted its damp neck reassuringly and rode on.

At midmorning, the four stopped at a lower clearing in the hill line where a stretch of land leveled for nearly a mile before jutting back up into the rocky hillside. Gazing at a short strip of weathered shacks and adobes, Shaw said, "There's Saltilo. Watch your step. It's the first water since Zarco for anybody traveling in a hurry."

The four spread wide as they rode down onto a dirt street filled with rock and sunken boulders. Halfway along the street before them, three sweat-streaked horses stood at an iron hitch rail. Nearby, on a wet spot of earth, an ancient donkey walked in a short circle turning the wooden spoke of a crude water wheel. Seeing the four men ride in, rifles in hand, an elderly woman grabbed the hand of a small boy and jerked him along into a darkened doorway.

"They know we're here," said Dawson, his thumb over his rifle hammer.

Almost before he'd gotten the words out of his mouth, a shot rang out from atop an adobe roof. Dawson and Caldwell veered their animals to one side of the street, Shaw to the other. Only as they hurried down from the horses' backs to take cover did they see that Tunis lay on the ground, his hands clasped to his bleeding chest.

Caldwell tried to run out to the downed lawman, but two shots from atop an adobe sent him scurrying back to cover. Shaw cut a sharp glance to the rooftop and said to Caldwell, "Go on now, I've got them."

Without hesitation Caldwell ran out to Tunis, grabbed him by his shoulders and dragged him out of the street. From a rooftop a gunman poked his head up to take another shot, but a bullet from Shaw's rifle nailed him between the eyes.

Dawson had seen a rifleman duck back out of sight. He gave Shaw a hand signal, asking for cover, then moved forward crouched until the gunman showed his face again. Dawson dropped him with a shot to the stomach. The gunman went backward and down with a deep grunt. He landed sitting down against the wall of an adobe, his boots spread wide, his hands clutching his lower belly. A string of saliva swung and bobbed from his parted lips.

"Fast Larry!" a voice called out from another adobe farther up the street. "This is Clell Butterfield, you son of a bitch! Who's that with you?"

"Just some cousins of mine," Shaw replied.

"Cousins my ass," Butterfield shouted. "You and your *cousins* are all dead if you don't turn around and walk away from here. We need them horses."

Shaw levered a fresh round into his rifle chamber. "Better come take them, Butterfield. The longer you wait, the less you're going to be needing them."

After a silence, Butterfield called out, "You know he jackpotted all of us, didn't he . . . him and his two hounds?"

"Yep, he did," Shaw replied, knowing that he meant Leeman, Bone and Waite.

"So, it turns out, Hatch was right, Leeman jackpotted him too, back in Julimez," Butterfield said. "You can't trust no son of a bitch anymore, can you?"

"That's my belief," Shaw replied, his eyes scanning the street for any more gunmen, knowing Butterfield was keeping him talking while whoever was with him took position. "Who's with you here, Butterfield?" he asked.

Before Butterfield could answer, another voice called out from across the street, "We're just some *cousins* of his, Fast Larry."

Shaw recognized the gravelly voice of Andy Mertz. That most likely meant Wallace Pearl was with them, hidden somewhere nearby.

"What about these horses?" Shaw asked. "Are you coming for them, or what?"

"Oh, we're coming," said Butterfield. As he replied he stepped out from the cover of a darkened doorway, firing a rifle from his hip. "I never was much impressed with you, *big-time gunman!*"

Shaw's shot hit him in the chest, knocking him backward. At the same time a shot from Dawson helped slam him to the ground.

Shaw swung toward Andy Mertz, who charged at them down the middle of the street. But before Shaw fired, a shot from Dawson stopped Mertz cold. From beyond the well, the sound of running boots resounded along a hard rocky path between two adobes. Shaw waited, watched, his rifle against his shoulder. When Pearl appeared back in sight from behind the adobe, headed for the cover of rock and brush, Shaw's shot nailed him.

"Think there's more?" Dawson asked as the two backed along the street to where Caldwell had leaned Tunis against a barrel sitting in the shade of a canvas overhang.

"No, but I wouldn't swear to it," Shaw said. He kept a wary eye on the street and rooftops while Dawson bent down over Tunis and looked at the wound in his chest.

"I'm sorry," said Tunis. "It seems that . . . once again I haven't made a good showing."

"Don't talk," said Dawson. He leaned him forward and looked down his back for an exit wound. Seeing it, he leaned Tunis back carefully and looked at Caldwell.

"It missed his lungs," Caldwell said. "He's not bleeding too fast."

"He still can't ride," said Dawson. "Riding will kill him."

"So will the army . . . when they find me here," Tunis said in a pained voice. "If I'm dying let me pick my spot." He gripped Dawson's forearm. "I won't hold us up."

Dawson considered it. Looking along the street, he said to Caldwell, "Get him patched up best you can. I'll go see about buying a cart."

"A cart." Shaw shook his head as he gathered the reins to the horses to lead them to the well. "If you ride from here to Metagore in a mule cart you'll wish that shot *had* killed you."

"That's encouraging, Shaw," Tunis said. "I'm . . . certainly looking forward to it." He managed a pained wry grin.

Metagore, Mexico

Deacon Lucas Leeman, Charlie Bone and Blackie Waite stood inside the small cantina, staring out through an open window toward a small adobe farther down the opposite side of the street. Earlier they'd watched Morgan Hatch and Engles go inside the adobe, Hatch shoving Engles ahead of him. "What the hell do you suppose happened to him?" Waite asked, seeing a bloody bandanna tied around Sonny's head, keeping his all but severed ear in place.

"Beats me," said Leeman. "I'm glad we tied our horses out back. They don't know. we're here. We could get the drop on them, kill them right now if we had a mind to." He seemed to think it over for a moment, then said, "But maybe it's time we called a truce with them instead."

"What for?" Bone asked, staring hard at the evicted couple who had walked only a few yards away and sat in the dirt staring back toward their home.

"What *for*?" Leeman gave a dark grin and said, "You know, for something to feed to the army when they get here? Something to keep them busy while we put some more distance between us and their damned cannons."

Bone shook his head. "Huh-uh. It won't work. Sonny might be stupid enough to get jackpotted a *third* time, but not Hatch," he said. "We'll need to fight and get on up and out of here before we've got soldiers down our backs."

"Don't tell me it won't work," Leeman said, his temper flaring a bit.

"No offense," said Bone, seeing he'd stepped out of line with Deacon Leeman. "I guess I just can't see it happening again."

"Want to make a wager?" Leeman asked. "Say, a hundred dollars?"

Just to settle Leman's cross attitude, Bone said, "Sure, why not?"

"Hold on, Deacon," said Waite. "You're going to walk out in the street and call them out and tell you want to make a truce, after us doing what we did to them?"

"That's right," Leeman said bravely. "Of course I want the two of yas covering my back, just in case I'm wrong."

Waite shook his head and said, "All right, Deacon, whatever you say." He slipped his Colt from its holster. Bone did the same.

In the adobe across the street, Hatch had seated Sonny at a wooden table and lowered the bloody bandanna from the side of his head, Sonny's ear clinging to the sticky cloth.

"Did it come off?" Sonny asked loudly, unable to gauge his voice without being able to hear it.

"No, it's still hanging on, and it's turning black and looking worse," said Hatch, before he realized Sonny couldn't hear him. "Damn it," he said to himself. He put the bandanna back in place and stepped around in front of the deaf gunman.

"How is it?" Sonny asked loudly.

"It's much better," said Hatch. Knowing Sonny couldn't hear him, he gave him a wink and a high sign, assuring him everything was just fine.

"Morgan Hatch," Deacon Leeman shouted from the middle of the street.

Hatch froze for a second; a dark gleam came into his eyes. "There's that rotten son of a bitch," he said quietly to himself.

Seeing the look on Hatch's face, Sonny said loudly, "What is it, Morgan?"

Hatch took him by his shoulders, pulled him up from the chair, laid his gun hand on the butt of his Colt and nudged him along toward the front door. "I expect a picture truly *is* worth a thousand words."

Chapter 26

—————

Topping a rise, Shaw stopped sharply and pulled the buckskin back out of sight.

Dawson, who rode right behind him, stopped rather than plow into him. "What is it?" he asked, knowing Shaw had come upon something.

"It's Leeman, Hatch and Engles, all three standing in the street." He settled his horse and said, "Maybe if we give them a minute or two they'll kill one another."

Behind Dawson, Caldwell brought the cart to a stop, Tunis' horse pulling the crude rig, Caldwell's horse hitched and tagging along behind it.

"But we're not going to count on it," Dawson said, checking his rifle.

"No," Shaw said somberly, "it's time we wash our hands of them."

On the street, Hatch had stepped in front of Sonny and stopped him with a raised hand when he saw Leeman holding his hands chest high, a white handkerchief dangling from his fingertips in a call for a truce. In the open window, Hatch could see the two gunmen watching every move they made. "A truce, huh?" he said with a tight, angry smile. "You've got to be joshing me." To his right side, three feet back, Sonny stood staring blankly, his hand closed tight around his gun butt.

"No, I'm not joshing," said Leeman with a serious look on his face.

"And what are those two for?" said Hatch, nodding toward Waite and Bone. "I suppose they're here in case I turn down your offer, sort of like a peace meeting between the cavalry and the Indians?"

Leeman chuckled and replied, "Yeah, I guess you could say that." He nodded at Sonny. "What's wrong with him? He looks like he doesn't know where he's at."

Seeing Leeman talking, nodding at him, Sonny bristled and took a step forward. But Hatch stopped him, putting a hand on his chest. "Shaw spurred him in both ears," he said. "Damn near ripped one off."

"Spurred him in both ears?" Leeman asked with a bemused look, as if having a hard time picturing it.

"Nailed Sonny between his spike spurs and shook his head like a cat shaking a ball of twine," Hatch said. "Poor Sonny is ruined—couldn't hear a freight train if it ran right over him."

"*What?*" Sonny asked loudly.

"Nothing, Sonny." Hatch settled him with a slight wave of his hand.

"Damn," said Leeman, looking at the blank expression on Sonny's face, the dried black blood down the lobe of his uncovered ear. After a pause he said, "See? That's a good reason why we need to settle our differences and pull together. We've got *soldados* on our trail, not to mention those lawmen from before. If there was ever five men who need one another, it's all of us."

"I trust you like I'd trust a rattlesnake, Leeman," Hatch said.

But Leeman realized that since Hatch hadn't hit the street shooting, it was a good possibility he could pull this truce off with him.

"You don't have to trust me, Morgan," he said. "Hell, you'd be a stone idiot to, after what I've done to you. But let's get real serious about staying alive. I've still got that gold station waiting for us in Durango. Now that our ranks have been thinned, I'll be needing some good riders. I always said you and Sonny there are the best." He paused and looked around the empty street. "Say, what happened to the woman, the one Sonny called Whore?"

"I don't know. Dead, I guess," said Hatch. "She just wandered off on the flats amid all the fighting."

"Too bad," said Leeman. "It might have been good to have a full-time woman around, a whore at that."

"Back to us, Leeman," said Hatch. "If we made a truce it would only be until after that Durango job. After that I might just have to go ahead and kill you—me or Sonny." He gestured toward Engles.

"I understand," said Leeman. "If you feel so moved to kill me, you'll be welcome to try."

"What you say?" Sonny asked, his voice twice as loud as it needed to be.

"Nothing, Sonny," Hatch said again, his own voice growing louder even though it made no difference whether he screamed or whispered. Seeing the added confusion in Sonny's eyes, he gave him another hand signal, settling him down.

"Then we've got a truce?" Leeman smiled. He'd won, he'd talked Hatch into a truce. He almost couldn't believe it himself. Maybe Morgan Hatch was not as smart as he'd thought him to be. Maybe that was why he and Sonny and Wild Dick always rode together. They could all three have been idiots seeking other idiots for company, he thought.

"Yeah," said Hatch, grudgingly. "Call your hounds on out here. We've got a truce."

Not a minute too soon, Shaw said to himself, standing around the corner of an adobe he'd crept up to, using a footpath that ran behind the small village. Looking across the street, he saw Dawson crouched beside a long-abandoned freight wagon. Giving Dawson a nod, Shaw stepped into the street without his rifle, and started walking calmly toward the five outlaws, Boone and Waite having stepped out of the adobe and walked up beside Leeman.

"Deacon, look who's coming here," said Bone, turning slowly toward Shaw.

"Well, I'll be, if it's not Fast Larry himself," Leeman said, finding something amusing about Shaw walking up, his broad sombrero darkening out his face, the ragged poncho hanging down hiding his gun belt.

Upon seeing Shaw, Sonny screamed in rage and tried to reach for his gun. But Hatch grabbed his hand, stopping him, and motioned for him to stand down. Holding on to Sonny's forearm, Hatch said to

Shaw, "You're a brazen bastard, I'll give you that, coming here, after what you did to Sonny."

"That was only a start," Shaw said. He kept walking closer.

"Yeah, he's brazen, this one," Leeman said jokingly, with no apparent fear or even concern, Shaw stalking toward him like a mountain cat. "But why shouldn't he be? He is the *fastest gun alive*, after all." Leeman's eyes widened, in mock astonishment. *"Whoooa!"*

Shaw ignored him.

"Careful, Deacon," Bone cautioned in a whisper, "you don't know this devil."

"Oh, hell, I know this kind of fool," Leeman said, unimpressed, loud enough for Shaw to hear every word. "Fast guns! Quick Draw Artist! Professional Shootist! That's all hot air and malarkey."

"Easy, Leeman," said Hatch.

But Leeman ignored him. He called out to Shaw, "What can we do for you, Fast Larry? What brings a big gun like you up into this poor village? Are you here to scare crows off their corn? If you are they'll starve to death." He laughed a little too loud at his own joke.

"What is wrong with you, Deacon? Bone's right," Waite said under his breath, "you don't want this man throwing down on you! He truly is the *fastest gun alive*! That's not some kind of made-up thing."

"Say fastest gun alive to me again and I'll backhand you, Waite," Deacon said, his mood turning ugly all of a sudden.

"You heard him, Shaw," said Hatch, seeing this

was no laughing matter. "What do you want here? You're not riding with us. I wouldn't trust you after what happened between us in Zarco."

"I'm not here to ride with you, Hatch," Shaw said, stopping in the street. "I'm here to kill you," he added flatly.

Leeman stared at him; so did the others, spreading out a little, putting some distance between them. Shaw reached over with his left hand and flipped his ragged poncho up over his shoulder.

"What?" Sonny blurted out loudly again, looking back and forth in confusion, his hand wrapped around his gun butt.

"All of yas take it easy," said Leeman. "Let me take him, I'll show you just how fast he—"

Shaw's hand came up too fast to see. His shot bored through Leeman's forehead and sent a spray of blood, brain and bone matter spilling along the middle of the street. Ten yards away, the couple Hatch had dragged out of their adobe shot across the street and back inside their home. A door slammed; a bolt slid quickly into place.

Dawson stepped onto the street, his Colt out and firing.

Shaw's second shot hit Charlie Bone, slamming him backward out of one boot. Bone did a wild broken flip and landed facedown. Shaw's third shot hit Waite squarely in the heart and sent him flying backward, both feet off the ground. He hit the ground and didn't make another move.

Dawson's first shot had hit Morgan Hatch, killing him instantly. Then he swung his gun toward Sonny Engles, who had come up with his gun toward Shaw.

But before Dawson could fire, Caldwell stepped out with a shotgun from beside an adobe where he'd been positioned to keep any of them from running away. He fired both barrels. Sonny blew apart in every direction, without hearing a sound.

"Everybody all right?" Shaw asked, looking around, dropping his spent bullets and replacing them with fresh rounds from his gun belt.

Dawson, always amazed at Shaw's speed and accuracy, shook his head and said, "You almost didn't need us."

"*Almost* is not a hand to bet on," Shaw replied.

In the open back gate of the mule cart where they had left him, Agent Ripley Tunis struggled and raised himself up onto his elbows, hearing the breaking of dried brush as someone ran toward the trail. The running footsteps had begun during the shooting and continued after it had stopped. *An animal . . . ?* It could be, but he didn't think so. *Get ready,* he told himself, none of them having had any idea how many raiders might be waiting in Metagore.

Raising the Colt that lay beside him, he held it out at arm's length and cocked the hammer. *But what if it's only some villager, even a child . . . ?*

"Stop. Who's there? *Detenga, quién está allí?*" he repeated quickly in Spanish, in case it was some innocent party fleeing the gunfire.

"*Por favor,* don't shoot!" a frightened voice called out as the running footsteps came to a halt near the edge of the trail, some twenty feet from him.

"Oh my God!" he said. His gun slumped, his gun hand trembling as he saw the nun in her black glow-

ing robes step onto the trail, her head bowed to him
as if in servitude. She stepped closer, her hands
raised. "*Sister*, lower your hands, and forgive me
please. I'm afraid I'm awfully edgy today."

"I understand," she said, her face still bowed
toward him. She stopped not more than fifteen feet
away.

"You have nothing to fear, ma'am—I mean, *Sister*,"
Tunis said, correcting himself. "I'm with the American government. We're here to—" His words
stopped short as she raised her face enough for him
to recognize her. "You!" he said.

With a war cry, the woman hurled herself onto
him like some wild bloodthirsty raven, a big knife
cocked above her head. She had stunned Tunis,
caught him off guard. He tried to raise the gun again
after having lowered it with such abandon. But the
gun didn't come up quick enough. She landed
astraddle his wounded chest, knocking him backward. She stabbed the knife down at his chest with
all her strength. Tunis caught her arm at the wrist
and held on tight, his sore wounded chest taking the
impact, the pain of it.

In the street, the three lawmen turned at the sound
of the woman's catlike scream. They looked at one
another. A silent second passed; then a shot exploded
from the direction of the mule cart, followed by another, another and another. "Tunis!" Caldwell
shouted before the four shots had finished.

Cutting straight through brush and rocks toward
the cart instead of taking the street back to the trail,
the lawmen slowed a bit, with their guns drawn,

when they heard Tunis whisper in a hoarse muffled voice, "Help me. . . ."

Caldwell was the first onto the trail. He stopped and stared at the woman's bare legs astraddle Tunis, the wounded agent lying beneath her with his Colt raised and smoking in his right hand.

"What the . . . ?" Dawson and Shaw spread out a little as they drew closer.

"Help me," Tunis cried out again.

Caldwell saw the four exit wounds in the woman's back as he grabbed her and rolled her off the wounded lawman. Then he saw the big knife fall from her dead hand and clatter on the floor of the cart.

"It's the woman who killed Carr," Caldwell said, seeing her blank eyes staring up at the wide Mexican sky.

"Oh my, thank you, Caldwell!" Tunis gulped air in relief, the weight of the dead woman finally off his wounded chest. "She— She—" His breath kept giving out on him.

"Don't talk, Tunis, just take it easy," said Dawson, "we get the picture."

Shaw looked at the woman's face, then back along the winding rocky trail. "No telling who died in order for her to get herself outfitted that way."

"Well, her killing is over now," said Caldwell, finally slipping his Colt back into his holster.

"So is theirs," Dawson said, gesturing back toward the village. "The best thing we can do is get out of here before the army shows up."

"Yep, that's us all right," Shaw said. "Four *ameri-*

canos, who rode in, killed four men and a nun. Then rode out again."

"It's not as bad as it sounds," Dawson said. "We could line their bodies all up along the street if you think that would make it look any better."

Shaw seemed to consider it. "No, I think we best just leave, let them make of it what they will until the army gets here and sorts it all out."

They gathered their horses. "We'll still have to dodge soldiers for a while," said Caldwell.

"We can live with it," said Dawson. "The main thing is we got the job done."

"For a little while," said Shaw. "As long as there's a border, there'll be outlaws taking advantage of it." He looked at Tunis. "Put that in your report to Messenger. Tell him I said it."

"It'll be a while before I write any sort of report on all of this," said Tunis as Caldwell crawled into the driver's seat and took up the cart reins. "I've got to find the best way to tell him how I managed to kill a woman . . . who I thought was a nun." He managed a dark chuckle in spite of the pain in his chest. "Shot her four times, while she was sitting atop me, with her knees spread."

"See why I find reports so hard to write?" said Dawson, swinging up into his saddle.

"I know," Tunis replied. "That's why I threw my paper and pencil away. I decided if I lived through this, I could always sit down when I get home and make it up to suit myself—the parts that are too hard to explain, that is. The main thing is we did it, right?"

"You're going to go far in government work,

Tunis," said Shaw, swinging into his saddle beside Dawson.

"Obliged, Shaw. Nice of you to say so," Tunis said.

"My pleasure," Shaw said, touching the brim of his dusty black sombrero. He tapped his boots to the buckskin's sides and nudged it forward at a walk.

"What about you, Shaw?" the wounded lawman asked as Shaw rode in front of the cart, out of his sight.

"What about me?" Shaw asked without looking back.

"Can I tell Messenger that you're going to keep the badge? That you'll be riding for us now?"

"Tell him I'm going to keep the badge," Shaw replied, nudging the buckskin into a quicker pace.

"And that you'll be riding for us down here?" Tunis persisted.

Shaw didn't answer; Tunis started to call out and ask him again. But Dawson cut in and said, loud enough for Shaw to hear him clearly, "Leave it alone, Tunis. I *know* Shaw. He's not going to *tell us anything.*"

Shaw rode on ahead of them onto a stretch of level, sandy ground, then into the wavering heat, man and animal appearing as one against the desert sky.

GRITTY HISTORICAL ACTION FROM

USA Today BESTSELLING AUTHOR

RALPH COTTON

BLOOD LANDS

GUNFIGHT AT COLD DEVIL

FAST GUNS OUT OF TEXAS

GUNS ON THE BORDER

KILLING TEXAS BOB

NIGHTFALL AT LITTLE ACES

AMBUSH AT SHADOW VALLEY

RIDE TO HELL'S GATE

*Available wherever books are sold or at
penguin.com*

"A writer in the tradition of Louis L'Amour
and Zane Grey!"
—*Huntsville Times*

National Bestselling Author
RALPH COMPTON

NOWHERE, TEXAS
AUTUMN OF THE GUN
THE KILLING SEASON
THE DAWN OF FURY
RIDERS OF JUDGMENT
BULLET CREEK
FOR THE BRAND
GUNS OF THE CANYONLANDS
RIO LARGO
DEADWOOD GULCH
A WOLF IN THE FOLD
TRAIL TO COTTONWOOD FALLS
BLUFF CITY
THE BLOODY TRAIL
WEST OF THE LAW
BLOOD DUEL
SHADOW OF THE GUN
DEATH OF A BAD MAN
RIDE THE HARD TRAIL
BLOOD ON THE GALLOWS

**Available wherever books are sold or at
penguin.com**

No other series packs this much heat!

THE TRAILSMAN

#307: MONTANA MARAUDERS
#308: BORDER BRAVADOS
#309: CALIFORNIA CARNAGE
#310: ALASKAN VENGEANCE
#311: IDAHO IMPACT
#312: SHANGHAIED SIX-GUNS
#313: TEXAS TIMBER WAR
#314: NORTH COUNTRY CUTTTHROATS
#315: MISSOURI MANHUNT
#316: BEYOND SQUAW CREEK
#317: MOUNTAIN MYSTERY
#318: NEVADA NEMESIS
#319: LOUISIANA LAYDOWN
#320: OREGON OUTRAGE
#321: FLATHEAD FURY
#322: APACHE AMBUSH
#323: WYOMING DEATHTRAP
#324: CALIFORNIA CRACKDOWN

**Follow the trail of the gun-slinging heroes of
Penguin's Action Westerns at
penguin.com/actionwesterns**

Charles G. West

**"RARELY HAS AN AUTHOR PAINTED THE
GREAT AMERICAN WEST IN STROKES SO
BOLD, VIVID AND TRUE."
—RALPH COMPTON**

TANNER'S LAW

Tanner Bland returns home from the Civil War to
find that everyone thought him dead, and that his
younger brother married Tanner's fiancée. So Tanner
heads west to join an old army buddy, Jeb Hawkins,
and hit the gold mines of Montana.

But the wagon train they join is not what they hoped
for. Because in the train with them are the four
good-for-nothing Leach brothers—and before they
hit Montana, there'll be more than enough blood
for all...

Also Available
Range War at Whiskey Hill
Duel at Low Hawk

Available wherever books are sold or at
penguin.com

From
Frank Leslie

THE WILD BREED

Yakima Henry ventures south of the border to
save an old flame's brother from a Mexican
prison—only to incur the wrath of deadly
Apaches, scalp-hunting Rurales, and zealous
revolutionaries.

THE THUNDER RIDERS

Yakima Henry left his ranch in the White
Mountains for supplies, and rode right into a
bloody shootout between Saber Creek
townsfolk and a gang of banditos who just
robbed a stagecoach. But what really riles
Yakima is the banditos making off with his
prized stallion, Wolf, and a pretty saloon girl.

**Available wherever books are sold or at
penguin.com**